Circus Maximus: Race to the Death

'This thrilling debut is the first in a new historical series
full of dazzling action, rich detail, fabulous horses
and an unforgettable heroine.'
Fiona Noble, *The Bookseller*

'Fantastic new historical novel that I'm reading to my daughter.
She's loving it... We are hoping there's a sequel!'
Dan Snow, historian

'Rich in period detail, with a few real historical characters —
its principal invention the idea that a woman might have been a
charioteer — this is an involving,
well characterised tale that feels original...'
Sunday Times, Children's Book of the Week

'... a gripping novel set in ancient Rome, centred
on the world of chariot racing... The story wears the
historical detail lightly but very convincingly.'
Five Books

'*Circus Maximus* swept me away to ancient Rome
and I didn't want to come back. What a thrilling
historical adventure!'
A.M. Howell, author of *The Garden of Lost Secrets*

'This is an action-packed adventure that will take you on a ride... There is fast-paced drama in each chapter, which keeps you gripped to the story. I love the historical element...'
The Teacher Bookworm, teacher blogger

'Full of great characters — both horses and humans — and Dido is a terrific heroine... Annelise Gray has written a story that is both historically convincing and heart-stoppingly exciting. I hope there are more to come.'
Gillian Cross, author of The Demon Headmaster series

'Lovers of history, horses and heart-stopping adventure will be gripped by this action-packed and fast-paced read which will sweep you off your feet, leave you breathless and wanting to know more of the history behind the fiction.'
Armadillo

'Gray transports the reader to Rome in a hoofbeat, places, people and the dangerous times vividly brought to life... A superb historical adventure story.'
LoveReading

'It's fantastic... I loved it and there's a sequel to look forward to also.'
Anne Thompson, The Library Lady, blogger

CIRCUS
MAXIMUS
Rivals on the Track

To Emer-Clare,

Annelise

Cray

Also by Annelise Gray

Circus Maximus: Race to the Death

CIRCUS MAXIMUS
Rivals on the Track

ANNELISE GRAY

ℨEPHYR

An imprint of Head of Zeus

Head of Zeus Ltd
First Floor East
5–8 Hardwick Street
London EC1R 4RG
WWW.HEADOFZEUS.COM

For my mother,
Samantha

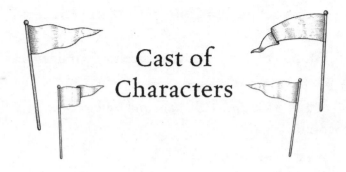

Cast of Characters

Utica (North Africa)

Dido – a brilliant young female charioteer, who also races in the guise of a boy called 'Leon'

Scorpus – Dido's uncle, a racehorse trainer and former charioteer

Hanno and Abibaal – Scorpus's sons

Parmenion – a charioteer in Scorpus's stable

Antigonus – Scorpus's assistant trainer

Anna – wife of Antigonus

Glarus – a racehorse trainer and friend of Scorpus

Thugga (south-west of Utica)

Muttumbaal – a legendary racehorse trainer and father of Scorpus

Barca – Muttumbaal's son and older brother of Scorpus

Ismene – wife of Barca

Bodo – Barca and Ismene's son, a promising charioteer

Elissa – Bodo's younger sister

Zeno – a racehorse trainer and rival of Muttumbaal

Danel – Zeno's son, one of the finest charioteers in north Africa

Amandio – younger brother of Danel

 ## The Romans

Gemellus Glabrio – a wealthy Roman, living in Thugga

Cassius Chaerea – a soldier in the Praetorian Guard

Scylax – a former charioteer for the Green faction, now one of their talent scouts

Caligula – the Emperor of Rome

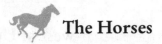 # The Horses

Porcellus – a fiery black stallion, owned by Dido but wanted by Emperor Caligula

Jewel – a one-eyed chestnut mare with the heart of a lioness

Cupid, Misty, Psyche and Storm – horses from Scorpus's stable

Atlas, Blaze, Brightfoot, Curly, Dagger, Eagle, Ocean, River and Thief – horses from Muttumbaal's stable

Centaur – the lead horse in Danel's team

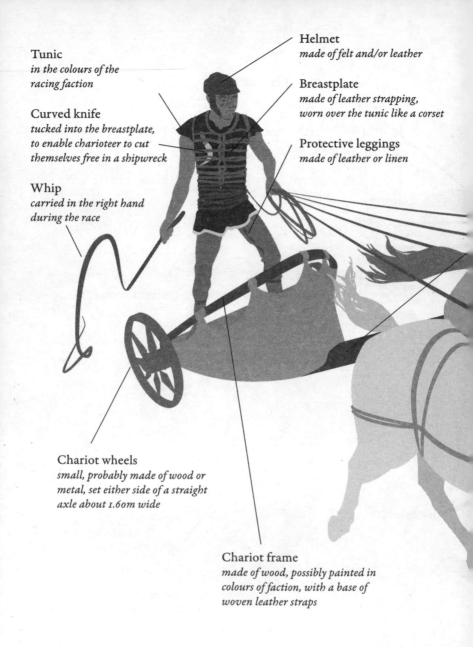

Tunic
in the colours of the racing faction

Curved knife
tucked into the breastplate, to enable charioteer to cut themselves free in a shipwreck

Whip
carried in the right hand during the race

Helmet
made of felt and/or leather

Breastplate
made of leather strapping, worn over the tunic like a corset

Protective leggings
made of leather or linen

Chariot wheels
small, probably made of wood or metal, set either side of a straight axle about 1.60m wide

Chariot frame
made of wood, possibly painted in colours of faction, with a base of woven leather straps

No racing chariot remains have survived the journey through time from the Roman world. This sketch is based on research into images of chariot racing in ancient art and literature.

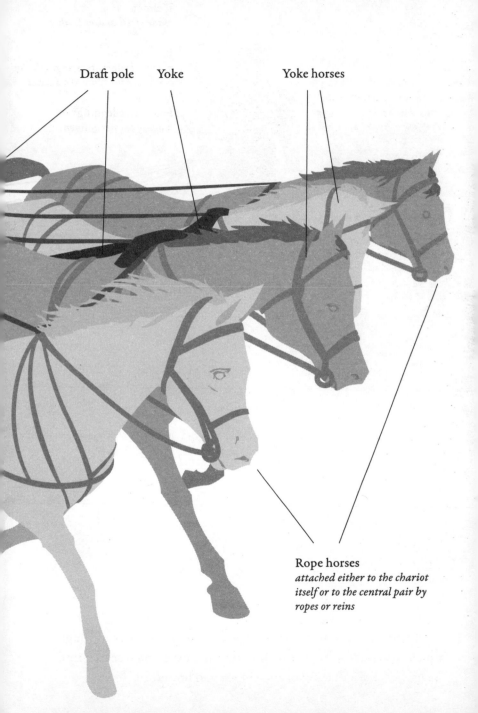

Draft pole   Yoke   Yoke horses

Rope horses
attached either to the chariot itself or to the central pair by ropes or reins

'Faster, come on boy, faster! We've got to get inside them at the turn!'

Porcellus's black ears were braced against the wind like shields raised for battle. His neck was tense, his bright eyes wide with excitement.

'Come on!'

The gap to the lead chariot was closing. Porcellus's flying hooves ate up the ground and my opponent looked fearfully over his shoulder.

Thought you had the beating of us, didn't you? I smiled. *But you underestimated me, my friend. Just like they all do.*

The other charioteer lashed his team's tiring rumps with the leather tongue of his whip. But it was too little, too late. Porcellus slid past them, curling around the turning post like a serpent. I felt the wind dragging through my hair as we galloped down the last straight. The finish line was in sight.

The Circus crowd was on their feet, roaring us home.

'Dido!' they chanted. 'Dido, Dido, Dido...'

'Dido!'

The roar faded from my ears and the excited faces lining the walls of the Circus Maximus disappeared along with the great stadium itself. It was just Porcellus and me on the practice track at my Uncle Scorpus's stable, racing for glory against an imaginary rival. But a lone voice was still calling my name.

'Dido!'

Scorpus was marching across the pasture. He looked furious and I knew why. I hauled back on the reins and Porcellus obeyed the command to slow down, snatching at the bit in his mouth. The wheels of my light training chariot crunched to a halt as Scorpus reached us.

'What do you think you're doing? Do you want people to see you?'

He pointed to the top of the valley, above the stables, where travellers passed along the coast road on their way to the nearby town of Utica.

'No one's going to get a good look at us from up there,' I said. 'Calm down, Scorpus, I was only giving Porcellus a run.'

'You're not even wearing a helmet! Has it slipped your mind that the emperor probably has half the Roman army out there, looking for a girl charioteer? And that you're driving a stolen horse?'

My hackles went up.

'Porcellus isn't stolen. He's mine, my father gave him to me.'

'I'm not sure that's how the emperor would see it.'

'You know how much I love Porcellus.' I was getting angry now. 'I'd never do anything to risk losing him again. But it's not fair to keep him locked in his stable all day. He's not even allowed to join the other horses when they come out for training. It's like when he was racing for the Greens, with Emperor Caligula keeping him chained up as if he was a pet dog.'

'So you're comparing me to Caligula now?'

'No. You're a bit less of a tyrant. But only a bit.'

I saw a reluctant smile tugging at the corner of his mouth and I felt better. I hated it when we argued.

'Honestly, Scorpus, where's the harm? It's been two months since Porcellus and I escaped from Rome. In that whole time, no one has come here looking for us. No one.'

'Well, that's where you're wrong. They just did. That's why I came out to warn you.'

Fear bubbled in my stomach.

'What do you mean? Who?'

'A messenger. He came from Rome. Bringing this.'

It was a picture, roughly painted on a square of yellow papyrus. Scorpus handed it to me and I studied the image of a female figure in a white tunic trimmed with gold. Her long dark hair flowed from under the helmet and in her raised hand was a whip. She was driving a chariot pulled by a galloping black horse with a white star clearly visible on his forehead.

'It's me at the Circus Maximus,' I said. 'When I raced for the Blues as Princess Sophonisba. And that's Porcellus.'

'Yes. And it came with this letter from Otho.' Scorpus held up another piece of papyrus. The red wax seal on its edge was broken. 'Get Porcellus back to the stable, then come inside and I'll read it to you.'

'What does it say? Wait, read it to me now – what does it say? Scorpus!'

'Horses first,' he said, walking back across the pasture towards the house.

I unhitched Porcellus from the chariot, leaped on to his back and galloped him to the stables. We passed Scorpus's one-time apprentice, now his assistant trainer, Antigonus, who gave us a brief wave. As soon as we reached the barn, Scorpus's old favourite, Sciron, ambled over to the gate. He'd already been retired from the circus track a long time when I first met him and his dark brown muzzle was heavily speckled with grey. Porcellus whickered at him in greeting. Sciron was the only friend he'd made since he got here.

Quickly, I rubbed Porcellus down before putting him in his stall. More horses had come up to the pasture fence, and although I was in a hurry to find out what was in Scorpus's letter, I went and gave their noses a rub. The red roan, Cupid, tried to hold me up by gently nipping at the pouch on my belt, where I sometimes kept sticky dates as a treat. From his stall, Porcellus screeched in protest. He regarded those dates as his special privilege.

Parmenion limped around the corner from the feed room, a bucket in his hand. He was still suffering with the leg injury from his crash in the Circus months before and couldn't manage much more than stable duties. His tawny hair was sticking up as usual and his sun-bronzed face was shiny with sweat. Porcellus's mood changed at once. His ears flapped forward and he kicked his door in excitement.

'Hello, you impatient viper. And hello to you too, Porcellus.' Parmenion grinned at me as he opened the door of Porcellus's stall.

'Very funny. Did you remember to put some olive oil in with his feed?'

'I certainly did, Princess.'

I rolled my eyes.

'Haven't you got tired of that joke yet?'

'I don't seem to have done, no.'

'Why that girl at the bakery likes you, I will never understand. You won't forget to fill up Porcellus's water, will you? It's hot in there and he's not going to get out again until nightfall.'

By the door which led into the kitchen, my young cousins, Hanno and Abibaal, were lingering beside the domed baking oven. A delicious smell of warm bread filled the air. Anna was making lunch for everyone. I could see her through the open door, her black hair escaping from its long plait and her teeth clenched as she heaved a vast pot towards the fire.

'Offer to help, you idiots,' I scolded the boys. 'She's got a baby inside her, remember. Antigonus would be furious if he saw you letting his wife lift a heavy thing like that on her own.'

I found Scorpus in the room where he did his accounts. He was sitting at a table, studying the square of crumpled papyrus. I saw the worry in his black eyes. My heart thudded uncomfortably.

'Is it… bad news?' I asked.

He sighed and started to read.

'My good friend, I write this in haste. Helvia

and I leave Rome tonight and there is little time, but much to tell you. You need to know, first of all, that I have sold the Blue faction and therefore our business relationship – though not, I hope, our friendship – must come to an end, for now at least. Betucius Barus will be the new faction master. I've told him you're the best trainer in the empire and that he'd be mad not to continue to buy horses from you. But Betucius favours the Spanish breeds over the African and I fear you may see fewer scouts from the Blues coming by than you used to. I know this will affect your livelihood and I am sorry.

'The reasons for our sudden departure will not surprise you. The emperor is in ill humour. Ever since the humiliating defeat of his favourite driver at the Circus Maximus by the mystery charioteer known only as Princess Sophonisba, Caligula has brooded with all the petulance of a child who has lost his favourite toy. He can never stomach the Green faction being defeated, of course. But he was keen to make the girl their new star so that he could fawn over her as he once did your former apprentice, Nicias. That she should flee Rome rather than accept the honour of that invitation, he regards as an insufferable insult.

'Caligula's advisors try to divert his mind. There is talk that the Greens have recruited a new driver, a precocious young talent who will arrive in Rome soon and hopefully restore some of the emperor's good humour. But the emperor nurses a grudge like a bloodhound guards a bone. He is determined to discover the princess's true identity and force her to return to Rome, along with the racehorse she took from under his nose. To that end, he sends the Praetorian Guard almost daily to the Blues' clubhouse to intimidate me. The water is a little hot for my liking. It seems prudent to remove myself from Rome.

'Please, my friend, do not be concerned for me. I have many friends around the empire and I shall build my fortune again elsewhere. Helvia is here now and tells me the boat is about to leave and I must finish writing. She bids me pass on her fond wishes to the princess.

'I trust we will meet again. Until then, may the gods protect you.

'Your friend, Opellius Otho.'

Scorpus finished reading and looked up. I sank on to a low stool. Scorpus came around the table and squatted in front of me.

'They'll be safe, Dido, I promise.'

'You don't know that. What if Caligula finds them and kills them?' I was struggling to speak. 'It'll be because of me, because they were protecting me.'

'He won't find them. They've got Otho's money and Helvia's cunning. That'll be more than enough to keep them out of trouble.'

My breathing steadied.

'What about you, though, Scorpus? How are you going to make a living if you can't sell horses to the Blues any more?'

'You can let me worry about that. I'll think of something. There's always the Red or White faction, although they don't send so many scouts this way. I'd rather not sell to the Greens, what with them being the emperor's favourite team. But, if there's no other choice, we'll see. It's you I'm worried about.'

He picked up the picture of me and Porcellus.

'This is a reward poster,' he explained. 'The emperor's offering ten million sesterces to anyone who can find you and Porcellus and bring you back to Rome.'

'Ten million?' I was astounded. 'That must be more prize money than the Greens win at the Circus in a year!'

'Probably. Just shows how much you're worth to him, Dido.'

'What do you think he would do to me? If I had to go back?'

Scorpus hesitated.

'I can't be sure. He might want to punish you for taking Porcellus. Caligula thinks of the horse as his own, even if he belonged to you first. But my best guess is he'll try to make you race for the Greens, as he intended before.'

I shook my head violently.

'Never. I won't ever do that. Not while the emperor's their biggest supporter. He's the reason my father's dead and he killed Icarus and I'll never forgive him. Never.'

'Well, now you know why I wanted you to stay out of sight.'

I hung my head. Scorpus squeezed my shoulder.

'I know, Dido. I know it's not been easy. You're a charioteer in your blood. You want to be out there, tearing around the track at a circus again. There is an obvious solution, you know.'

'You mean go back to being Leon.'

He nodded. I sighed in frustration.

'That means starting again at the beginning, competing at the local games in Utica.' I tapped the poster in his hand. 'I won at the Circus Maximus, Scorpus! I had hundreds of thousands of people screaming my name! Well, not *my* name. But they were cheering for me all the same.'

'They also cheered for you at the Circus when you raced for the Blues as Leon.'

'I know. But when I was Princess Sophonisba, I was allowed to be a girl so I was a little bit myself. When I'm Leon, I have to be a boy, somebody completely different. I have to keep my hair short and put on that dye Anna makes for me and not speak too much. It's not fair. Why can't I be Dido?'

'You know why,' said Scorpus gently. 'I wish it was different, Dido. But chariot racing is a man's world. Always has been, always will be.'

II

Green was spreading across the landscape around Utica, like an emerald wave rippling across a grey shore. They were planting the spring wheat in the fields and the smell of freshly dug soil mingled with the salt tang of the distant sea.

I fanned the hem of my skirt to let some cool air in. Scorpus had said I could go into Utica with Parmenion and Abibaal to pick up the new horses arriving by boat from Carthage. The downside was that I couldn't wear the stable clothes in which I was most comfortable. Instead I had to pretend to be a slave girl, going to shop for food at the market. It was a warm day and the long-sleeved woollen tunic I'd borrowed from Anna was sticking to me. I sat in the back of the cart, a basket wedged beside my feet. The boys were taking it in turns to drive the mules. Abibaal was chewing on a piece of straw. He was almost thirteen, a year behind his brother

Hanno. The soft childish flesh on his face was starting to mould itself to his jaw and cheekbones. Sometimes I would catch him playing with the toy horses that Scorpus had once made for him out of brushwood. But he was keen to grow up. Straggly dark-brown curls crept down the nape of his neck. He had been wearing it like that ever since we came back from Rome, and Parmenion had told him that it was the fashion among a lot of the charioteers at the Circus Maximus.

A long strand of my fair hair escaped from behind my ear and I pushed it back. It had lightened in the spring sun over the last two months.

'You and Porcellus were having a great run out there this morning, Dido,' said Abibaal over his shoulder to me. 'I was watching you. I think maybe you were a bit off balance on some of the turns, though.'

'Really?' I said. 'Interesting. And you only a two-horse charioteer, still racing in the boys' events at Utica. Do you have any other advice you'd like to give me?'

Abibaal shifted uncomfortably. I relented and poked him playfully in the back. Although I didn't want to admit it, he was right. I hadn't been at my best that morning. Ever since we'd come back from Rome, in fact, it felt as though my timing was off on the turns. It was probably the lack of training. I winced as I pinched the top of my arms which were covered by the long sleeves of the tunic. I definitely needed to start building muscle there again.

We arrived in Utica to find the broad main street busy with shoppers, travellers and traders as usual. I longed to go with Abibaal and Parmenion into the port area to see the horses being unloaded off the boats. But I'd made a promise to Scorpus not to draw attention to myself. After agreeing to meet Abibaal and Parmenion back by the cart, I went to the market, muttering Anna's list of ingredients under my breath. I bought onions, apples and cabbages from the greengrocer, a piece of bacon from the butcher and cumin seeds from the spice trader. Then I stood in line by the miller's stall, waiting for him to weigh some flour. A nearby wall was covered with advertisements for the next circus games at Utica which were going to be held the following month. There was a poster too, with black lettering on it and a drawing of a huge oval racetrack which caught my eye. Two men were looking at it, one of whom I recognised from the back of his bald head as Glarus, Scorpus's friend and fellow trainer. He'd only ever met me when I was dressed as Leon, but I pulled some of my hair across my face, just in case. The other man wore a leather cape over his shoulders and had greasy dark hair. He nodded at Glarus.

'I see you're looking at the new circus being built at Thugga.'

'Quite something, isn't it? They say it's going to be as big as the Circus Maximus, but I'll believe it when I see it.'

'You're in the racing business?'

'I am. Taking a team of drivers to compete at the opening of that circus, in fact. Late summer.'

The man took a piece of a papyrus from the leather pouch on his belt. I had to stop a gasp escaping. It was the reward poster of me and Porcellus.

'Don't suppose you know anything about this girl, do you?'

Glarus studied the picture and made a scoffing noise.

'You're not the first to show that to me. There's a lot of you fellows around, asking questions, trying to be the one to claim the reward. Sorry. Can't help. But if you ask me, it's all a hoax. No girl would be strong enough to hold a circus team of four chariot horses. I'll lay you money your princess is a man in a dress.'

The man in the leather cape looked disgruntled. At that moment, the miller handed me the flour and I hurried back to the cart, thoughts bumping into each other in my head. How many other bounty hunters were there, trying to find me and Porcellus? I cursed myself for being so stupid as to drive him that morning. From now on, I would do exactly what Scorpus said and only let Porcellus into the pasture at night. He would hate it, but anything was better than the chance of the emperor taking him away from me again. At the back of my mind, another thought tickled me. That new circus. Glarus had said it was being built at Thugga, which I knew was the town where Scorpus and my mother had grown up. If Glarus had been invited to games there, surely Scorpus must have been too. Why hadn't he said so?

Abibaal and Parmenion weren't back with the horses. As I waited by the cart on the edge of the market, a few men glanced at me and made comments which brought the blood to my cheeks. I cursed my girls' clothing and scowled at a man who whistled at me. His expression changed and he started to come towards me. I bolted at once, running down the street with the shopping basket banging against my knees. Thankfully, he didn't follow and after getting my breath back in the shelter of a portico, I decided to go down to the port to find out what was keeping Parmenion and Abibaal.

It was a breezy afternoon and the vessels tied to the quayside lurched and dipped in the harbour.

At the far end, beyond the cargo boats, were the animal transports with their deep hulls. Horses were being led on and off. As I walked towards them through the swarm of dock workers, I heard the clip of hooves and turned to find a dishevelled-looking man in soldier's uniform behind me, leading a chestnut mare. She was sturdy and well-muscled with a beautiful red-gold mane. But she had bad scarring on her shoulders and there was a sunken hollow in her face where her right eye should have been.

'You,' the soldier called to a sailor on the quay. 'Where are you headed?'

'Rome,' I heard the sailor say. 'Taking some animals over for the Circus Maximus.'

'Any room in your hold for another?'

The sailor laughed.

'You're joking, right? Look at the sight of her.'

'Don't let her appearance fool you. This is one of the fastest horses in the Third Legion. Took an arrow in the face during a skirmish with some rebels on the border. Carried me to safety all the same, never once lost her footing.'

'Very touching. But there's no market for blind horses at the Circus.'

'You could get a few sesterces for her somewhere, couldn't you?' pleaded the soldier. He looked dirty and desperate. 'Help me out. I've been discharged from the army. I need money to get back to Rome.'

The sailor rubbed his chin, looking critically at the one-eyed mare. Then he took out a pouch, counted some coins and gave them to the soldier who accepted them greedily. He stroked the chestnut on her back.

'See you, old girl. We had some great runs, didn't we? Be good, Jewel.'

He gave her another pat then walked away, counting the money in his palm. The mare turned and, with her good eye, watched him go. A mournful sound of protest escaped her. I stared after the soldier in disbelief. How could anyone do that? Sell the horse that had saved his life and abandon her like that.

The sailor took hold of the mare's rope and peered at her disfigured face with his flinty eyes.

'Circus horse. What a joke. Sicily. That's the place for you, ugly beast. They always need horses to work in the mines there.'

He tried to lead her down to the boat. But the mare resisted. When the sailor swore and pulled harder, she tugged herself free and took off along the quayside. I dropped the basket where I stood and ran after her. Dock workers were trying to grab her trailing rope but she dodged round them, her hooves skipping like a deer's. The soldier hadn't lied. She was lightning-fast, despite only having half her sight. At the end of the port, she rounded a corner and disappeared.

It took me a long time to find her in Utica's warren of side streets. An upturned souvenir stall gave me my first clue, followed by a woman complaining about her ruined laundry, and then some children gabbling excitedly about a one-eyed demon horse. Eventually, I found the chestnut, skulking at the end of a deserted alleyway. She was sipping filthy water from a puddle and she lifted her head as she saw me, snorting warily.

'It's all right,' I said, moving very slowly, keeping my voice as soothing as I could. 'Yes, I know. You've had a nasty time. But you can trust me.'

The mare stared at me in suspicion. I made a soft neighing sound in my throat. She skittered backwards and I cursed myself for dropping the basket earlier. I could have used the apples to tempt her. Changing tactic, I turned and started to walk away. I hadn't gone far when I heard the clip of her hooves again. *Yes.* She came up to me and let me take the rope.

'Hello, Jewel,' I said, stroking her gently on her cheek with my knuckles. 'Don't you worry. Everything's going to be fine.'

Back at the cart, I found Parmenion and Abibaal waiting with six horses roped together.

'Finally!' said Parmenion. 'We've been looking everywhere for you. What is *that*?'

'Well, where were you?' I asked, avoiding his question about Jewel. 'I waited ages and then a horrible man came and I had to run away.'

'Parmenion was talking to his girlfriend at the bakery,' piped up Abibaal. 'She was giggling and he was saying things about her eyes. It made me feel a bit sick, to be honest.'

Parmenion ignored him. 'I repeat, *what* is that?'

He nodded at Jewel, who sniffed him with interest.

'I found her. She needs a home. Tie her to the back of the cart with the others.'

Parmenion stared at me in disbelief. Then he sighed and took Jewel's rope.

'Scorpus is not going to be happy. But it's your funeral.'

III

Orange light dappled the sky as the sun slowly sank below the horizon. The rich stew on our plates was laced with the scent of thyme from the surrounding hills. Hanno tore off another piece of cheese bread and chewed on it, closing his eyes in bliss. Abibaal glowered at his older brother. He had been forbidden by Scorpus from having more of his favourite treat after stealing rolls from the oven.

'Thank you, Anna,' said Scorpus, passing his plate for a second helping. 'An excellent meal, given that you had to do without half the ingredients.'

He gave me a withering look.

'I know. I really am sorry,' I said, wiping up the sauce on my plate with some bread. 'But look what we got in exchange for cabbages and onions.'

'A horse with one eye,' said Scorpus in a dry voice.

'Wrong. A *fast* horse with one eye. I think she might even be able to race on the inside of a four.'

'You're mad, Dido.'

'I'm not! She's got great balance, exactly what you need for an inside horse. You should have seen her twisting and turning around all of those dock workers, Scorpus, she was so—'

'All right, all right,' said Scorpus, holding up a hand. 'I should know by now never to argue with you, Dido. We'll put her through her paces tomorrow. But you're dreaming if you think she'll make an inside horse.'

He glanced down the table at Parmenion, who winced as he shifted his badly scarred leg under the table.

'How's the pain today, lad?'

'It's been worse,' said Parmenion.

'Make sure you do those exercises I gave you. They'll help.'

Parmenion nodded as if he agreed. But I could see Scorpus was watching him, a frown in his eyes. Guilt flicked a claw across my heart. I never forgot that Parmenion had hurt himself saving my life. A glimpse of the crash flashed through my mind… Scylax leering down at me as I was dragged along the Circus floor… Quickly, I banished the memory. Anna brought in a plate of dates. I took one and began to nibble, letting the sweetness bring me back to myself.

'Scorpus,' I said. 'Have you heard about a new circus being built at Thugga?'

My uncle carried on eating his stew, giving me a sideways glance as he did so.

'Where did you hear about that?'

'The man I told you about earlier, the one asking about me. He and Glarus were looking at a poster on the wall. It said there are going to be games later in the summer, with big prizes on offer.'

'How big?' asked Abibaal, distracted from his sulk.

'I don't know. I just wondered if your papa was thinking of taking some horses to compete. It might be an answer to some of our money worries, while we try to find new buyers for our horses.'

Scorpus took his time replying.

'I know about the new circus,' he said. 'But I've no intention of going back to Thugga.'

'Why not, Papa?' asked Hanno.

'Because it's a long way.' He caught my eye. 'And to tell the truth, I don't have especially fond memories of the place.'

'You mean like, your father dying?' suggested Abibaal.

Scorpus hesitated.

'That's one of them.'

'Grandpa Muttumbaal was a trainer like you, wasn't he, Papa?'

'Yes. A great one.'

'What did he die of?'

Scorpus dropped his spoon on the plate with a clatter and sat back, an irritable look on his face.

'Why are we even talking about it? We're not going to Thugga and that's the end of it. Enough questions.'

Abibaal lapsed into sullen silence.

I went to the pasture to say goodnight to Porcellus. He was grazing next to Sciron, but he trotted over as soon as he saw me and greedily sucked up the date I was holding out for him. I noticed the new horse, Jewel, was standing on her own under a tree. She was hanging her head, blinking her one good eye forlornly.

'You should be nicer to her,' I said to Porcellus, combing my fingers through his forelock and smoothing it neatly over the white star on his forehead. 'It wasn't long ago that you were new here too.'

I heard a footstep behind me and almost jumped out of my skin. A tall figure ambled from the shadows.

'Sorry,' said Parmenion. He took a long swig from the canister in his hand.

'You're having too much of that stuff,' I told him. 'It's no wonder you can't sleep. Scorpus knows about that tavern you go to in Utica.'

'That's because Antigonus is a sneak. Scorpus can talk about his exercises all he wants, but this is the only thing that really helps with the pain in my leg. So put your disapproving face away, Princess.'

He eased himself on to the ground, using a fencepost for support, and patted the grass next to him.

'That girl from the bakery wouldn't be very happy,' I said.

'Ah, Chloe,' said Parmenion dreamily.

'Phoebe.'

'Phoebe, that's her. Which one's Chloe again?'

I shook my head as I lay down. 'You're inexcusable.'

We looked at the stars, scattered across the indigo heavens like fragments of shattered glass. From the forests nearby and the surrounding hills, I could hear the rustle of wild boar and deer above the rattling chant of the cicadas singing in the trees. Parmenion took occasional gulps from the canister while I tasted the air, so much cleaner and sweeter than what I had grown up with in Rome. There, night-time smelled of cook shops and sewers and the tan yards where animal skins were dried into leather, and above it all, the yellow stink of the River Tiber. Here the breeze was warm, fragrant with wild herbs and pomegranates. It smelled like home to me now.

'So,' slurred Parmenion. 'When are you going to cut your hair and get back to racing?'

'Not you as well. Scorpus was saying the same thing. How do you know I even want to go back? Why should I, if I have to pretend to be someone else?'

'Because you were born to be a charioteer, Dido. It's who you are.'

'You don't understand.'

'Try me,' said Parmenion.

I sighed and tried to find the words for what I felt.

'All those boys in Utica, you know, the ones I used to beat at the local games. They believe the story Otho spread after my last race for the Blues as Leon. That I got shipwrecked, lost my nerve and came home. We made it up so that no one would make the connection between me and Princess Sophonisba and know how to find me afterwards.'

'And?'

'Don't you see? If I go back to being Leon, everyone in Utica's going to think I'm a loser,

Parmenion. That I had my chance at the Circus Maximus and failed. I don't think I can bear to have them laughing at me.'

'So? Go and wipe the smiles off their faces.'

'I can't explain. It's not so simple.'

'Of course it is. Besides,' he added, 'there's another reason you have to start racing again. Porcellus. You're not planning on keeping him caged up for the rest of his life like the emperor did, are you?'

'I don't want to. But what choice do I have? There's going to be more of those men like I saw today. Bounty hunters, combing the empire, searching for me and him.'

'Exactly,' said Parmenion. 'Which is why the circus track is the best hiding place for both of you. No one's going to believe that anyone would have the guts to put in plain view a stolen horse the entire empire is looking for.'

I gazed into the stars. Now that he had planted the idea, it was hard to let it go. It had been my dream to race Porcellus, ever since I'd broken him into harness as a young stallion. Could I really do it? Then I shook my head.

'I can't. What if someone from Rome's in Utica, a faction scout for the Greens, maybe? They'd be bound to know him.'

'Well, I still reckon you should think it over. Otherwise, Porcellus is going to be stuck in that stable for a long time. It'll be like when Scorpus wouldn't let you drive horses and tried to force you to work with Anna in the kitchen when you first came here.'

I grinned. 'She couldn't believe I'd never cooked an egg before. I was so unhappy.'

'So will that horse be, if you don't let him do what's in his blood – as much as it is in yours, Dido. You'll break his spirit. Trust me.'

I glanced at him, that guilty feeling troubling my heart again. But Parmenion was humming a cheerful tune to the moon.

IV

I stroked Jewel's rust-coloured cheek, keeping to her left side so that she could see me. Her ears were flicking back and forth and her skin twitched as Scorpus buckled the harness over her withers and attached the draft pole of the chariot. On Jewel's other side, Cupid waited patiently.

'Well,' said Scorpus, stepping back. 'Come on then. Let's try her out.'

I stepped up on to the base of the chariot and wound the reins a few times around my waist to give me control in case I needed it. Jewel arched her tail as we set off. She was strong and, at first, I struggled to hold her. But after a couple of laps, she settled. Cupid seemed to understand that her companion needed guidance, and soon I had them cantering in a good rhythm. Every time we took a turn, I could see the bright orb of Jewel's left eye, alert and interested. I quickened the pace, relishing the feel of the wind in my face. Eventually, Scorpus called us in.

'I hate to admit it,' he said, looking critically at Jewel. 'But you might be right about that mare, Dido.'

I beamed in triumph.

'I said she was quick on her feet, didn't I? I suppose you have to be if you're a cavalry horse.'

'What's remarkable is that it doesn't seem to affect her, only having one eye.'

'I know. I think she could be an inside horse, Scorpus. She's so responsive on the rein. And she really noses around the turn – did you see that? Almost as if she's sniffing her way...'

As I babbled on, I saw the smile in my uncle's eyes deepen.

'Does this mean you're going to be the one who trains her?' he asked when I finished. 'And takes her to Utica for her first race?'

I hesitated. I thought about all the excuses I'd made to Parmenion. But the feeling of being up on the chariot again, training a new horse, was so good.

'I'll think about it,' I said, although I was already imagining the view from the start line, thrilling to the idea of being in a race again.

We turned Jewel into the field with Sciron. In the barn behind us, Porcellus was restless, pacing about his stall. He and Sciron called to each other plaintively. They hated being apart.

'Have you thought any more about that idea of Parmenion's that I told you about?' I asked Scorpus.

'I'll admit you're right about the one-eyed mare, Dido. But I'm sorry. I think it's far too risky trying to race Porcellus as well, especially now we know there are already people here, asking questions about you. That horse's speed is going to draw attention as much as anything.'

I knew he was right. But I couldn't stop thinking about it.

In my room, I stared at the picture of me and Porcellus on the reward poster, which I'd taken from Scorpus's desk. Then I opened the citrus-wood chest next to my bed, where I kept my most treasured possessions. The green tunic I'd worn for most of my childhood, growing up under my father's care in Rome. A wooden carving Scorpus had made in his youth of an old horse called Tigris, which I used to wear around my neck for luck until its tail broke off. A long silver-blue strand from the tail of my darling Icarus, the horse I'd loved most in the world after Porcellus. I'd found it not long after we came back from Rome, in the stall he once occupied. I ran my finger along its length then replaced it carefully in the cloth wrapping I'd made for it. Finally, I reached into the bottom of the chest. A faint smell of lavender drifted up as I lifted the soft folds of the white, gold-trimmed tunic.

Gently, I stroked the fraying gold threads on the garment's hem. So often, I had imagined the first time my father must have seen my mother wearing it. Standing astride galloping horses, her dark hair flowing behind her as she and her acrobat troupe entertained and dazzled the Circus crowd in between races. That was the image I'd carried in my head, ever since I'd been old enough for Papa to tell me about her. Had they shouted her name – *Sophonisba* – as they did for me at the Circus Maximus that day? Probably not. They only did that for charioteers. My other hand went to the chain around my neck, to the pouch where I carried the precious lock of her hair which my father, Antonius, had kept for me.

And that's when it dawned on me. I was almost fifteen, the same age as my mother had been when she ran away from her home in Thugga. A year younger than when she'd met Antonius and had me. And I had no idea what my future held. For most girls, I knew there was only one choice. Get married and start a family. I didn't feel ready for either of those things and I knew my mother hadn't either, or she wouldn't have run away when my grandfather tried to force her into a marriage she didn't want. But I also knew that before too long, I might not be able to pass as a boy – which would mean I wouldn't be able to race. What then? Maybe that's what Scorpus had been trying to tell me when he tried to persuade me to be Leon again.

I picked up the reward poster.

I stared at the white of Porcellus's star, glimmering against his black coat. And an idea came to me as if a god had whispered in my ear.

'What do you think?' I asked nervously.

Scorpus surveyed Porcellus, who was tethered loosely to the pasture fence and eating pieces of dried fig from my hand.

'I don't understand. How did you do it?'

'I used the hair dye Anna makes for me when I'm pretending to be Leon. It covers the star well, doesn't it? It's not quite dry yet but I can put some more on tomorrow.'

Scorpus shook his head as he stared at Porcellus's forehead, which was completely black.

'It's clever,' he admitted. 'And it does make him unrecognisable as the horse on that poster. But I don't know, Dido.'

'Well, I do. I thought about what you said and you're right. It's silly for me to be missing the chance to do what I love because I can't have things exactly the way I want them. So I'm going to train Jewel and teach her how to run on the inside of a four-horse team with Porcellus on the outside trace. She's got the foot speed to keep pace with him and all the attention is going to be on her, because of how she looks. Who knows, maybe I can get her to the Circus Maximus one day, even if I can't go back myself.' I nodded. 'I've made up my mind, Scorpus. I'm going to be Leon again.'

Jewel came ambling up to the fence. Hearing her approach, Porcellus's ears went back. He flicked his tail crossly, like a cat.

'Porcellus…' I warned.

Undeterred, Jewel extended her nose greedily towards the fig I was holding. Porcellus bared his teeth and prepared to defend his territory. Quicker than a cobra, Jewel bit him.

Porcellus skittered back to the end of his rope, an expression of utter shock on his face, which turned to outrage as he watched Jewel take the remaining fig from my palm and lazily chew it up. She lifted her upper lip in what looked almost like a grin.

'Looks like you've met your match, Porcellus,' said Scorpus, unable to control his laughter.

Sitting on my mattress later that night, I picked up a mirror Anna had left behind when she moved out and looked at my reflection in the dull silver surface. For a long time, I studied the green eyes and thick mane of bright hair I had inherited from Antonius. I knew my strong nose and high cheekbones came from my mother's family. Then I picked up the scissors I had taken from Anna's sewing basket.

'Goodbye, Dido. For now. I'll see you again.'

Opening the sharp blades, I gathered a handful of my hair and scythed neatly through the wheat-coloured strands.

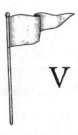

V

The racetrack at Utica was less than half the size of the Circus Maximus. It had none of the grandeur of Rome's famous stadium, where bronze turning posts at either end of the channel split the track in two, and golden dolphins plunged their noses to signal the start of each new lap. But the roar of the local crowd could still make the hairs on my arm stand up. Even though this was only the two-horse race and most of the drivers were novice charioteers – young boys of twelve or thirteen, excited to be wearing their first racing breastplate – there was loud and fierce support among the spectators, who clenched their fists and spat encouragement at the horses and drivers hurtling around the narrow dirt track.

I had to stuff my knuckles into my mouth to stop myself from yelling along with them. My voice could give me away when I was dressed as Leon in my charioteer's uniform of tunic, breastplate and thick leg-wrappings, and with my hair short and dark as it was now. Next to me, Scorpus was roaring like a lion, hands cupped around his mouth.

'Get forward, Hanno!' He made a gesture with his arm. 'Move up!'

Hanno, who had been in third place, obeyed his father, hurling the end of his long whip like a fisherman trying to hook a mullet. Cupid and Psyche obediently lifted their red roan heads and quickened their stride. A length behind, Abibaal, steering the dark grey Misty and Storm, was shadowing his brother with the look of an excitable puppy in pursuit of its first rat. They were promising charioteers, both of them. Hanno was the more careful and tactical of the two, Abibaal the all-out racer. If he could learn to be patient, I was sure that Abibaal would be the stronger as they got older and I knew Scorpus thought so too.

'Come on, boys,' bellowed Scorpus, banging his fist into his palm. 'Move, move, move.'

As if they'd heard him, both Hanno and Abibaal overtook the chariot in second. They were coming to the final lap and Hanno still had the edge on his younger brother as they made up ground on the lead charioteer. The rest of the field was scattered behind them. As they came to the turning post,

Abibaal recklessly tried to go around Hanno on the outside, a move that almost never works unless you're driving a much faster pair. For a moment I thought he was actually going to make it, but then the wheels of his chariot locked as he forced his horses to cut back inside too sharply. Scorpus groaned. Hanno now had a length's advantage and the lead charioteer in his sights. Cupid and Psyche picked up speed on the long straight and they made a beautiful passing move on the right.

'Good boy,' crowed Scorpus. 'Now come on, Abibaal, where are you?'

The dark greys were galloping at full tilt. Abibaal was squatting so low, we could barely see the peak of his leather helmet above the guard rail of the chariot. A lash of his whip and Misty and Storm's noses stretched forward even further. There was one more turn to go. Hanno rounded it safely and the second charioteer, hearing the thunder of hooves behind him, hugged the inside line to give Abibaal no chance of surprising him on the left. But Misty and Storm didn't change course. I glanced at Scorpus.

'He's not going to…? Is he?'

Wordless in response, Scorpus folded his arms and rested his forehead on them.

The charioteer in second glanced over his

shoulder. It was always the temptation when you sensed another driver coming up behind you just before the turn, but it was so often a fatal mistake. The wheels of his chariot drifted slightly right, leaving a small gap between him and the central barrier. I bit down on my knuckles. For so many charioteers, that tantalising gap was the pathway that forked in two directions. Glory. Or the Underworld. Abibaal pointed his horses straight at it.

I covered my face with both hands. There was a roar from the big crowd of Blue supporters around us. I peered between my fingers and realised that somehow Misty and Storm had shouldered their way through. Abibaal was now in second place. Hanno was already cantering over the finish line to applause from the crowd. When Abibaal crossed moments later, he got an even bigger cheer than his brother. But I could see he looked downcast.

I followed Scorpus to the stalls where the horses were sheltered between races. Hanno, caked in dust and beaming with pride, was being congratulated by Glarus.

'Well done, son,' said Scorpus, grasping Hanno by the shoulder. 'You paced that well. Where's your brother?'

'In there,' said Hanno, pointing to an empty stall with a slight roll of his eyes.

While Scorpus paused to exchange a few words with Glarus, I went into the stall to find Abibaal sitting in the corner, his helmet discarded on the ground next to him.

'Great race,' I said. 'What a last turn.'

'I lost. I was terrible.'

'Don't be so hard on yourself. You recovered from a difficult position and you got second place. That's good race-craft.'

'Second place is losing. Would you be happy with second? Would Papa? And why do I always have to lose to Hanno?'

'You'll beat him one day. Soon, in fact. You're going to be a great driver, Abibaal.'

His answer was to get to his feet and kick at the soiled straw bedding. Unfortunately, he wasn't to know there was a hoof-pick lying in it. It flew like a slingshot and almost hit Scorpus in the eye as he came into the stall. The sympathetic look on his face vanished, replaced by a thunderous stare.

'Is this what you're going to be like, after every race? Go and congratulate your brother right now.'

Abibaal's face was red. He stormed past his father. A muscle pulsed in Scorpus's cheek.

'He didn't mean it,' I said. 'I'm sure he'll talk to Hanno; he'll get over it.'

'He's got to learn how to lose. I'm not having

him turn out like Nicias, thinking that he's owed the win just because he wants it.'

'Well,' I said after a pause, 'I suppose I'd better get out there myself.'

'Have you got your knife?'

I patted the front pocket of my breastplate which stored the curved blade I would use to cut myself free of the reins in case of a shipwreck.

'Hopefully I won't need it.'

Scorpus shook his head.

'I'm not sure this is a good idea. Glarus said he's had another visit from someone sniffing around for information about the princess.'

I hesitated, but only for a moment.

'All the more reason for me to get out there and throw sand in their eyes. Parmenion's right. If Porcellus isn't going to be like an animal in a cage for the rest of his life, we have to be able to hide him in plain sight of everyone. I've got my race plan worked out. I'm not going for the win. I'll hold them back so that we finish somewhere in the middle of the pack. That should mean no one gets suspicious.'

'Just as long as you're sure and as long as Porcellus agrees to that too. I know you and that horse have a special bond, Dido, but he's a strong-willed animal, remember. He might not like the idea of racing to lose.'

'Well, neither do I. But Porcellus will do what I tell him.'

Scorpus nodded.

'I'd better go and find that stubborn son of mine. See you on the track. Good luck.'

I headed to the warm-up area, where Parmenion was waiting with the horses. It was Jewel's first race. In a month, she'd picked up the art of chariot racing faster than any horse I'd trained. I was excited to put her to the test and to finally get the chance to drive Porcellus before a circus crowd.

As I passed the other stalls, I sensed some of the charioteers from rival stables were watching me. Just as I'd expected, there were a lot of nudges and several mocking looks. An apprentice from Glarus's stable, whom I had beaten in my last race as Leon, before Otho bought me to race for the Blues in Rome, shouted as I went past.

'So you're back. Circus Maximus spat you out, hey?'

I ground my teeth but said nothing.

'What happened to that little blue roan of yours?' taunted my opponent. 'I heard he didn't make it. Didn't have the heart for the big races either, maybe.'

I was prepared for them making fun of me. But the insult to Icarus was too much. Rage flooded my veins, turning my blood hot. I was about to turn round and say something. But the words died on my lips.

A horribly familiar figure had stepped into my path. A small brute of a person with a thick neck and canine jaw. One sleeve of his green tunic hung flat and empty against his torso.

'Well, well, well,' said Scylax. 'We meet again, Leon of the Blues.'

VI

Numbness crept through my body as I gazed at him. Scylax looked heavier and unhealthier than when he'd been one of the top charioteers for the Greens. His skin was grey and he was chewing something tucked inside his cheek, like a cow with toothache.

'So this is where you ended up,' he said, brown spittle escaping his lips. 'Scurried back home to your local track with your tail between your legs, did you?'

I didn't answer. Something strange was happening to me. My heart was beating loudly. I felt as if I was about to be sick. Suddenly my surroundings dissolved and instantly reformed. I was back in the Circus Maximus, surrounded by heat and noise. It was my last race as Leon, the race that changed everything. Pain was ripping through my body, sand was being kicked into my face, filling my lungs. I was being dragged along the track, tethered to my bolting horses by the reins wrapped around my waist. As I slashed at them with the curved blade of my knife, I saw Scylax peering at me over the side of his chariot, his eyes narrowed in murderous concentration. One of his horses' hooves struck my flailing legs and I heard myself cry out. Then a shadow flitted across the sand as Parmenion leaped from his own chariot into Scylax's. They started to struggle. Wildly, I swiped at the reins again and felt the blade sever the leather. The last thing I heard before hitting the ground was the sound of a crash. Then nothing… until I opened my eyes and saw the body of my darling Icarus lying broken on the track up ahead. I felt as if I was disappearing into a long black tunnel. Terrible screams echoed through my head. Were they mine? Or were they Scylax's, down in the medical cells below the Circus afterwards?

Scylax's mean voice was grating like the teeth of a saw. I snapped back into the present.

'… ruined my career, you and that friend of yours. You have any idea what it's like to have a surgeon's scalpel hacking through your own flesh and bone? I can still feel it, you know.' He flexed the stump of his arm beneath his tunic, still chewing viciously.

A steward with a tablet in his hand came running up.

'Aren't you in the next race?' he said to me, checking his tablet. 'Leon and lead horse, Jewel. Come on, hurry up, they're waiting for you.'

He was about to scurry off again, but Scylax stopped him.

'Have you sorted out those front row seats I asked for? I'm here in an official capacity, I'll have you know, head racing scout for the Green faction. Got my authority from the emperor himself, see?' He produced a roll of papyrus, bound with a wax disc, and waved it in the face of the steward, before turning back to me, savage hatred in his eyes.

'Don't think *you'll* ever get a second chance at the Circus Maximus. Not with the Greens, anyway. Emperor Caligula wouldn't want me wasting his money on some washed-up Blues driver. But you tell your trainer he can be sure of a visit from me in a day or two. I'm expecting a good welcome from all the stables around here, and trainers who are prepared to sell their horses to the Greens at the right price. Make sure you pass the message to Scorpus.'

He spat and the contents of his mouth landed in a regurgitated mess on the ground. Then he lurched away towards the spectator stands.

I looked at the bare skin of my arms. It felt as if a swarm of wasps was crawling all over my body, creeping under the surface of my flesh. Somewhere in the distance, I heard the race officials shouting for me.

Porcellus greeted me with an ear-shattering whinny which drew amused looks from the surrounding spectators. Jewel was chewing placidly on her bit. She and Porcellus and my two yoke horses were all beautifully turned out, with glossy coats and long blue ribbons plaited into their manes and tails.

'He's pretty full of pepper,' said Parmenion, struggling to keep Porcellus still. 'You'd better make sure he doesn't out-jump the other three at the start.' He looked at me curiously. 'Anything the matter?'

'No. I'm fine,' I heard myself say and took the reins from him, hoping that he didn't notice my hands were trembling.

'Good. Remember. Wipe the smiles off those idiots' faces.' He patted Porcellus before winking at me and stepping back.

Almost blindly, I drove to the warm-up track. As I'd planned, Jewel drew a lot of attention from the spectators. There were unkind comments about her one eye. Porcellus's ears were pricked. He seemed happy and excited to know he was about to race again and to feel my hand on his reins. But confusion raged in my head. Should I back out? If there was one person in the crowd that day who was going to see through Porcellus's disguise, it was Scylax. He had seen him every day in his marble stall at the Greens' clubhouse. On the other hand, if Scylax was planning on visiting our stables, the danger was just as great. He'd be bound to ask to see Porcellus put through his paces, along with our other horses. What if he wanted to buy him for the Greens and got suspicious when Scorpus refused to sell?

'Charioteers to the gates!'

I had to make the decision quickly. Heart thumping, I steered Porcellus to the starting gate.

Just do what you planned, lose the race and Scylax won't guess it's him. It's your best chance.

But as I lined up alongside the other teams, I realised it wasn't Porcellus I was thinking about. I couldn't get the image of Icarus's lifeless body out of my head. A trumpet sounded, making me jump.

'Charioteers, ready?' yelled the starter over the noise of the crowd as he raised his flag. The boys holding the six gates shut prepared to leap aside. I crouched in my usual starting position, legs braced in preparation for the sudden acceleration and

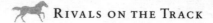

gripping the reins. Then I realised that the leather was sliding between my fingers. My palms were damp with sweat.

The starter's flag dropped.

VII

The wind blew hot on my face as the chariots launched across the start line. I tasted dirt on my tongue as the horses' hooves churned up the track, and felt the wheels picking up speed under my feet. But for the first time in my life, I didn't get a thrill from it. It was as if I was a child waking from sleep to discover myself in unfamiliar and frightening surroundings. The crowd was sliding past me so fast. Instinctively, I found myself doing the correct things with my hands and feet, squeezing the reins at the right moment so that we took the first turn in style, Porcellus well up to the bit, Jewel's feet dancing around the posts like a satyr's hooves.

On the second lap, the field started to spread out. Glarus's apprentice edged into the lead, glancing behind to track where I was. I held my team back, settling into fifth place. It was a new experience, deliberately racing to lose, and there was a voice inside my head protesting that only cheats did this. But my heart was still fluttering strangely around my chest, like a bird trapped in a cage, and I found myself grateful for the opportunity to slow down. I knew the spectators wouldn't suspect anything was wrong at this stage. I was known for making my run late, waiting until the final laps before I started to overtake the other teams.

Porcellus wasn't used to the tactic, though. When he was the number one racehorse for the Greens, he was used to going straight to the front and staying there. Seeing four other chariots ahead of him, he snorted and started to pull.

'Steady, boy,' I muttered. 'Steady.'

We approached the turn into the third lap. The field was bunching again and I tightened my grip on the reins to ensure we didn't run into the back of the chariot in front. Porcellus tossed his head impatiently and the leather slipped straight through my fingers. There was an intake of breath from the crowd as Jewel stumbled, almost landing on her knees. I hauled her up and managed to get my four back into a rhythm. But I couldn't shake off my encounter with Scylax. It was making my arms and legs feel heavy and numb.

As we caught up to the fifth-placed charioteer, the crowd started to cheer. 'Leon! Leon!'

I blinked rapidly. That buzzing sound was in my ears again. My opponent glanced back and moved towards the channel, clearly expecting me to try to overtake him on the inside. I hesitated, torn between my instinct to make the pass and another voice urging caution.

Then something jolted me. The driver behind had caught up and rammed the corner of my chariot. My wheels skittered off course as the other two charioteers fought for position. I was now in last place. Porcellus started straining again, eager to show off his pace and fighting against my attempts to hold him in check. Once again, Jewel almost tripped.

The crowd screeched and I flinched at the noise. The two chariots ahead of me had collided on the sharp turn into the fifth lap. One driver managed to stay on his feet and kept his team going. The other was hanging off the back of his chariot, his legs scrabbling to find a foothold. He grabbed at his knife to cut himself free of his reins. I swerved past his bolting horses and caught a glimpse of his eyes as he sawed frantically. The leather coil around my own waist seemed to tighten. I couldn't breathe.

With clear sand in front of him, Porcellus stretched out his nose gleefully, trying to drag his three teammates with him. Thinking that I was at last making my move, the crowd was cheering again. Their faces bled into one, like colours running down a damp wall-painting.

'Leon! Leon!'

My temples were throbbing. The last time I'd heard that chant, it had been Icarus whose pricked ears were directly ahead of me, his ashen mane dancing along the crest of his silver-blue neck…

The reins went slack in my hands.

'Porcellus,' I croaked, 'slow down. Please, slow down.'

Maybe he understood the fear in my voice. Or maybe the feel of the reins slack across his back told him something was wrong. Either way, the chariot slowed and the other three horses followed Porcellus's lead. To anyone watching, it must have looked like that burst of acceleration had taken the speed out of their legs. The chants of 'Leon' gradually stopped and I sensed the disappointment in the crowd as we fell towards the back of the field.

Somehow, I stayed upright for the final two laps. The pressure on my lungs had eased. With a shaking hand, I even cracked my whip over my team's heads once or twice to make it look as if I was trying to win. Jewel took her lead from Porcellus, who kept the pace steady. I was dimly aware of Glarus's apprentice taking the victory on the other side of the track and milking the applause of the crowd. He caught up with me after I crossed the line in last place.

'Good race. Look forward to the next one,' he said with a smirk. 'I guess we learned a few things around here while you were away racing with the big boys.'

As I followed the other beaten charioteers out of the arena, I spotted Scylax in the front row reserved for the most important spectators. He was talking to someone next to him and as I drove past, he shook his head mockingly.

Back at the stables, I told Parmenion I could unharness my team myself. As I slipped the bridle off his head, I kissed Porcellus gently on the cheek.

'Thank you,' I whispered.

But even the understanding blink of his dark brown eyes couldn't do anything to soothe the confusion raging inside my head.

'It's so annoying you had to lose,' complained Abibaal. 'You could have beaten any of those charioteers easily if you'd wanted to, Dido.'

It was the second time since we'd set off from Utica for home that he'd said it. When he repeated himself moments later, I lost my temper.

'Give it a rest, will you,' I snapped.

Abibaal looked hurt. He and Hanno still weren't speaking either. For the next half mile there was a subdued atmosphere as we led the horses along the road.

'Rain coming,' said Parmenion, breaking the silence and nodding to the dark clouds on the horizon. 'Better hope we get home before it sets in.'

Ahead of us, Scorpus was driving the wagon with the chariots. I'd already told him about seeing Scylax, but not about what had happened during the race. I hoped I'd be able to sit down with him after supper without the boys around. Maybe he would be able to explain the strange feelings I'd had. But as our convoy turned off the road down the long farm track, Anna came out of the house to meet us. She was flustered and had clearly been waiting for our arrival.

'Master Scorpus, there's someone here to see you. He arrived this afternoon and he has been waiting. I made sure he had some refreshment.'

She gestured towards the end of the porch. A man was sitting in one of the chairs there, a drinking cup on the low table next to him. For an awful moment, I thought Scylax might have beaten us back along the road from Utica. Then, as the man stood and stepped forward into the early evening light, I clutched Porcellus's rein in disbelief. Were the gods playing some strange trick on us? For it seemed as though Scorpus was now in two places at once – on the driving seat of the cart and also standing on the porch. The clothes were different, but the two faces were so alike – the same hard, piercing eyes and strong jaw, the same beard flecked with grey.

The visitor nodded.

'Scorpus.' Even his voice matched my uncle's, deep and a little sullen. 'It's been a long time. I'd like to talk, if you don't mind.'

Scorpus looked as if the shock of seeing his own reflection had made him lose the ability to speak. Then he turned to me and the boys and I saw the warning look in his eyes.

'Hanno, Abibaal… Leon.' He stressed my name slightly as he said it. 'Meet your Uncle Barca. My brother.'

VIII

I t felt like hours since anyone had spoken. A light
breeze plucked at the wind chimes which swung
from the tiled edge of the porch roof. The heat
was dense and there was a smell of rain in the air.
Thunder rumbled angrily over the horizon. I could
feel the sweat pooling under the bandages wrapped
tightly around my chest. In his usual chair to my left,
Scorpus was pushing vegetables around in the broth
in his bowl, his spoon scraping the red earthenware.

'An excellent soup,' said Barca. 'My compliments
to your daughter, Scorpus.'

Anna, who was going around the table offering
second helpings, looked uncertainly at Scorpus. But
it was Hanno who came to her rescue.

'Anna's not our sister,' he explained. 'She's
married to Antigonus. He's Papa's assistant.'

'Forgive my mistake,' said Barca. 'I'm
embarrassed not to know my own brother's family

better.' His searching eyes came to rest on me. 'I must confess, Scorpus, that word had reached us down the years, via our mutual friend Otho of the Blue faction, that your wife had given you two sons. I was unaware until now of the existence of a third.'

I looked apprehensively at Scorpus. How would he explain the fact that I looked so similar to both him and the boys? Scorpus took his time wiping his mouth with his napkin before speaking.

'Leon is half-brother to Hanno and Abibaal,' he grunted. 'I knew his mother before I married theirs. He came looking for me, about a year ago, and when I saw his skill with a chariot, I was happy to accept him as my son.'

His eyes flickered around the rest of the table as if to say, 'Play along.'

Barca's expression cleared.

'Ah. That explains it. And also why I heard him call you Scorpus before. I suppose the relationship is still new to you both. Good of you to take the boy in. I hope you'll meet my own children one day soon.' He took a sip from his cup, peering over the top of it at Scorpus as he did so. 'Ismene asked me to send you her regards, by the way.'

Scorpus nodded, still digging through his soup.

'Who's Ismene?' asked Abibaal, unable to

suppress his curiosity. 'And why haven't we ever met *you* before, Uncle Barca?'

'Ismene is my wife, which makes her your aunt. As for why we haven't met, well, that's a good question. I suppose it's because Thugga is some way away and your father and I are both very busy running our stables.'

'Are you a trainer, then?'

'I am. In fact, I still manage the stable where your father and I grew up.'

'Were you a charioteer too?' asked Abibaal eagerly. 'Did you race at the Circus Maximus like Papa?'

Barca smiled, thinly, I thought.

'No. I was never quite good enough to get to the Circus Maximus. Your father was always the star charioteer in our family. I'm three years his senior so I used to have the beating of him when we were young. But after his first victory over me, he never let me win again.'

Abibaal grinned at his brother across the table. 'You hear that, Hanno? You'd better watch out.'

Scorpus pushed his bowl away, so forcibly that some of the broth spilled over the side. Barca picked up his napkin to mop away the sweat that had gathered in the deep furrows on his forehead. I noticed that his fingernails were gnawed down to the flesh. Raindrops had started to fall softly on the porch roof.

'I'm sure you must be wondering what brings me here, brother,' said Barca. 'What has it been? Fifteen years?'

'Something like that,' said Scorpus. His face was like a rock.

'It's difficult to know the best way to begin in these circumstances. But I have news you deserve to know, and so do your sons. I came to tell you that our father is ill. I'm not sure he has another winter in him.'

My eyes flew to Scorpus. Hanno and Abibaal were looking at their father too.

'But, I don't understand,' said Hanno, clearly puzzled. 'I thought Grandpa Muttumbaal was dead already. You told us he was, Papa.'

Barca looked shocked. Scorpus drummed his fingers on the table. I stared accusingly at him and saw guilt on his face, as well as anger.

'Ever since he decided to disown my sister and forbade us even to mention her name, he's been dead to me. That's all that needs to concern anyone else.'

'It was a question of honour, Scorpus,' said Barca, an edge to his voice. 'You were the one who came back from Rome and told us what our sister had been doing after she ran away from home. Performing horse-riding tricks in the Circus Maximus, for public entertainment. How is that a decent way for any female to behave?'

The silence was punctured only by the rapid patter of the rain over our heads and the gentle lament of the wind chimes. In the face of Scorpus's scrutiny, Barca seemed to flinch. He took a long drink of water.

'I'm sorry. I didn't come here to rake up an old family quarrel. As I said, our father is very sick. But the business he built is also in trouble. You don't need me to remind you, Scorpus, that the factions at Rome used to pay a fortune for any animal trained by Muttumbaal of Thugga. But with the emperor so keen on the sport, the demand in Rome for horses to race at the Circus Maximus is greater than it has ever been. There are trainers with half the skill of our father, but they'll also sell their horses for half the price. You must have run into this problem yourself, Scorpus.'

'I'm not as stubborn as my father. I take what I can get to make a living and look after my family.'

'I am of the same view as you, brother. But you know our father. We used to joke that if you cut his veins, they would bleed blue. He has always refused to sell to anyone other than Otho. But now the

Blues have a new faction master, one who favours Spanish horses. We are running out of money and if things don't change, we'll have to sell up after he dies. Leaving me with nothing to pass on to my children.'

Scorpus was silent. Barca leaned forward.

'Have you heard about the new circus being built at Thugga?'

'Perhaps.'

'It's magnificent, Scorpus. It will rival the Circus Maximus itself when it's finished, mark my words. The man building it is Gemellus Glabrio, a friend of the emperor. He's planning circus games in August to mark the opening of the stadium in time for Caligula's birthday. But they won't be like any games you or I have ever seen before, Scorpus.'

He produced a large piece of papyrus and spread it on the table. Hanno and Abibaal got up and went to stand on either side of their uncle so that they could get a proper look. It was the race programme I'd seen Glarus and the bounty hunter looking at in Utica.

'That's what it will look like, when it's finished,' said Barca, tracing his finger around the drawing of the vast oval circus. 'Just imagine it, boys! It's to be a contest between trainers, not factions. Two full days of chariot racing and the best young drivers in Africa invited to compete. Glabrio wants new blood. There'll be scouts there from the four factions of Rome – Green, Blue, Red and White – all looking for new talent. And the prize money will be spectacular. More than you'd get at the Circus Maximus! Glabrio's fortune is enormous and he's keen to impress the emperor. On the final afternoon, the two stables with the most victories nominate their best driver and their best team of horses. One race. Two charioteers. Winner takes all.'

'How much is all?'

'A million sesterces.'

Abibaal's jaw dropped. He turned to his father, a pleading look in his eyes, but Scorpus spoke before his son could.

'Tell me once and for all what it is that you want me to do for you, Barca.'

Barca folded up the race programme.

'I want you to come to Thugga and join forces with us for the games,' he said bluntly. 'We have great horses at our stable. Easily good enough for the Circus Maximus. Our father has lost none of his skills as a trainer. But we had to sell our last apprentice driver several months ago when there wasn't any money left to pay for his upkeep. My son, Bodo, shows promise but he's inexperienced.

We need your help, Scorpus, and we need your
sons. Bring them, bring your best horses too and
help restore our family's fortunes before Papa dies
and it's too late.'

IX

The storm broke in the night and didn't wear itself out until the early hours. As the rain pummelled the roof tiles, I lay awake, huddled under my blankets, only drifting off as the dawn light began to seep into the room.

When I woke, I realised I was late for my morning stable duties and hurried outside. Dark blue clouds were retreating into the distance, but the air was still soft and damp with the promise of more rain. Anna's honeybees were emerging from their hive to peer at their reflection in the surrounding pools of water. In the pasture, most of the horses were still under shelter. I spied Porcellus with Sciron below a dripping tree and was pleased to see that the black dye on his forehead was holding. Jewel was grazing quietly not too far from them.

The stable block appeared deserted and the hatch door that led to Parmenion's quarters was closed.

He had gone to Utica last night to see his friends at the tavern and was probably hoping I'd cover up for his absence this morning. He'd be in trouble if Scorpus found out. I was about to go and start sorting out the feed when I heard a noise in the harness room and discovered Scorpus with one of the racing chariots tipped on its side in front of him. He was repairing the base, using a sharp needle to re-stitch the frayed leather strapping. I felt his eyes rest heavily on me as I took a stool next to him, but I deliberately ignored him. Picking up a pile of reins, discarded after the races at Utica yesterday, I started to clean off the dust with a cloth.

'I'm sorry, Dido.' Scorpus's voice was rough with lack of sleep. 'I should have told you. I suppose I've spent so long pretending that he was dead that I'd almost convinced myself it was true.' He set the chariot upright and tested the stitching with his own weight.

'Do I have any other relatives I should know about?' I asked, not bothering to keep the sarcasm out of my voice.

'No. Your grandmother's dead. It would have been much harder for me to cut myself off from the family if she was still alive. But a sickness took her.'

I used my fingernail to pick some dirt from a buckle on the reins.

'When my papa was killed,' I said, getting the words out with difficulty, 'when I realised I'd never see him again, it was the worst day of my life. I suppose it isn't easy for me to understand how it wouldn't be the same for someone else.'

Scorpus was silent for a moment.

'Not everyone's lucky enough to have as good a father as Antonius was to you.'

He turned the chariot on its side again and began to examine the linchpins. I saw the guilt and pain in his eyes and I felt my heart soften.

'Didn't you and he ever get on?' I asked. 'You and Muttumbaal, I mean?'

Scorpus nodded.

'There were times when we did. I thought he was like a god, when I was a boy. He never showed us much affection, but he could handle the most difficult horse. Barca was right. All the factions tried to buy from him, everyone wanted their horses trained by him. He was a brilliant charioteer too; he had a great career at the Circus Maximus. But he wasn't a good father. I sometimes worry I'm turning into him.'

I was still cross with him, but I wasn't going to let that go.

'Don't be silly. You've raised Hanno and Abibaal by yourself after your wife died; you're wonderful with them.'

'I'm not so sure. I worry that I'm hard on Abibaal because I see a lot of myself in him. I used to lose my temper when I lost a race, just like he did yesterday. Your grandfather once thrashed me for it.'

'But you wouldn't do that. Besides, Muttumbaal could be sorry now for the way things turned out between you. Why else would he send your brother here to ask for your help? Are you sure you don't want to go back home and find out?'

'No. It's too late. I sent Barca away this morning. That sob story about not being able to pass the stable on to his children didn't fool me. I know what he and Papa are up to.'

'What do you mean? No more secrets, remember.'

Scorpus sighed, nodded and picked up a cloth to clean the wheels of the chariot.

'Years ago, my father was great friends with another trainer. A man named Zeno. They were Circus rivals in their youth but they liked and respected each other. Zeno bought the land next to our stable and our families were close growing up. But that all fell apart when Sophonisba ran away to Rome.'

'Why?'

Scorpus flipped the wheel, watching it spin.

'Because Zeno was the man your mother was supposed to marry.'

I blinked in surprise. I'd always known the reason for my mother's escape from Thugga to Rome. But I'd never really pictured the man she'd rejected, the man her father had chosen for her.

'How did that make Zeno and Muttumbaal fall out?'

'Zeno was a widower. He had one child, a daughter – Ismene – who was a good friend of Sophonisba's. But Zeno was always desperate for sons to carry on his racing business. So when Sophonisba turned fifteen, my father suggested her as a bride.'

'And didn't even give Mama a choice? Zeno was so much older than her.'

'Yes,' admitted Scorpus. 'It's not so unusual, you know. There's not much for a girl to do except get married once she's at a certain age. It's different for men.'

I made a face. 'It's still unfair.'

'Well, Sophonisba felt the same way you did. She begged not to have go through with it, but my father wouldn't listen. When she ran away the day before the wedding, Zeno was humiliated. He accused Muttumbaal of failing to rear a dutiful daughter and demanded the bride price she would have brought to the marriage. My father was furious with Sophonisba for what she'd done. But he wouldn't accept the insult to his family and he refused to pay. It was war between him and Zeno from that day on.'

'So these circus games aren't just going to be about which stable wins. It'll be about settling an old score?'

'Exactly.' Scorpus nodded. 'I'm not getting involved.'

I picked up another length of harness for cleaning, sifting through everything in my mind as I worked.

'You said Ismene, Zeno's daughter, was friends with Mama. Is she the same Ismene who's married to Uncle Barca?'

The wheels of the chariot rattled violently as Scorpus set it upright.

'Yes. Their wedding was arranged when they were young, before the two families fell out. After Sophonisba ran away, Zeno wanted Ismene to divorce Barca. Ismene wouldn't do it. She felt her loyalty should be to her husband's family.'

I heard a strange tightness in his voice. But I had too many questions to make room for another.

'Did Zeno find himself another wife?' I asked.

'He did, and got the sons he always wanted into the bargain. Barca was telling me this morning, before he left, that the eldest, Danel, is the finest young charioteer he's ever seen. If Barca thinks that, you can trust his judgement. That's why he's so desperate to recruit you, Dido. He'd heard all about Leon of Utica, the wonder boy who raced for the Blues in Rome. He's hoping you might be able to beat Danel.'

I felt a thud of dread in my heart. *No more secrets.*

'Scorpus, there's something I need to tell you. About what happened yesterday, in my race.'

Haltingly, I explained what had happened after I saw Scylax – the numbness, the buzzing in my ears, the image of Icarus's death repeating in my head. Scorpus stopped working and listened. When I had finished, he reached to squeeze my hand.

'I'm sorry, Dido. I thought you didn't seem yourself afterwards. I should have realised something like that might happen.'

'Why?' I tried to laugh, but it came out shakily. 'I don't understand. I was looking forward to the race so much. I was ready! I didn't have any of those feelings when I drove my big race as the princess in the Circus Maximus and that was after Icarus died.'

'But you hadn't seen Scylax since the accident, had you?'

'No. What difference would that make?'

'All those months of training we did afterwards at Otho's villa, you were focused on winning and taking revenge on the emperor, for Icarus and for your father. That drove you. I expect you tried everything you could not to think about what happened to Icarus, didn't you? But seeing Scylax yesterday brought it all back.'

My stomach lurched. I knew there was truth in what he said.

'Do you think it'll happen again?'

Scorpus's answer didn't come at once.

'I don't know,' he said. 'I felt something like you describe, after Sophonisba's accident. Seeing her body lying on the track, I knew I'd never be able to race in the Circus Maximus again. I tried a few times at the games in Utica, when I was setting up my stable here and I couldn't afford apprentices. But somehow, I'd lost the burning desire to win that I'd always had. It didn't seem important any more.'

I let his words sink in. A month ago, I hadn't been sure when, or if, I wanted to race again. Now I had a glimpse of what it might be like to have the choice taken from me. It terrified me. Who would I be, if I wasn't a charioteer?

Scorpus ruffled my hair.

'Let's not despair yet, Dido. A lot of charioteers have thoughts like this after a bad shipwreck. It's known as seasickness. But it usually passes, with time. Maybe that's all you need. Come on, let's go and feed those horses.'

As we were mixing buckets of oats and wheat bran in the feed room, I thought about the other problem facing us.

'If Scylax comes here today or tomorrow like he said, wanting to buy horses for the Greens, what are you going to do?'

'If he offers the right price, I'll have to sell to him. I'm sorry, Dido. It sticks in my gullet after what he did to you. But I haven't got many other choices if I can't sell to the Blues any more. The Reds and the Whites don't send many scouts this way. Unlike my father, I won't destroy my sons' inheritance for the sake of pride. I realise that doesn't solve the problem about how we make sure Scylax doesn't recognise Porcellus, though.'

'I know. I thought about going off with him somewhere for a few days. But then we're out in the open and anyone could see us and get suspicious. If we stay here, though, I'm worried Porcellus might attack Scylax if he sees him. He's bound to remember him from when he was with the Greens.'

Scorpus looked thoughtful.

'There is something we could do. But you won't like it.'

We both heard whistling and looked up to see Parmenion weaving down the pebble track that led to the stable from the road. Scorpus looked grim.

'Don't be too hard on him,' I pleaded. 'He's in pain, Scorpus. And you said yourself, people go through strange things after a bad shipwreck.'

'I did say it and I can forgive him for what's in his head. But not for how stubborn he's being, refusing to take advice.'

'He saved me from Scylax, remember. I'd be dead if it wasn't for him. And his dream of glory has been destroyed because of it. Sometimes, I worry that...'

'What?' asked Scorpus.

But I bit back the words on the tip of my tongue and instead said, 'Even if his leg doesn't get better, you won't let him go, will you? He can stay and work for you?'

'Of course. But he needs to face up to his responsibilities. Maybe he doesn't have a future in chariot racing. That doesn't mean he's got no future at all.'

I wasn't so sure. Now that I knew what it meant to face giving up on the only life I'd ever wanted to live, I understood much better how Parmenion felt.

X

'Papa! Papa!'
It was Hanno who alerted us to the danger. Parmenion and I were training in the small lunging paddock. He and Scorpus had talked after his late return from Utica. It was a difficult conversation but it ended with Parmenion agreeing to stop drinking and to follow Scorpus's rules for rebuilding the strength in his leg. I suspected that Parmenion didn't know himself whether he could keep his promise. But I'd offered to help and was now holding one end of a long set of reins while Parmenion used the other for support as he squatted and then straightened again, before repeating the exercise. He was sweating and cursing with the effort. Then we both heard Hanno's yell, which brought Scorpus out of the stables. Three horsemen were riding down the long pebble track to the farm.

Scorpus hurried over to us.

'Here we go,' he said. 'Parmenion, up that ladder into the barn and keep out of sight, as we agreed. Go on, it's for your own safety.'

Scorpus hurried away to greet his unwelcome guests. Parmenion lingered, staring keenly at the distant figure of Scylax. The look in his eye worried me.

'Go on, Parmenion,' I said. 'You won't help Scorpus if you pick a fight.'

I went to join Antigonus by the gate to the paddock where we usually trotted up horses for Otho and other buyers. We watched as Scylax dismounted and motioned to the men on either side of him to do the same. They wore sword belts and had stony faces and thick arms.

'Who are those two with him, do you think?' I asked Antigonus.

'Third Legion soldiers, by the look of them. I imagine they're here to persuade anyone who doesn't like the prices Scylax is offering.'

I glanced anxiously into the pasture. Porcellus was standing under a tree next to Sciron, his head hanging, looking listless. It had broken my heart to watch him eat the feed Scorpus had given him, knowing what was in it. But as Scorpus told me, it was the only way. 'Opium,' he'd said. 'My father taught me how to use it on a horse that needs sedating and, whatever else I might say about him, he knew more about herbs and their effect on horses than any vet. Porcellus might be sleepy for a while, Dido, but it won't hurt him.'

I still felt as though I'd betrayed him.

Scorpus brought Scylax into our yard. He was chewing, just as he had been in Utica.

'So this is where Otho came to buy horses for the Blues. Not much of a place, is it? But then Otho wasn't much of a businessman. Suppose you heard he had to sell up and get out of Rome. Course you have. Wouldn't be so desperate to do business with the Greens otherwise, would you?'

Scorpus said nothing. Scylax's eyes lighted on me.

'There he is. The reason I'm here with you instead of at the Circus Maximus, where I belong.' He laughed unpleasantly. 'Still, we're all charioteers. We know the rules of the game. Accidents happen. No hard feelings.'

But I could see the venom in his eyes.

'Where's the other one?' he said. 'Tawny-haired lad with a mouth on him. He was one of yours too, or so I heard.'

'Not now,' replied Scorpus. 'His leg didn't heal and I'm not interested in carrying dead weight. I let him go.'

Scylax nodded in approval. Scorpus snapped his fingers at me.

'Leon. Don't just stand there. Fetch our guests some refreshment.'

He gave me a meaningful look and I took the hint. As I headed to the kitchen to alert Anna, I glanced anxiously into the pasture again. Sciron was gnawing on Porcellus's mane, as if trying to wake him up. Porcellus blinked and looked reproachfully at me.

When I returned to the stables, the boys were trotting horses up and down in front of Scylax. Scorpus introduced each one, listing their circus victories and talking up their strengths. It was difficult to think of Cupid, Psyche, Misty and Storm – good friends all of them – going to race for the Greens. But this was the business, and I knew I couldn't get sentimental about it. What mattered was Scorpus making the right deal. Scylax sat in a folding chair, propping his dirty sandals on a footstool. He chewed and spat out the contents of his mouth, barking orders as if we were slaves. Every now and then he said something to one of the silent soldiers, who scratched a note on a tablet.

Anna emerged from the kitchen with a plate of honey cakes and a wine jar. I didn't like the way the soldiers looked at her as she crossed the yard and was glad Antigonus was at the other end of the paddock.

'Sweet things from a sweet lady.' Scylax winked at Scorpus as Anna set the food down. 'That's good salesmanship. Can't stand most of what passes for food around these parts.' He poured himself a large measure of raisin wine and drank it in a gulp. As his eyes wandered lazily around his surroundings, they came to rest on Porcellus.

'Saw that horse yesterday, didn't I? Came in last.' He shot me a malicious glance.

'Yes,' said Scorpus. 'I bought him a year or so back, but he's not been as promising as I'd hoped.'

'Not surprised. Looks like he's about to fall asleep. What you going to use him for now, pulling a cart?'

He laughed and as the sound drifted across the yard, Porcellus's head lifted. His cloudy gaze focused on Scylax and a menacing rumble rippled from his belly. Scylax heard it and he sat up straight, his expression suddenly keen. I exchanged an anguished glance with Scorpus. At that moment, Sciron started nibbling on Porcellus's mane and his black head drooped again, as if a fog of sleep had blown into his face. Scylax leaned back in his chair, the suspicion in his eyes fading as quickly as it had dawned.

'Well, I've seen enough.' He let out a loud burp. 'Let's talk business. You can have thirty thousand apiece for the roans, another thirty thousand each for the dark greys and I'll take that team of chestnuts for eighty thousand.'

Two hundred thousand sesterces. It was less than half what the horses were worth, barely more than Scorpus had paid for them as untrained colts at the market in Carthage.

'Those chestnuts are some of my best stock,' said Scorpus. I could tell he was working to keep the rage out of his voice.

A smile played around the edges of Scylax's mouth. He picked at his back teeth with a dirty fingernail.

'I like you, my friend. You're hospitable. So I'm going to be generous. Two hundred and fifty thousand for the lot – payable on delivery at the docks in Utica – and don't push your luck. It's the best you're going to do.' He detached the scroll with the imperial seal from his belt and waved it as if making practice sweeps with the blade of a dagger. 'Just remember, it's the emperor of Rome you're going to be upsetting if you don't make this deal with me.'

The two soldiers watched Scorpus closely. Finally, he nodded. Scylax poured another measure of wine.

'Let's have a drink. To new business.' He nodded dismissively at the silent soldiers. 'You two, back to Utica and tell them to make room for eight more horses on the transport boat. I'll follow later.'

But an hour after the soldiers had left, Scylax was still there. He had finished the wine and wolfed the food Anna had brought, but he was still talking and showing no sign of leaving. Scorpus had no choice but to invite him to stay for supper. They ate alone on the porch while Anna fed the boys and I in the kitchen. When I'd finished, I crept along to the atrium where I could see them through the gap in the door.

'You used to race at the Circus Maximus, didn't you?' said Scylax with a loud belch. 'Back in Emperor Tiberius's day? That neighbour of yours, Glarus, he mentioned you had.'

'Yes. I didn't last long though,' replied Scorpus.

'Well, most don't. Takes a special sort of something, in here, you know?' Scylax banged on his chest with his knuckles. 'You still think about it?'

'The Circus? I don't know.'

'Come on.' Scylax squinted at my uncle. 'You hear the noise of that crowd in your sleep sometimes. Admit it.'

There was a pause.

'Maybe,' said Scorpus, thoughtfully. 'I suppose you have to find a purpose for yourself afterwards. You can't go on living a young man's dream. But it can be hard. Knowing you'll never get to drink from that cup again.'

'I know what you mean.' Scylax nodded as if he really felt Scorpus's words. 'Never saw myself doing anything else, not since I was a lad. I was on my way to becoming the best, you know, before the accident that lost me this arm. Who knows... might even have taken over as the Greens' number one someday...'

His voice trailed off. The wind chimes rippled. Scylax downed his wine and set the cup down with a snap.

'I'll tell you this for certain,' he said. 'If I had got to the top, you can bet I wouldn't have lost to that girl. The one calling herself a princess.'

'Oh. Yes,' Scorpus sounded vague. 'I've seen some of the reward posters in town. All seems very mysterious.'

Scylax toyed with the cup, rolling the base along the table.

'Haven't told anyone what I know about that business.' He was slurring his words now as the wine caught his tongue. 'But I reckon the reward money's the least I deserve, after what happened to me. Just following team orders and look what I get for it.' He tugged angrily at the empty sleeve of his tunic.

'I'm intrigued. What's this information of yours that's going to win you the money?'

The wood creaked under Scylax's weight as he leaned forward to whisper to Scorpus.

'The girl. I know who she is.'

XI

There was a long silence, broken only by the clink of the wind chimes. I was scared to breathe in case they heard me.

'After the race, see, I was up in the Greens sanatorium,' continued Scylax. He was babbling now, excited to share his secret. 'My arm was bleeding again and it needed tying up. They brought Nicias in while I was there; you know, the driver she beat. Bloody mess, he was. The emperor went for him right there in the Circus, you know, after he lost to her. He was the golden boy, used to dine at the palace sometimes. But Caligula turns on anyone who lets him down. Nicias was muttering something, trying to tell the medics. They didn't understand him. But I was in the bed next to him and I caught it. *Dido.* Just kept repeating it over and over. *Dido. Dido.*'

I blinked, a picture of Nicias coming into my mind. Scorpus's apprentice, the boy with so much anger in his heart, who had hated me and wanted so badly to defeat me on the track.

'He croaked a few hours later,' continued Scylax. 'But by then, it had all come back to me. Her father, Antonius, was the head trainer for the Greens, see. She used to drive that horse around the practice track, pretending like she was a charioteer. I remember how she fawned over the animal. Visiting it every night, taking it treats. Apples, figs, sweet things like that. If she could, she'd probably have tucked the horse in with a blanket, like it was her doll or something.'

Scylax shook his head scornfully and emptied the rest of the wine jar into his cup.

'Still, she had some skill with the reins, no doubt about that,' he said grudgingly. 'She disappeared at the same time as her father. No one ever knew where they went, though I heard rumours the father was dead. But I talked to the old cook at the Greens' clubhouse and he remembered that young Dido was bred from some woman who used to entertain the crowd between races, before she broke her neck doing it. And – get this – the cook remembered her name. *Sophonisba.* What do you think about that?'

'Interesting. Very interesting. So what do you plan to do next?'

'That reward money's tempted a lot of bounty hunters. They're searching all over the empire for the girl. But the way I see it, I've got the inside track. I know what the wench really looks like when she's not in her princess costume. Scrappy, scrawny sort of girl with yellow hair. She'd be two years older now, but how different can she look? And if I find her before those people-scavengers do, I can take her back to Rome and collect the reward for myself.' He tapped Scorpus on the arm. 'You sure you don't know how to reach your old friend, Otho? He's disappeared, but if anyone's going to know where to start looking for her, it's him. I could share some of that money with you if you set me on the right path. We're alike, you and I. Old warriors of the track. Important we look out for each other.'

There was a pause.

'I wish I could help you,' said Scorpus. 'But I wouldn't know where to find Otho. If I hear of anything though, I'll certainly get word to you.'

'Make sure you do,' grunted Scylax. 'And you'd better not tell anyone what I said. That money's mine and I'll kill any man who tries to cheat me, you understand?' He finished his wine and swayed to his feet, stumbling slightly. 'Where's my horse?'

Scorpus called down the atrium for Hanno and told him to fetch the grey horse. Shortly after, I heard the sound of hooves.

'What the…?'

Scylax swore. I peeped around the door and, to my horror, saw that it wasn't Hanno who had brought the grey over.

'Evening,' said Parmenion, a lopsided smile on his face. 'Someone call for a horse?'

It was obvious he was even drunker than Scylax, who was now gripping the porch railing, looking as if he might spring over it. He turned to Scorpus.

'Let him go, eh?' he growled. 'You filthy liar.'

'At least he's not a filthy cheat,' said Parmenion. 'Which is more than can be said for you.'

'You did this!' shouted Scylax, jabbing at the stump under his tunic. 'You're the reason I can't race.'

'Painful, is it? I know some exercises you can do if that helps.'

That did it. Scylax went for him. Parmenion let go of the grey horse and fended off the first punch before landing one of his own. The mockery in his eyes was gone and in its place was wild anger. Then he overbalanced and tripped. Scylax was about go in with his feet, but Scorpus wrestled him away. Grabbing his horse by the reins, Scylax spat on Parmenion's leg.

'Don't think you've heard the last from me. Either of you.'

Later, long after Scylax had ridden off into the darkness, I found Scorpus in his study, doing his accounts by the light of an oil lamp, his elbow resting on the table as he stared at the tablet in front of him. Its wax surface was covered with scribbled markings from the flat-edged stilus in his hand. He looked up as the door creaked.

'Eight horses for less than half their worth,' he said. 'I'm trying to work out how many more I'd have to sell to make up for it. And thanks to that crazy young idiot Parmenion, my bridge to the Greens is now burned.'

I picked up an ink-well shaped like a chariot, fiddling with it as I watched Scorpus make a few more marks on the tablet.

'Scorpus? I think we should go to Thugga. Help your father, like your brother wanted.'

I was expecting him to dismiss the idea. Instead, he threw down the stilus and rubbed both palms over his face.

'I've been trying, but I can't think of what else to do myself. I could pray to the gods, but what do they know about running a racing stable?'

'So why don't we just go?'

'For one thing, because I built this place with my

own hands, without any help from anyone, least of all my father. I don't want to have to crawl to him on my knees and beg for his help.'

'You wouldn't be begging,' I said. 'He came to you first, remember. He needs your help as much as you need his.'

'It's complicated. There are other things that make it difficult for me to go back, things I haven't...' He stopped.

'What? More secrets. I thought we'd talked about that.'

Scorpus studied me.

'Tell me the truth, Dido. Do you want to meet him? Was I wrong to deny you the chance before?'

'I don't know if I want to meet him or not,' I said, honestly. 'I would like to see where you and Mama grew up. I never had the chance to know her. But that's not why I want to go. You've done everything for me, Scorpus. You took me in when I was lost and alone, and you gave me a home. And you encouraged me to be the person I really am. You taught me to be a charioteer. Now, this is something I can do to help you. If we win good money at those games, you'll be able to keep your business and Hanno and Abibaal will have something to inherit. I know I had a bad race in Utica, but I think you're right. I just need time to get over that.'

Scorpus was silent for a while.

'I always swore I'd never go back there… There's so much bad blood…'

I watched him stare broodingly at his scribbled sums. Then he shook his head.

'My head's too full. We don't have to decide anything right away. Let's talk about it tomorrow. Goodnight, Dido.'

As I passed Hanno and Abibaal's room, I was relieved to hear them laughing. At least they'd made up. The door between the atrium and the porch was closed. I checked that the shutters were open to allow air in then left the door to my own room ajar as I lay down on my mattress, threw off the blanket and tried to let myself drift off. But biting insects and stifling heat made sleep impossible. I went into the kitchen to retrieve the bottle of castor oil Anna kept there for repelling mosquitoes. Opening the back door, I let the night breeze cool my face for a moment, listening to the hum of the cicadas. The thud of hooves caught my ear. The horses must be agitated by the heat. Then I smelled the bitter tang of smoke.

I tore through the house, hammering first on Anna and Antigonus's door and then on Scorpus's, screaming at them to wake up before I ran outside. In the moonlight, I could see a line of horses on the pebble track leading to the road. I thought for a moment that they were escaping the smoke, wherever it was coming from. Then I realised there were men with torches leading them. I would have raced up the track to stop them. But I had already seen the molten flames licking at the space above the stables where Parmenion slept.

'Parmenion!' I shrieked. 'Parmenion!'

XII

I tried to get to the ladder that led to the hatch door. But the smoke was too thick. So I grabbed the rope pull for the bell which Scorpus used to wake up the apprentices and frantically started ringing it. Someone started coughing. Then Parmenion's confused face appeared in a gap in the timbers.

'You have to get out!' I yelled.

He disappeared. Moments later, I heard the thud of the hatch door swinging open and more coughing. There was a clattering sound followed by a howl of pain.

Covering my mouth with the neck of my tunic, I plunged into the smouldering darkness of the stable. My eyes were watering, my lungs filling. I stumbled over something. It was Parmenion, trying to drag himself across the floor. His hand grabbed for mine in panic and I started to try to haul him towards the door. But I was choking on the fumes now. To my relief, Antigonus and Scorpus arrived to help. Together, we pulled Parmenion to safety.

Gasping for breath, I clutched Scorpus by the tunic.

'The horses! They're stealing them, all of them!'

'I know, I saw.'

'Where's Porcellus? Did they take Porcellus?'

Not bothering to wait for an answer, I tore towards the pasture. Scylax was standing by the open gate with a torch in his hand, directing soldiers.

'Come on, I want every animal he's got. Don't leave him anything.'

I saw Porcellus. A soldier had managed to get a noose around his neck. He was tossing his head, trying to slip the rope. But the drug we had given him had weakened him and he didn't have the strength to fight. His grey-muzzled friend Sciron was trying to help, rearing and kicking the soldier with his front hooves like a boxer. But Sciron's best years were behind him and he was struggling to keep up the assault.

I ran towards them, thinking of nothing except stopping them from taking Porcellus, no matter what. Then, in the darkness, I heard hoofbeats, moving fast. Something red and gold streaked past me. Jewel descended on the soldiers like a vulture swooping for prey. Trying to bite them, she chased two out of the pasture. Then she sank her teeth into the arm of the soldier holding Porcellus. He howled and dropped the rope before running away.

Scylax swore.

'Crazy beast. Fine, let it go. We've got the best ones anyway.'

Leaving the gate swinging, they hurried to join the soldiers leading the other horses. Jewel and Sciron pursued them, skidding to a halt beside the gate. Sciron stood for a moment, proud and defiant as he watched his vanquished foe flee. Then, his knees suddenly buckled. Like a hulled ship slowly capsizing, he sank to the ground.

Scorpus was the first to reach him. Abibaal and Hanno caught up and we crouched around Sciron as he made a futile attempt to stand. Then, moving his nose slightly so that it rested in Scorpus's palm, his ribs rose and fell for the last time.

I looked at Scorpus, whose eyes were glistening.

'Quick... isn't there something you can give him? One of your medicines, to help him breathe...'

'Not this time, Dido.' My uncle's voice was heavy. 'There's nothing we can do for him. He's gone.'

From the safety of the villa porch, we sat watching in silent despair as the stable was relentlessly eaten from the inside by the fiery monster in its belly. On the roof above us, Antigonus was dousing the tiles with water to stop them catching alight from the hot smoke still wafting across the yard. Only Porcellus and Jewel remained of the horses we had turned out for the night a few hours before. Jewel was grazing, but Porcellus was standing like a mournful sentry beside the dark shape lying on the ground next to the gate.

'Will you bury Sciron, Papa?' asked Abibaal, who was red-eyed both from the smoke and from crying.

'Yes, son. We'll put him on the edge of the wood. Near your mother. Just like one of the family.'

Parmenion was huddled in a blanket, shivering as Anna wrapped a thick bandage around his leg.

'I'm so sorry, Scorpus,' he croaked. 'I should have kept my stupid mouth shut. I won't blame you if you want to let me go.'

Scorpus didn't say anything. I saw the orange flames reflected in his dark eyes. All his work, the stable he had built, going up in flames. And Sciron… his oldest friend. I felt helpless rage. Not towards Parmenion and not even towards Scylax – who I hated but who had been made what he was by pain and the brutality of the world he came from. It was Emperor Caligula who had done this. He had ordered the ambush at the Circus which should have killed me, but ended up ruining Parmenion's life as well as Scylax's. It was because of Caligula that Icarus was dead. And it was because of Caligula that I had lost my beloved papa. In that moment, I wished the emperor was in front of me, so I could accuse him to his face.

'We have to go to Thugga and compete in those games,' I said at last, to Scorpus. 'Don't we?'

He nodded grimly.

'Yes, Dido. I can't see any other way, now.'

XIII

'Is that it, Papa? Up there?'

Abibaal pointed to a shelf of land above a distant slope dotted with olive groves. The outline of a town stood against the bright blue sky.

'That's it,' said Scorpus. 'That's Thugga.'

The landscape around us had changed gradually since we left Utica. Mountains loomed larger beneath their crown of purple cloud, and wheat fields, rippling in the afternoon breeze, stretched as far as the eye could see. It had been a slow, tiring journey, first by river then by road. But now we were almost there. As we rounded a corner, the entire floor of the valley opened below us. Abibaal cried out again.

'Look! Over there. Do you see it?'

Parmenion, Hanno and I came alongside to look. Scorpus had pulled the cart to a halt, clearly also startled by what we were seeing.

'That's… big,' said Hanno in awe.

A thrill charged through the pit of my stomach. Rising from the valley floor below Thugga, a vast circus was under construction. It was like looking at some buried warship being dug out of a silted seabed.

'What do you think, Papa? Is it as big as the Circus Maximus?' demanded Abibaal.

'Hard to tell at this distance,' said Scorpus. 'But it's certainly not far off.'

'Do you suppose that house behind it belongs to Gemellus Glabrio? asked Hanno. 'The one Uncle Barca was talking about, the man who's building it?' He pointed to a sprawling villa on the hillside above the construction site.

'Probably,' said Scorpus. 'I think his grandfather lived there when I was a boy. He must have inherited it, along with his fortune.'

Abibaal squinted. 'Why is the new circus… moving?'

I saw what he meant. It was as if a vast cobweb covered the stadium and it shimmered every time the breeze caught it. I shielded my hands with my eyes. Then I realised what was causing the effect.

'They're people,' said Scorpus, echoing the thought in my mind. 'Slaves. There must be thousands of them, working on scaffolds, bringing in construction materials, laying the sand for the track. Brought to Carthage specially by the boatload, I should think.'

We stayed there a while, listening to the rattling of tools echoing across the valley, before driving on.

Another mile along the road and we passed through the town gate into Thugga. We attracted some attention as we clattered along the winding main street. There were a few inquisitive stares from people who recognised Scorpus, including three old men playing dice outside a shoemaker's. They paused their game and peered at us through clouded eyes, their gnarled hands hovering over the gaming board. Scorpus did no more than nod to them. I stared at the shops and houses and temples, thinking about how all these places must once have been familiar to my mother. Maybe she used to play in that fountain like those children were doing. Or peer through the doorway of that bakery, sniffing that same sweet scent of pastry that I could smell now.

At the end of the street, we turned and followed Scorpus along a dusty track that meandered down the hillside. Just visible through the avenue of olive trees was a long, low villa with a tiled roof. At the bottom of the track, the view opened and I gazed for the first time on my mother's childhood home. It was built from the same honeyed brick as Scorpus's villa, though it looked as if the roof was in poor repair. Chickens roamed, strutting and pecking at the ground and I spied a yellow cat crouching beneath a bush, watching us in suspicion. To one side of the house was a messy vegetable garden. A woman was kneeling there, digging lettuces out of the ground and setting them in a basket at her side. As she worked, strands of her dark, curly hair fell across her cheek. Near the woman, a young girl of ten or eleven was patting soil in a pot. A doll lay next to her. The girl looked up when she heard the crunch of our wheels and called excitedly to her mother. A look of shock passed across the woman's face when she saw us. She stood, wiping her hands on the skirt of her tunic and shaking her head.

'I can't believe it,' she said, coming forward, delight replacing the disbelief in her eyes, as we climbed down from the cart. 'Barca told me you'd sent him away and I told him he shouldn't have expected any different. Is it really you?'

Scorpus smiled.

'It really is, I'm afraid. It's good to see you again, Ismene. How are you?'

'Older. Older and greyer, as you can tell.' She sighed and tugged at a few strands of her hair.

'You haven't changed at all as far as I can see.'

A giggle escaped her.

'Whereas you've become *much* more charming since you left. What was it you used to call me? Spiderlegs?'

'Me? Never. That was…' He paused. 'That was someone else's name for you, I think.'

I saw a sad moment of understanding pass between them. Then Scorpus stretched back an arm.

'Let me introduce you to my boys. This is Abibaal, my youngest, and Hanno and Leon.'

'My, my. They didn't fall far from the tree,' said Ismene, her warm eyes travelling to each of our faces in turn, though they lingered on mine the longest and I wondered if she'd seen a trace there of her old friend. 'And this is…?'

'My apprentice and stable manager, Parmenion,' said Scorpus shortly.

Parmenion gave a respectful nod. He was exhausted from the journey, I could tell, but determined to hide from Scorpus how much his leg was hurting. But when Ismene twinkled at him, he responded with a smile that made him look like the old Parmenion.

'An apprentice in charm, by the looks of him,' said Ismene. 'I imagine they'll be seeing that smile in half the taverns around town. The Thugga girls had best be on their guard.'

She glanced at her daughter, who was clinging to her side.

'Elissa, this is your uncle and your cousins. They're going to try and help your papa and Grandpa Muttumbaal win at the new circus.'

Elissa eyed us in wordless curiosity.

'She's not nearly as shy as she's pretending to be,' said Ismene, stroking the girl's soft brown hair. 'Her big brother, Bodo, is at the practice track with his father and grandfather. I think Muttumbaal's giving him a lesson.'

'Tell me something, Ismene,' said Scorpus. 'I know I can rely on you to speak the truth. Does my father know Barca came to see me?'

Ismene hesitated.

'He knows, yes. Whether he was happy about it, I couldn't tell you.'

'Barca told me he's sick. Was that a lie too?'

'No. I'm afraid not. It's his lungs. The apothecary has given him ephedron to try to help open them up, but he has trouble breathing most days. Go over and see them, Scorpus. Elissa and I will make supper and get some beds ready for you all. It will be a bit of a squeeze, but we'll manage.'

Scorpus looked back at our horses. Porcellus was sniffing at Jewel, who was ignoring him.

'I should help Parmenion get these animals

settled first. They're tired. We would have brought more, but we had a visit from some horse thieves.'

'I can help Parmenion,' Ismene offered. 'Don't forget, I grew up in a racing stable. I think I know one end of a horse from the other. Go on. You can't put it off forever, you know. He might not admit it, but I know he's missed you, Scorpus.' She hesitated. 'We all have.'

And once again, I saw that sad look pass between them.

XIV

The stables behind my grandfather's house had clearly seen better days. Some of the stalls had loose hinges and the harness room was full of battered chariots and tangles of dirty reins. But the grazing land beyond was rich, well-watered and full of horses, beautiful creatures with glossy coats and finely honed muscles. In the centre was an oval practice track. Two figures were standing beside the fence. One of them came hurrying across the field towards us.

'You changed your mind.' Barca was beaming, his arms open wide. 'Welcome home, brother. I can't tell you how happy this makes me.'

As the two of them embraced, I looked towards the practice track where the other spectator, a boy in a faded blue tunic, was watching a chariot drawn by four black horses with a mixture of white markings. They were driven by a sinewy but frail figure with thinning grey hair.

'Is that Grandpa Muttumbaal?' asked Abibaal.

'That's him,' said Barca. I didn't miss the pride in his voice. 'Now you'll see where your father learned everything.'

Throughout our journey here, I had wondered what it would be like to finally set eyes on this man, my grandfather, whose fame as a trainer I had boasted of when I was small – until I'd understood how cruelly he had treated my mother. In the end, all I felt was bewildered awe. Muttumbaal's gnarled hands held the reins so loosely that I was convinced they were going to slip through his fingers. But the way he drove those black horses was like nothing I'd ever seen. His hunched body moved like a reed in the wind, swaying effortlessly with the motion of the chariot, never once veering off balance. He didn't carry a whip but I could see his lips moving and somehow the horses responded to his direction. I glanced at Scorpus. He was watching his father with an expression that was difficult to read.

The boy beside the fence greeted us with a smile. He was about my age and had wavy chestnut hair, freckled olive skin and a sweet, dreamy expression.

'Who's this, Papa?' the boy asked. Barca ignored him and cupped a hand around his mouth.

'Father,' he called. 'Look who it is. I told you he'd come.'

The black horses picked up speed. Four enormous wine jars had been set up to form the corners of a rectangle in the centre of the track and the horses were being driven around the outside of them.

'Grandfather is teaching me how to take my turns better,' said the boy, still smiling at me and the boys. 'I'm Bodo, by the way. You must be my new cousins. I'm so glad you've come to help us.'

The chariot continued to accelerate.

'Watch this,' said Barca, nudging his brother. 'Remember how he used to make us do this?'

My grandfather was doing nothing that I could see to communicate with his horses. Then, as they curved around one of the wine jars, the chariot's wheels suddenly changed direction, carving a new path in the sand, like a chisel cutting cleanly through a plane of wood. They crossed the rectangle on a diagonal, hurtling towards the opposite jar, only slowing at the very last moment to loop around it, the inside horse's shoulder almost brushing the lip of the jar. Again and again, the horses switched course, crossing the rectangle from opposite corners. It was the most controlled display of horsemanship I'd ever seen. Finally, they eased to a walk and were allowed to stretch their necks before coming to a halt in front of us.

'Look at the markings in the dirt,' said Barca triumphantly. 'You see that? There's only a single track. He's kept to exactly the same line. That takes some skill, I can tell you.'

Bodo ducked under the fence and picked up a knobbled wooden stick that was leaning against it.

'Thank you, Grandfather,' said Bodo. 'That was wonderful. I understand what you were talking about now. Look, Uncle Scorpus has come and he has brought my cousins too.'

Muttumbaal clung to the low guard-rail at the front of the chariot as he lowered himself to the ground. He seemed to be having trouble with his breath and remained bent over for a while as he drew air into his lungs. Then he straightened, took the stick from Bodo and leaned on it as he turned towards us. He had an unforgettable face. His eyes were like chips of black flint, glittering above hollow cheeks. His high, bronze forehead was marked by the sun. There was a long silence which Scorpus eventually broke.

'Father. I thought it was time you met your grandchildren. This is Hanno and Abibaal. And this... this is Leon.'

Muttumbaal's cutting glare flickered between me and the boys. Barca went forward, putting a hand on his father's wrinkled arm.

'Scorpus has come here to help us, Father. He wants to make peace. We can save both our stables if we join forces as a family. It's time to put the past behind us.'

Muttumbaal twitched his arm out of his son's clasp.

'You're a fool, Barca. You always were. Your brother doesn't want peace. I can see it in his face.' He started to shuffle away, pausing long enough to look back over his shoulder. 'Besides... don't want his help. You ignored me... went to Utica against my wishes.'

'But, Father...'

'Enough. He's not racing for us. I won't forgive a son who betrayed me.'

XV

We ate supper in the courtyard at the back of the house, squashed together on wooden settles around a low table. There was a high-backed wicker chair piled with cushions at one end, where I guessed my grandfather usually sat. But he didn't appear.

'Did you see the new circus on your way in?' asked Ismene as she started to ladle a spicy-smelling bean stew on to our plates.

'It's an impressive construction,' said Scorpus, picking up a spoon. 'How have the locals reacted to it?'

'Enthusiastically, for the most part,' said Barca. 'It'll bring a lot of money into Thugga. Some of the local tradesmen have been complaining, mind. They think Glabrio's cut corners on the construction and short-changed them on the cost of labour and materials. But it'll be ready on time, don't worry about that.'

'I don't see how it does us any good, if our father's going to be stubborn.'

'Don't worry, brother,' said Barca. 'He'll come around. He has to.'

From the bench next to her mother, Elissa regarded us with silent interest. Her keenest fascination, though, seemed reserved for me and I worried that she had seen through my disguise with her girl's instinct.

After supper, Barca said Bodo could take us to see the horses. As Bodo opened the gate into the pasture, he whistled to a pair of glossy bays. I noticed the pleasure with which they greeted him and the gentle way he handled them.

'This is Eagle and this is Dagger. They're one of our best pairs. And here comes Atlas,' he said as a powerful dark brown horse with a white blaze cantered up. 'He's built like a siege machine but he's got the quickest legs in the stable. These two coming over now are Brightfoot and Blaze, they're the yoke horses you saw Grandpa Muttumbaal driving earlier… that blue roan following them is River. And this beautiful boy here is Ocean… he's my favourite.'

As he stroked the nose of an elegant silver-grey with sleepy eyes, Jewel and Porcellus came trotting up. Porcellus barged rudely past the others and poked his nose into the folds of my tunic. When I didn't produce a fig or date for him, he pushed me irritably with his nose. I rubbed his neck and took the chance to check his forehead to make sure there was no white showing through.

'What did you think of the new circus?' asked Bodo. 'Is it anything like the Circus Maximus?'

I realised his eyes were on me, eager and bright.

'Papa told me all about you,' he explained shyly. 'About how you became a champion at Utica and then Opellius Otho bought you to race for the Blues in Rome. That's my greatest dream. Only, I'm not sure I'll ever be good enough. Is the Circus Maximus as grand as everyone says it is? Why didn't you keep racing there?'

A picture came into my head of Icarus lying motionless on the track and I quickly pushed it away.

'I was injured. I had to come home.'

'Oh. Are you better now?' Bodo looked anxious. 'It's just that we really need you if we're going to beat Amandio and Danel.'

'Who are they?' asked Hanno.

Bodo pointed to the other side of the valley where there was a large estate, dotted with grazing horses.

'That's where they live. Their father, Zeno, is Mama's father too, so we're actually related, only

I've never been to their house. Zeno and Grandpa Muttumbaal used to be friends but they fell out about something. Nobody will tell me what. So they don't speak and we're not supposed to talk to Amandio and Danel either.'

'Your father told Scorpus that Danel's a great charioteer,' I said. 'Is that true?'

Bodo sighed, as if in awe.

'Wait until you see him. That's all I can say. He drives the most amazing team too. His inside horse, Centaur, is a *beast*. As soon as Glabrio's games are over, Danel's going to Rome to race at the Circus Maximus for the Greens. Apparently, their best charioteer was killed recently and Danel is going to replace him as the Greens' new number one.'

This news startled me. So, Danel was the precocious young charioteer Otho had spoken of in his letter.

'Bodo! Bodo!'

Elissa was gambolling towards us like a foal determined to keep up with the herd. Her hair was escaping from its pins.

'You didn't wait for me,' she chided her older brother. 'I wanted to help you show them the horses.'

'Why?' asked Bodo in some surprise. 'You're never interested in them.'

Elissa looked embarrassed. Her eyes flickered in my direction. Realisation dawned on me. *Oh no*, I thought.

'Of *course* I'm interested,' she said crossly to Bodo. 'You just never include me.'

She held a tentative hand towards Jewel then withdrew it in horror.

'Urgh! What happened to her eye?'

'She used to be a soldier's horse. She lost it protecting him,' I said, stroking Jewel soothingly and hoping that Elissa hadn't hurt her feelings. 'But she sees well enough with the other one.'

Elissa's lips puckered, but she tried to hide her disgust, giving Jewel an awkward pat.

Back at the villa, Ismene showed us to our sleeping quarters.

'Hanno, Abibaal, I've put you in here with Bodo.' She pulled back a curtain that led to a messy little room in which two straw pallets had been squashed against the far wall. 'It's small, but Scorpus tells me you're used to sharing.'

Hanno immediately claimed the bed on the left and was challenged by Abibaal.

'Leon, Parmenion, you're down here.' Ismene led us down the corridor and pulled back another curtain. 'I'm afraid it's been used as a storeroom for a while so it's a bit musty. I've cleared it as best I can and there are some more blankets in that chest between the mattresses if you need them...'

She stopped, suddenly aware that Parmenion was struggling to keep a straight face.

'Have I made a mistake?' she asked hesitantly. 'Scorpus said that Parmenion usually sleeps in the stable, but I thought this would be more comfortable.'

'That's very kind.' I narrowed my eyes slightly at Parmenion. *Shut up.* 'Thank you for going to so much trouble for us.'

'Oh, it's no trouble at all. I'm glad to have the house full and happy young faces around us. I used to visit here often when I was a child, you know. We were all such good friends, me and your father and...' She paused, a wistful look in her eye. 'Well, goodnight.'

As soon as her footsteps had faded, Parmenion lay down on the nearest pallet, put his hands behind his head and closed his eyes.

'I hope you don't snore,' he murmured. 'Because I'm going to be a much less forgiving room-mate than Anna if you do.'

Ismene had left the shutters open so that the breeze blew through. I caught the fresh tang of olives. Exploring the room, I found a cupboard set into the wall and opened it. There seemed to be nothing inside but dusty shelves and cobwebs. I was about to close the door when I caught sight of a small wooden box on the top shelf.

Parmenion yawned. 'This is comfortable, I have to say. But you can throw me out into that filthy old barn if you want. Just say the word. I'm sure the rats here are friendly.'

I was too distracted by the collection of objects inside the box to answer him. Most were horses, the kind sold by craftsmen as souvenirs for children on race days. I poked my finger among them and found more treasures. A ticket token for a day of circus games. A race card too, with the name of the horses competing in the different events. Someone had filled it in, marking the winners in ink now faded. Finally, wrapped inside a piece of cloth, were several figurines of the same charioteer. He had curly black hair and a handsome profile, rather like my old hero, Fabius of the Greens. I felt a smile stretching across my face. Whoever owned this box had obviously liked this charioteer very much.

'Dido?' Parmenion had opened one eye and was squinting at me. 'I am joking. You know that, don't you? I'll be happy to sleep in the stable if you want.'

A warm feeling was spreading through me from top to toe. I was certain that I knew whose room this had once been and who had owned this box of treasures.

'No,' I said to Parmenion, closing the lid of the box. 'Stay here. I don't mind. It's nice having the company.'

I went to sleep that night with a hopeful feeling in my heart. It wasn't just that I was certain they were my mother's things in that box, or that finding them made me feel as though I was seeing her as a real person for the first time, more than a goddess in a glittering costume. It was that for all my grandfather's efforts to banish Sophonisba's memory from his house, she was here. The little box – preserved, I was sure, by her childhood friend, Ismene – was like a softly beating heart, keeping a part of her alive. Somehow, it made me feel safe and I slept deeply for the first time since Scylax had appeared in front of me at the track in Utica.

XVI

I woke early, as I'd hoped. The sun's first light seeped through the shutters. Glancing at Parmenion, under his blanket, I noticed that the lines of pain around his mouth had softened in sleep. Dressing as quietly as I could, I went outside.

It was a beautiful morning with the promise of a hot day to come. Porcellus looked up as soon as he heard my whistle and he trotted to the pasture gate. But he stopped short, eyeing me suspiciously, as I held out the apple to him that I'd kept back from supper the night before.

'Oh, stop it,' I said. 'You know I'd never poison you. It was to keep you safe from Scylax. Come on, don't be like that, Porcellus.'

Wrinkling his lip, he bit into the sweet flesh of the apple. Jewel wandered up, swishing her yellow tail. Porcellus flattened his ears, but he didn't object when I offered Jewel a morsel of fruit.

'There,' I said. 'That's much better. You two have to stick together. You've got more in common than you think.'

Ocean, Brightfoot and Atlas all came to the gate too and I was greeting them in turn, watched jealously by Porcellus, when I heard a hacking cough behind me. A menacing grumble rippled through Porcellus's nostrils. He pushed against the fence aggressively.

'You've got a lot to say for yourself, haven't you?' grunted Muttumbaal.

He reached the fence and extended a gnarled fist. Porcellus quivered. Protective instinct kicked in and I was about to knock my grandfather's hand out of harm's way. But to my astonishment, Porcellus stretched out his nose and began licking the liver-spotted knuckles in front of him. Muttumbaal opened his fingers, revealing a handful of squashed raisins inside his palm.

'What's your story, then?' said Muttumbaal, as Porcellus sucked up the raisins. 'Libyan by the look of you… maybe a little Spanish blood. That's a good combination in a chariot horse.' He let Porcellus lick his fingers and for an anxious moment I thought I saw his black eyes lingering on Porcellus's forehead.

'So, you're my grandson.' Muttumbaal's voice was drier than a twig snapping. 'The wonder boy from Utica. Didn't expect you to be so weedy.'

I wasn't sure how to reply, so I didn't.

'Modest as well as skinny, are you?' Another fit of coughing made him retch. 'Well, let's find out if you're good enough to race for me. Harness your little black horse with Atlas there. Then bring them to the practice track.'

'I've been racing him in a team with Jewel,' I blurted out as Muttumbaal began to hobble away. 'The other horse we brought. They go well together, him on the outside, her on the inside.'

'Maybe that's how Scorpus runs things. But not in my stable, you don't.'

'If you're worried about her eye, you don't have to be…'

Muttumbaal shook his head.

'Mares,' he spat. 'They don't make inside horses. Too stubborn. Don't do as they're told. You need them under the yoke where they can be kept in line.'

I stared at him, feeling a deep resentment kindle inside me. Muttumbaal's eyes glowed.

'My stable. My rules. Now, are you coming, or aren't you?'

'Turn… turn now… you're too slow!'

Sweat was pouring off me, trickling down the

back of my neck and pooling in the pits of my arms. I pulled on the inside rein. Atlas threw up his brown head as we looped around the massive wine jar in the tightest circle I could manage. On the outside trace, Porcellus matched him stride for stride, eager to force the pace.

'Now drive hard out of the turn, this isn't the time to take a rest. This is where you destroy your opponent's hopes and dreams!'

Muttumbaal stood in the centre of the track, jabbing his walking stick as if it was a sword he was about to plunge into an opponent. Raising my exhausted arms, I brought the reins down. Porcellus and Atlas responded, scrapping to outdo each other. We hurtled past the frail figure of my grandfather. But only a few strides later I had to rein them in again as we reached the other wine jar and pivoted around it. Backward and forward we went across the diagonal between the same two jars, the pattern made by my chariot's wheels etched into the dirt like warp thread on a loom. I had done this sort of exercise before, but never for so long, or at such a relentless pace. Every muscle in my body was screaming and I longed to be allowed to rest. But Muttumbaal kept bellowing, demanding more from me, and I couldn't give up. I wouldn't.

'They're coming for you now! They can see you're beaten! What have you got left?'

Unsure if my legs would hold me up much longer, I was sucking in air, gasping for breath in my lungs.

'Are you giving up? Are you?'

My emotions bubbled at the surface but I concentrated on the next turn with all my might. My left wheel curved neatly around the base of the jar. As soon as I had rounded it, relief was offered.

'Now let them go,' barked Muttumbaal, waving his stick. 'All the way to the far end of the track and back, as if it's the last lap in the Circus Maximus. Imagine the Sun God is on your tail!'

Joyfully, Porcellus and Atlas surged into a gallop. Dark manes flying, they tore towards the distant turning post like a flight of arrows. I crouched behind them, my knees absorbing the pummelling of the wheels on the hard ground, the wind blowing in my face. For a moment, it was as if I was back at the Circus. As soon as the thought entered my head, I felt my heart pound. They were chanting Icarus's name and I knew what was about to happen.

No, not again. I can't let it happen again.

I pulled hard on the rein. Porcellus gnawed on his bit in frustration, but I forced him and Atlas to steer wide around the post, taking no chances. On the home straight, I let them go again and, as we passed Muttumbaal, he waved a weary hand for us to stop. I leaned over the low guard rail of the chariot, trying to get my breath back as we slowed to a walk. Muttumbaal met us in the middle of the track. He seemed almost as exhausted as I was.

'Your trainer's been soft on you,' he wheezed. 'You're out of condition. You shouldn't be as tired as you are, you need to build more muscle.'

'I know… I just… haven't been training as much recently,' I said, as soon as I was able.

'Why? You carrying an injury?'

'No. I've… not been in a big race for a while.'

'You think the best charioteers only train for the big races?' He snorted. 'I can see what your trouble is already, Leon of Utica. To you, the winning habit is like a pair of shoes you put on from time to time. Well, think again. Plenty of charioteers came out of this stable who've achieved greater things than you and none of them did it without blood and sweat and working their hearts out.'

I was nettled. Did he have any idea what I'd gone through to get to the Circus Maximus? Having to fight to persuade Scorpus to agree to train me when I first went to live with him. Pretending to be a boy in order to get the chance to compete. Losing my father, losing Icarus…

'I know about hard work,' I said. 'Barca came to

Utica because he said you needed me. I can go back there if you want me to.'

My grandfather's eyes glinted.

'You think because you've been to the Circus Maximus, there's nothing left for you to learn? Is that what it is, you arrogant puppy?'

I was torn between a retort and an apology. Muttumbaal leaned on his stick.

'That last turn... what happened?'

'Nothing, I just misjudged it.'

'No use trying to hide it from me. You held back. You're thinking about the shipwreck you had.'

I stared at him in surprise.

'Did Scorpus tell you?'

'He didn't have to. Like I said, I've trained more charioteers than you've seen sunrises. I can spot a case of seasickness at fifty paces.'

I hesitated.

'It was a few months ago. At the Circus.'

'What happened?'

'There was another driver, one of the Greens... they'd taken the pin out of my wheel and drugged my inside horse.'

'And he got killed, did he?'

I nodded, feeling my throat tighten. 'I keep seeing him... lying on the track after the crash... not moving...'

Muttumbaal nodded. There was no sympathy in his face. But I didn't feel as if he was mocking me either.

'To be the best, you have to be able to win even when you're not driving great horses. But no charioteer ever rises to greatness without them. You lose one, it can feel like losing a friend. The pain makes you afraid. But in the end, you have to see that fear is just another opponent. To be faced down, then defeated.'

I spied a figure on the bank above the practice track and realised it was Scorpus. He was sitting on the grass, elbows resting on his knees, watching us.

'There's another fight you need to settle within yourself though,' said Muttumbaal and my attention snapped back to him. 'How much do you want to win? Really want it?'

I was startled.

'Of course I want it. I want it more than anything.'

'Are you sure?' He was studying me. 'They tell me you've won at the Circus Maximus. That's a sweet taste. But are you still hungry for it? Be honest with yourself.'

I thought back to the race at Utica. Ever since then, I had been refusing to think about what I'd felt, unwilling to consider the possibility that something inside me had changed in that moment. That I cared about not getting hurt more than I cared about winning. Muttumbaal nodded as if he could read my thoughts.

'You understand? It's not enough to want to win because you're up against the top charioteers at the Circus Maximus. Great champions want to win no matter how small the stakes, no matter who the opposition is. More importantly, you have to know what you're prepared to sacrifice to get there. There will always be other charioteers coming up behind you, wanting to beat you, wanting to shipwreck you if that's what it takes. Are you prepared to accept the risk and the pain as well as the glory? Is it enough for you to be remembered as a good charioteer? Or do you need to be remembered as the greatest?'

All of a sudden, I was back on the practice track in front of the Greens' clubhouse, driving around it with my father, Antonius, beside me. I could feel his touch on my hand, the tug of the breeze in my hair, the pulse of Porcellus's hooves and the rush of the wheels beneath my feet. But there was another memory, gnawing at the edges of the picture. It was the sound of laughter. Scylax had been standing on the balcony that evening with some other Green drivers, watching us. It was so ridiculous to them, the sight of me, a girl in a green tunic too big for her, trying to be a charioteer.

'The greatest,' I said. 'I want to be the greatest.'

'Then you need to work harder,' said Muttumbaal bluntly. 'Great charioteers have one thought in their mind, every single time they pick up the reins, whether it's in a race or in training. Win. Win. Win.' He rapped the ground with his stick in time with the words. 'There is nothing else. Now go. I've seen enough.'

XVII

After breakfast, Barca told Bodo to take me and the boys into town to look around.

The streets of Thugga were busy. At the town fullery, slaves were hard at work in the laundry vats, trampling the grease and dirt out of the clothes with their feet. On a bench beneath an awning, an elderly schoolteacher was delivering a lesson to a group of boys whose brows were creased in concentration as they practised their numbers, scratching carefully on tablets propped against their knees. The market was full of women with baskets over their arms, chattering while they waited for their fruit and vegetables to be weighed. The three old men I'd seen the day before were in the same spot outside the shoemakers, absorbed in their game of dice. From the open door of a cook shop, a delicious smell wafted temptingly into the street. The owner was standing at the counter, spooning a pale, creamy batter on to the blackened surface of the griddle. We watched, fascinated by the way the cakes bubbled and browned.

By the cook shop was a wall covered in notices and graffiti. Bodo beckoned us.

'Look,' he said. 'These are the winners' lists from the last games they held at the old circus. You can see some of the other charioteers who'll be competing against us. This driver's trained by Hector of Bulla Regia. They're a tough stable, so watch out for them. If they can shipwreck you, they will.'

'Can't be worse than the Greens in Rome,' I said.

'Well, I don't know about that, but I can tell you, there's a lot of bad blood between the Bulla Regia supporters and the Thugga crowd. There was almost a riot when they came here for the last games.'

'Who are they?' asked Hanno, pointing at another pair of winners.

'They're from Carthage, they've got some good drivers there. No one as good as Danel, but Papa says some of them will definitely end up at the Circus Maximus.'

As I listened to him, my eyes slid over to another poster, a newer one, obviously recently added. The white of my mother's tunic stood out next to Porcellus's dark coat.

'Oh, yes, that,' said Bodo enthusiastically, as he

saw what I was looking at. 'Can you believe it? A girl winning at the Circus Maximus? Everyone's wondering who she could be. Were you in Rome for the race?'

Behind Bodo's back, I could see Abibaal trying not to smirk.

'No… no, I wasn't. It was after I had my accident, I'd already come back home to Utica.'

I hoped my voice didn't sound too high.

'The funny thing is,' said Bodo. 'People are saying her name was Sophonis—'

He stopped, biting his lip as if worried he had said too much. Anxious for him to continue, I prompted him.

'Go on.'

'Well… I think we *might* have had an aunt called that. Sophonisba.' He lowered his voice, mouthing the word under his breath. 'Has Uncle Scorpus ever talked about her?'

'I… don't think so.' I raised an eyebrow at the boys who took the hint and obediently shook their heads. Bodo shrugged.

'I could be wrong, of course. It's just that, I was with Mama in the market once, about a year ago. There was an older lady waiting next to us for the greengrocer. They were talking about Elissa. She was being naughty back then, refusing to go to bed, not wanting to help Mama in the house. All of a sudden, this older lady laughed and said something like, "Reminds me of Sophonisba when she was small. Never did anything she couldn't see a reason for." Mama went white, as though she'd seen a ghost. The old lady apologised and said she'd forgotten. But I remember her last words to Mama. "Muttumbaal was lucky to have a daughter like her. Old fool." Mama didn't say anything. I wanted to ask her afterwards what the woman meant. But something told me not to.' Bodo stared at the poster of me and Porcellus. 'It's so odd that no one can find her.'

A rattling noise made us all look back down the street, past the old men at their dice game. A rib-thin dog was racing towards us, ears flat to its skull, a piece of metal tied to its tail. The schoolboys having their lesson craned their necks to watch. Behind the fleeing animal, a laughing group came striding in pursuit. The boy leading them was about the same age as Bodo and me, tall and loose-limbed, with black hair and a confident smile.

'Oh no,' I heard Bodo say.

'Who are they?' I asked.

'The one in front's Amandio,' said Bodo, muttering out of the side of his mouth, his eyes fixed on the shop wall. 'Danel's brother. The others are Zeno's apprentices. Don't look at them; maybe they won't notice us.'

But it was too late.

'Well, look who it is,' said Amandio, sauntering up to Bodo, draping an arm around his shoulder and ruffling his hair with his knuckles. 'How are you, Bodo?'

Bodo looked uncomfortable, but he didn't try to free himself.

'Found yourself some friends to play with? That's nice.' Amandio grinned at me and the boys. 'Poor old Bodo here's usually by himself unless he's got his little sister with him. To tell the truth, he's the type who prefers spending time with girls rather than boys... aren't you, Bodo?'

The lads behind him laughed. They were unmistakably charioteers, you could tell by their calloused hands and bulging calf muscles. Bodo stared at the ground, a glow in his cheeks.

'We're his cousins,' I said coolly.

Amandio cocked an eyebrow at me.

'Really? How's that then?'

'Our father, Scorpus, is Bodo's uncle,' chimed in Hanno. 'He trains horses for the Blue faction in Rome.'

'And we're not here to play,' added Abibaal,

his chin tilted in a bold challenge to the older boy. 'We're here for the games.'

Amandio and his friends exchanged glances.

'Old Muttumbaal's bringing in outside re-inforcements, is he? That should amuse my father when I tell him. Especially when he sees the size of them.'

Abibaal's face turned red.

'Ah. Wait. *Now* I know who you all are,' said Amandio in a teasing voice. 'Your papa's Muttumbaal's son, the one who went off to race for the Blues at the Circus Maximus. My father told us all about it. Everyone talked about how he was going to be a legend and beat all the Circus records. But then he came back home, took off again and nobody in Thugga ever heard from him since. The rumour is, he got seasick.'

I sensed Abibaal's temper flaring.

'He did *not*. Our father's one of the best trainers in all Africa and you're going to find out just how good when that new circus opens.'

'If you say so, little man,' said Amandio, still smiling. 'I expect Bodo's mama was pleased to see Scorpus again, wasn't she?'

I tried to grab Bodo, but I was too late. He launched himself at Amandio, who was ready for him. The schoolboys having their lesson threw down their tablets and ran over, ignoring the protests of their teacher. They yelled encouragingly to Bodo who was now trying to prise Amandio's arm away from his neck.

'Let him go, Amandio.'

I turned to find an older boy of about Parmenion's age loping towards us. The schoolboys parted like water for him, a look of awe on their faces. It was as if a god had walked into our midst.

Reluctantly, Amandio took his arm off Bodo, who rubbed his throat.

'Thank you, Danel,' he muttered.

So this was him, the boy everyone said was going to be the next star of the Circus Maximus. He looked the part, I had to admit. Tall, muscular, with wavy dark hair and a face that looked as if it had been sculpted from bronze.

'Father wants us at the stable,' he said to Amandio. 'We've got some new horses in.' He glanced at us and nodded. 'Friends of yours, Bodo?'

I didn't get the impression he was particularly interested in the answer.

'Yes,' stammered Bodo. Like the schoolboys, he was clearly nervous in the presence of this heroic figure. 'I mean, no, actually... they're my cousins from Utica. This is Hanno and Abibaal and Leon.'

133

'They're here for the games,' said Amandio, giving his brother a meaningful look. 'They're all sons of Scorpus. Muttumbaal's son, you know, the one who disappeared?'

The bored look on Danel's face suddenly lifted.

'Wait,' he said, peering at me. 'You're Leon of Utica? The charioteer who went to race for the Blues in Rome?'

'Yes,' I said cautiously.

'I've heard of you. A friend of mine went to compete at your local games. You beat him by almost five lengths and he said you were the best he'd driven against, other than me.'

'Oh,' I said.

'This is excellent.' He was smiling now. 'You'll have to tell me all about the Circus Maximus. I'll be there soon myself, to race for the Greens. It'd be good to talk to someone who knows it.'

I stared at him, taken aback by his interest, which seemed genuine. He was obviously annoyingly confident in his own talent. But he also wasn't the Danel I'd been expecting. I wondered for a moment if he was making fun of me. Just then, a loud voice interrupted us.

'Danel! Amandio!'

Amandio swore under his breath. A man in a striped tunic was marching towards us.

'What are you doing standing around in the street?' he barked. 'Do you know how much work there is to do at the stable?'

'Sorry, Father,' said Danel. 'It took me a while to find him.'

Zeno came up to us. He was a small man, with the lean figure of an ex-charioteer. His long hair was receding and he had angry, watchful eyes, like a hawk.

No wonder my mother ran away rather than be forced to marry you, I thought.

'Who's this you're talking to?' asked Zeno.

'This is Leon of Utica, Father. You remember, the one we heard about? He's Muttumbaal's grandson, and these are his brothers. They're here for the games.'

Zeno's thick eyebrows drew together.

'So. Muttumbaal's playing dirty. Bringing in outside help from another stable. I could raise an objection with Glabrio if I wanted, but it doesn't surprise me. Doesn't matter, either.' He nodded at me and the boys. 'You tell that stubborn cuss you call Grandfather that I don't care what kind of tricks he pulls. He's finished in this town. If he knows what's good for him, he'll sell his stables and his land to me. I'd give him a good price and—'

'Father, let them be,' said a quiet voice. 'It's not their quarrel.'

Ismene had come out of the shoemakers a few doors down from the cook shop and was standing behind us. Zeno frowned.

'Stay out of what doesn't concern you, Ismene.'

'Doesn't concern me?' She shook her head – half in sorrow, half in anger, so it seemed. 'You and Muttumbaal have carried on this feud for more than fifteen years. It's trapped all of us between you.' She gestured towards Danel and Amandio. 'Now my own brothers are almost strangers to me.'

Zeno was silent. I noticed that the old men playing dice by the shoemaker's shop were listening in on us. Ismene walked up to her father.

'I miss you too, Papa. Please. Isn't it time to end this?'

Her warm eyes pleaded with him. She laid a hand on his forearm, but Zeno shook it off almost at once.

'You made your choice, Ismene. You picked Muttumbaal's family over your own. You have to live with the consequences.'

He signalled to Danel and Amandio to follow him.

'See you on the track,' said Danel, nodding to me as he went.

Back at the house, Barca was waiting to greet us, a grin on his face.

'I don't know what you did on that track this morning, Leon. But you've changed your grandfather's mind. He says he'll do it. He'll train you and the boys. And he wants to start right away.'

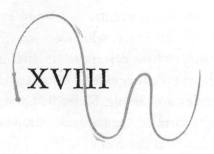

XVIII

'No charioteer – not me, not Scorpus, not even your grandfather – has ever competed in games like the ones we're about to prepare you boys for,' said Barca. 'So pay attention.'

We were perching in a row on the fence of the practice track. Hanno and Abibaal were squashed in between me and Bodo. Barca, Scorpus and Muttumbaal were facing us, my grandfather leaning on his stick. It reminded me of being back among the Blue faction charioteers on the Field of Mars in Rome, sitting in the stands above the practice track while the trainers and their assistants talked tactics. In front of us, four chariots with peeling paintwork were drawn up on the edge of the track, their long draft poles resting in the sand. Parmenion was bringing the horses and tying them to the fence.

'Glabrio wants a spectacle that will spread Emperor Caligula's glory throughout the province, and inspire awe in his subjects,' said Barca. 'As well as the four-horse and two-horse events, there's to be a new kind of race, the channel race, which is a test of pure speed – two teams of four drivers in single chariots, going head to head on either side of the channel. But otherwise the rules are simple. Sixteen stables. Two full days of competition. One winning trainer and one champion driver at the end of it. There's money on offer for each victory we win, and for second and third place too. But we're not interested in second place, are we?' His eyes swept over us. 'Are we?'

'No,' we chorused.

'Good. It's victory money we need if both our stables are going to stay alive. That means each of you has to step up to the challenge. We can't have any weak links.'

I felt the fence underneath me creak as Bodo shifted awkwardly.

'We've been working out the best strategy for us as a stable,' said Scorpus, holding up a tablet covered in his scrawl. 'We're at a disadvantage only having four drivers, when other stables will have at least six or seven apprentices to choose from. It means none of you can get injured, or we won't have a full team for the channel race. So, your fitness is going to be as important as your charioteering skills.'

'Which horses are we going to be driving, Papa?' asked Hanno.

'That's what we're going to decide now. The two-horse races are for boys, so that's you and your brother. Bodo and Leon will be our four-horse drivers. We're going to get to work this afternoon, putting together the right teams for you all.'

'Who actually decides, though?' demanded Abibaal. 'I mean, there's three of you. Who's in charge?'

Scorpus paused and glanced at his father.

'Your Uncle Barca and I will be in charge of your strength and conditioning. But this is your grandfather's stable. He's your trainer and you take your race orders from him.'

The boys and I all looked at Muttumbaal, silent and still as an eagle on a branch. Barca clapped his hands, drawing our attention back to him.

'There are going to be some good teams out there when those games begin. But none with a trainer as skilled as your grandfather. Not to mention the fact that we've got Leon.' Barca smiled at me. 'So, unless anyone has questions, let's get—'

'You haven't told them the most important thing,' interrupted Muttumbaal.

Barca paused. Muttumbaal pointed with a claw-like finger. His eyes swept over each of us in turn. I felt his gaze linger on me the longest.

'The stakes are as high as they can be. You all have

to train like you've never trained before. I expect
the best from you. Because when you go into that
circus, remember what it is you're competing for.
It's not money, or a faction, or your own pride. It's
your family's honour. There are only two things that
matter in this life. Winning and family. Remember
that.' I saw him and Scorpus exchange the briefest
of glances. 'Now. Let's begin.'

The first practice didn't go well.

Since Muttumbaal hadn't yet seen Hanno and
Abibaal race, he insisted on pitting them against
each other over three laps of the track. Eagle and
Dagger, the glossy bays Bodo had shown us the
night before, were matched with Hanno. After
some deliberation, my grandfather gave a pair of
frisky chestnuts called Thief and Curly to Abibaal.
Parmenion harnessed the teams and after a few laps
to get used to their new horses, the boys went head
to head. Abibaal, keen to impress his grandfather,
took an early lead which he held for most of the
race. But it was Hanno who snatched the win after
Abibaal misjudged the last turn, veering wide and
conceding his two-length advantage. For the rest of
the afternoon, Abibaal's face was like thunder. He

complained that Hanno had been given the better horses and nothing would coax him out of his bad temper.

Now Muttumbaal, Scorpus and Barca huddled together, discussing the best four for me. Barca was trying to convince his father to put Atlas on the outside of the team. 'That inside horse of Danel's is such a brute of an animal. If he and Leon end up going shoulder to shoulder around the turns, surely it would be better to match strength with strength.'

But Muttumbaal shook his head dismissively.

'Atlas might be strong, but he's a coward. He'll give way if Centaur muscles in on him.' He nodded at Porcellus. 'That little black horse has the right spirit. Let's try him on the outside. Brightfoot and Blaze can go under the yoke in the middle.'

While Parmenion harnessed the horses, I went up to Scorpus.

'What about Jewel? Can't we try her in the inside position?'

Scorpus shrugged apologetically.

'If I thought it would do any good, I'd argue her case. But he's always been prejudiced against mares and it's no good trying to convince him otherwise. To be fair, you don't see many of them on the winners' lists at the Circus.'

'What do you expect, if no one gives them a chance,' I grumbled.

Porcellus also seemed disgruntled at leaving Jewel behind in the pasture. He stared at her over the fence, whinnying urgently as Parmenion buckled his bridle. But Jewel had found a patch of grass and was ignoring him. Grumpily, he nipped Parmenion on the wrist.

'Easy, viper,' said Parmenion, tapping Porcellus on the nose. 'Don't forget this is the hand that feeds you.'

For the first few laps of the track, Porcellus rolled his eyes and wouldn't settle. But as we picked up speed, his eyes brightened and soon he was enjoying bullying the other horses into keeping pace with him. Brightfoot and Blaze were ideally matched yoke horses with exactly the same length of stride, while Atlas had amazing agility for such a solidly built horse. It would take time, yet they had the makings of a perfect team. I felt myself relaxing, confidence coming back as I dared to take the turns at increasing speed. *I can do this. It's going to be all right.*

Barca beamed in satisfaction.

'You're going to give that arrogant cub Danel something to think about for once, Leon.'

On the other side of the track, Bodo was driving a four which included the silver-grey, Ocean. From the picture both Bodo and his father had painted of his driving skills, I wasn't expecting to be that impressed. But it was easy to see how talented he was, with light, sympathetic hands and good balance. His real problem was obvious.

'Get closer to the posts, Bodo,' shouted Barca. 'You're leaving too much room for someone to blow past you on the inside.'

Bodo nodded hastily but his father's criticism had disrupted his concentration and at the start of his next lap, he clouted the post with his inside wheel. Barca frowned.

It was then I noticed that my grandfather had limped over to speak to Parmenion, who was watching our practice. Muttumbaal was gesturing towards Parmenion's leg and after some discussion between them, Parmenion went and harnessed a pair of spotted ponies.

'Your grandfather wants to put me through my paces,' he said when I asked him what he was doing. 'Says he's seen a lot of injuries like mine and thinks I might not be beyond repair.'

He said it lightly, as if it was a joke, but I could hear the enthusiasm in his voice. It made me uneasy and I noticed Scorpus also watching with a frown as Parmenion made his way down to the other end of the track where Muttumbaal was waiting. Soon the spotted ponies were circling the wine jars at a slow canter.

Not long afterwards, Scorpus called me and the boys in and told us to unharness our horses. He and Barca then put us through the most gruelling physical training session I'd ever experienced. They made us walk half-way down the track then sprint back, repeating the cycle over and over until we were almost throwing up from the effort. Then they gave us heavy ropes and made us hold them in either hand and shake them in an endless rippling movement along the sand. Finally, they laid sandbags across our shoulders and made us do repeated squats and jumps. Bodo was the last of us to collapse.

'That'll do for day one,' said Scorpus, regarding us critically as we lay on our backs, panting in the late afternoon sun. 'You all need a lot of work if you're going to survive two straight days of racing without your bodies falling apart. Bodo's probably the fittest of any of you.'

Bodo wiped the sweat from his brow and beamed. I noticed Barca didn't congratulate his son.

Parmenion's training had come to an end too. He and my grandfather were deep in conversation. I saw Muttumbaal reach to squeeze the flesh around Parmenion's knee and heard Parmenion yelp.

The boys were trudging off the track, Hanno and Abibaal arguing about who had lasted the longest in the sandbag exercise. But I waited for Parmenion, who soon came limping back, alone.

'What did he say?' I asked as soon as he was in earshot. When he didn't answer, I repeated myself.

'He says he can help me with the pain. Henbane's the best thing, according to him. And he thinks Scorpus is right about those exercises. They'll help strengthen the muscles so it's easier for me to walk.'

'That's good. Isn't it?'

'He also said I'll never be a charioteer again. Not at the Circus Maximus, anyway.'

I stared at him in dismay. Parmenion smiled ruefully but I could see the agony he was in.

'You want to know what the funny thing is? He says it probably wasn't the accident at the Circus that did the worst damage. It was when I fell down the ladder during the fire. I suppose Scylax got his revenge after all.'

'I'm so sorry, Parmenion. But you shouldn't give up. You probably just need more time, there are lots of charioteers who—'

Parmenion held up a hand and spoke in a sharp voice I'd never heard him use.

'Stop feeding me hope. It was a nice dream, while it lasted.'

XIX

I sat on the window ledge, looking through the open shutters at the dusk gently draping itself over the landscape. Next door, I could hear the muffled voices of Hanno and Abibaal bickering. It had gone on all through supper and eventually Scorpus sent them away from the table.

On the other side of the room, Parmenion's mattress was empty. I hadn't seen him since he walked away from me at the practice track earlier. I wished that he would talk to Scorpus. But things hadn't been the same between them since the night of the stable fire. I knew Parmenion thought Scorpus was still angry with him. And Parmenion felt too guilty to ask him for help. Watching the flies dart and tussle in the fading light, I had a heaviness in my chest. All the people I cared about were fighting. And there didn't seem to be anything I could do to stop it.

A crunch of footsteps disturbed my thoughts. Bodo came around the side of the villa and approached my window.

'I wondered if you wanted to come out and see the new circus before it gets too dark?' he asked. 'It looks amazing with the evening sun over it and you can get quite close to the construction site.'

I swung my legs over the ledge, eager for distraction. Elissa suddenly appeared. She had followed Bodo outside.

'Can I come too?' she asked eagerly. But Bodo crushed her hopes.

'No, you can't, stupid. Mama would kill us and you're supposed to be in bed, anyway.'

Elissa looked at me and her face reddened. Silently, she watched us walk down a narrow track that led away from the house. Bodo glanced over his shoulder.

'Just making sure she doesn't follow,' he said gruffly. 'She's a nuisance when she wants something she can't have. You know what girls are like.'

I was annoyed. Then it occurred to me that it wasn't like Bodo to say something unkind, and I realised he was trying to cover up for what Amandio had said in town the day before, about him preferring his sister's company to that of other boys.

We reached the edge of the olive grove that surrounded Muttumbaal's land and began to cross the fields of wheat which rolled across the valley like waves.

'Who are those people?' I asked, pointing to a group of bobbing heads half-way across the field in front of us.

'Sightseers, probably. Papa says there are hawkers making money by selling tours of the new circus. No one's allowed to see the inside while it's still being built, though.'

The amber sun was dipping low now. Ahead, the dark outline of the new circus looked like the prow of a warship advancing across the flaming horizon. Like the Circus Maximus, it had a towering archway at one end. A group of men were directing the operators of a huge wooden crane which was winching something on to the plinth above the arch. A small crowd watched from the ground. As my eyes adjusted to the light, I realised that the object being lifted was an enormous bronze sculpture of four horses, their legs frozen in mid-stride. The crests of their manes glowed as if on fire, illuminated by the torches surrounding them. Their necks were arched and their mouths gagged on their bits. A charioteer came into view behind them, a crown of laurel resting on his head. I saw his face and stopped dead.

'I saw them bringing it across the fields,' said Bodo. 'It took about thirty slaves to drag it. Do you think it's meant to be the Sun God?'

A cloak billowed behind the driver as he leaned back on the reins, flexing the muscles in his thin arms. Even though I knew it was only a statue, there was something so true to life about that slender frame, with the babyish curve to his chin. It sent a chill through me.

'No,' I said. 'It's the emperor. It's Caligula.'

A wooden fence blocked our view through the mouth of the arch, on to the track itself. Guards directed the tour hawker – a fast-talking man in a striped cap – to go around the outside of the circus with his group, which included a family with small children. We followed at a short distance and I was glad to leave the sculpture of Caligula behind. Even though I knew he must be sitting in his palace in Rome, hundreds of miles away across the sea, it felt as if he could see me through the flat, sightless eyes of the statue. I kept glancing back, half-expecting to hear that awful, childish laugh.

We walked the entire length of the track, peering over the fence at the looming arcade of the upper storey, with its honeycomb of archways. An army of slaves clung to the web of scaffolding covering the circus, labouring to finish the building. Their skinny bodies and exhausted faces were evidence of the toll the work took. Collars around their necks marked them as slaves, as did the churlish way they were spoken to by the guards supervising their work. I saw a man struggling to carry an enormous block of stone, his face screwed up in pain. A foreman shouted and brought a stick down on his shoulders. The slave stumbled, his knees buckling with the effort of staying on his feet. The foreman struck again and this time the slave fell, coughing up a long trail of spit. He stumbled to his feet, still clutching the heavy stone.

'Keep moving,' muttered Bodo to me as I paused, wanting to help in some way. 'They'll punish him twice as hard if you interfere.'

We'd reached the end of the track, where the outer wall curved round towards the first of the twelve starting gates. Blazing torches illuminated the ornate metal grilles which would snap open under starter's orders. The family we'd been following had stopped and were gazing at them with smiles of delighted wonder.

'Look,' said Bodo, tugging my arm and pointing to a group of men by the gates. 'That's Gemellus Glabrio. The man who's paying for the circus.'

It was easy to tell who he meant. Compared to the sweating labourers surrounding him, Gemellus

Glabrio was the image of well-groomed wealth. He was younger than I'd expected, with cropped sandy hair and a boyish figure. He was listening with a bored look on his face to a man with a tool belt slung around his waist who was gesturing at the starting gates. Glabrio's loud, confident voice carried to us on the evening breeze.

'... there's no more discussion to be had, fool. They have to open more quickly. This isn't some third-rate provincial racetrack I'm building here. I want those gates to be as fast as they are at the Circus Maximus. You're the engineer, you make it work.'

The engineer shook his head and said something, but Glabrio cut across him.

'I'm not interested in risks. I'm interested in results. This circus is opening in sixty days and those had better be working properly, or you won't be paid.'

Turning his back on the engineer, Glabrio called to a foreman who was directing timber carts.

'You. Are those stables going to be finished on time?'

'Should be, master,' grunted the foreman. 'We've got these men on reduced rations to hurry them along.'

'Good, good,' said Glabrio, nodding in satisfaction. 'Don't let up on them.'

He turned and looked at the officials' box above the starting gates and for the first time I noticed a man standing there by himself with his back to us. He was watching the statue of Caligula being guided into position at the other end of the circus. My skin prickled. Something about that tall, prowling figure seemed unpleasantly familiar.

'You see, Cassius? Everything is going the way I promised.'

The man turned, revealing a sharp profile. He spoke in a light, high voice that I remembered all too well.

'Are you sure your archway is strong enough to support the weight of that thing?'

Glabrio chuckled.

'Still trying to find fault? Admit it, Cassius. This stadium is the equal of the Circus Maximus. I shouldn't wonder if people come all the way from Rome, just to see it.'

'That's a rather brave statement,' drawled Cassius Chaerea. 'Setting yourself up in competition with the emperor of Rome.'

'Competition?' Glabrio laughed again, uneasily this time. 'No, you misunderstand me, Cassius. I wouldn't dream of comparing myself to the emperor.'

'Then I suggest you don't brag about the size of your circus. Caligula doesn't care to be upstaged.'

'But I'm trying to glorify him, Cassius! This is for him, to show my reverence. Look at that sculpture! It cost me almost half as much as the stadium itself, but it was worth every sesterce.'

Bodo tapped me on the arm, making me jump.

'Leon? It's pretty dark now. We'd better leave if we don't want to get lost going back across the field.'

I hesitated. I was desperate to know what Cassius Chaerea, tribune of the Praetorian Guard and probably the most dangerous man I knew, other than the emperor himself, could possibly be doing here. But I had no desire for him to see me.

'Yes, let's go,' I said.

Before Bodo and I could set off, the hawker in the striped cap accosted us.

'Magnificent, don't you think? Why don't you two join the tour? Only five sesterces.'

His voice was piercingly loud. I glanced nervously at Cassius Chaerea, who was still listening to Glabrio.

'No, thank you,' said Bodo, before adding with a hint of pride, 'we're not tourists. We're charioteers. From Muttumbaal's stable.'

The hawker's eyes widened.

'Everyone! Over here.' He beckoned to his gaggle of sightseers. 'Got a special treat for you

– two young heroes of the track, might even be legends of the Circus Maximus one day. Speak up, lads, tell them your names.'

I tried to pull Bodo away but he was already being pawed at in excitement by the small children we'd seen earlier.

'Hello. I'm Bodo,' he said with a bashful smile. 'And this is my cousin. Leon of Utica. He's actually raced at the Circus Maximus already.'

'You hear that, everyone?' screeched the hawker. 'This is Leon of Utica! Champion of the Circus Maximus!'

Sharp as a whip-crack, Cassius Chaerea turned.

'Who did you race for then, young Leon?' prompted the hawker. 'Greens? Blues? Come on, share some stories with us.'

'We need to go now, Bodo,' I said, trying to keep the desperation out of my voice. 'They'll be expecting us.'

Abandoning the protesting hawker, I hurried away into the darkness of the surrounding field, leaving Bodo almost tripping over his own feet as he tried to catch up. Like a field mouse trying to escape the snare of an eagle's glare, I could feel Cassius Chaerea's cold blue eyes boring into the back of my neck.

XX

Scorpus looked troubled.

'And you're sure he saw you?'

'I think so. Yes.'

Cursing softly, Scorpus threw down the leather harness he was mending.

'Well. That's it then, isn't it? We need to get out of here and back to Utica.'

'What?' I protested. 'How's that going to help?'

'Dido, you're telling me that a member of the emperor's own bodyguard is here in Thugga and you think we should wait around and find out what his intentions are?'

'All I'm saying is, what good is it going to do us to go back to Utica? Cassius knows who I am and where I live, Scorpus. If he is here looking for me, he'll just follow us home.'

Scorpus ran a hand over the top of his head. He knew I was right.

'I don't see why he would be here for me, though,' I said, trying to reassure him. 'Yes, Cassius is dangerous. But he hates Caligula as much as we do, Scorpus. That's why he let me escape from Rome when he saw me and Porcellus on that boat. He could easily have told the other soldiers we were there. Why would he let me go then, only to come and find me now?'

'I'll tell you why. Money. What if he wants to claim that bounty on your head?'

'I did think of that,' I admitted. 'I stayed awake for ages last night, expecting him to suddenly appear at my window. But he never showed up and it's not as though it would be that difficult for him to find me.'

'I don't suppose we've got any choice but to wait and see if he tries. But no sneaking out again at night, you hear me? It's a good thing you've got Parmenion in there with you.'

I agreed, not mentioning that Parmenion had climbed back through our window in the early hours of the morning. Part of me thought I should tell Scorpus. But I was afraid that his promise not to kick Parmenion out might not stand if he knew he'd started drinking again.

There was something else I was keeping from him, and that was how frightened I was by Cassius

Chaerea's unexplained appearance in Thugga. Although he had helped me in the past, I knew from experience that Cassius wouldn't think twice about hurting me if it helped him achieve his own ends. I had no intention of running into him if I could avoid it.

I went to bring Porcellus in from the pasture and was surprised to see him already by the fence, being fed pieces of apple by my grandfather. Muttumbaal was stroking his neck and murmuring something. He stopped as soon as he heard me approach.

'We're going to work on turns today,' he grunted as Porcellus greeted me with a happy squeal. 'You're still creeping up to the end of the channel as if you're trying not to wake someone. Atlas can be lazy if you don't push him along, so you need to get him working better with your little black horse here.'

I looked towards the far end of the pasture at the rust-coloured shape of Jewel grazing by herself.

'You know,' I ventured, 'Jewel, the mare we brought with us, is quicker on the straight than Atlas, and she and Porcellus already know each other. Why don't you let me try her on the inside today, just to show you what—'

'No,' said Muttumbaal and he began to shuffle away.

'Why not?' I called.

'Never question your trainer,' he snapped. 'Mares don't make inside horses. Told you so yesterday. Now get the rest of those animals in.'

I glared after him. Then I put my fingers in my mouth and blew. Jewel's head came up just as Muttumbaal hunched his shoulders and cursed.

'What in the name of…'

His voice trailed off as a rumble of hooves thundered across the landscape. My whistle had attracted the attention of several horses in the field, including Atlas. But Jewel was bursting through the middle of them as if she was leading a cavalry charge. She picked up speed as she came closer and skidded up to the fence, barging Porcellus to one side. I gave her a piece of apple that Porcellus had dropped.

'Good girl, Jewel,' I said.

Muttumbaal glowered at me.

'So?' he snapped. 'She's greedy.'

'Just give her a chance. That's all I'm asking.'

Muttumbaal's mouth moved as he if was chewing on something.

'She can go in the channel race,' he muttered at last.

'But—'

'Don't push me. You want to beat Danel, you'll do what I tell you. The channel race is a test of pure

159

speed. That's where your one-eyed mare might come in useful.'

On the small oval track in the middle of the pasture, Scorpus had hitched Blaze and Brightfoot to a practice chariot so that he could test the harness he had mended. I leaned against the fence, excited as always to see my uncle drive. My father had once described him to me as the greatest charioteer he'd ever seen compete at the Circus Maximus. Watching Scorpus now, I felt nothing but pride. He had that same extraordinary balance as Muttumbaal, an ability to shift his weight effortlessly, to communicate with his horses with the slightest pressure on the reins. I was certain that if he had gone into the Circus Maximus that very day, he could have defeated almost any driver who came up against him.

'He could have been the best there ever was.' Muttumbaal had muttered to himself as if I wasn't there. His eyes were fixed on Scorpus.

'He had the hunger and everything else I gave him. I taught him to be a circus warrior, to take the race to his opponent, never accept defeat. When he left this place to race at the Circus Maximus, I thought to myself, "Next time I see that face, everyone else in the empire will know it too. They'll put up statues in his honour. And everyone will know that he's my blood. Scorpus, son of Muttumbaal, the greatest charioteer in the empire."' He watched a while longer as Brightfoot and Blaze cantered around the track. 'Now, I suppose it'll be Danel, son of Zeno, whose name they remember.'

His black eyes locked with mine and I knew that a challenge had been thrown down.

'You did really well today, Jewel,' I murmured, squeezing water from the cloth and letting it trickle down her golden forelock. 'We showed Grandpa Muttumbaal, didn't we?'

Jewel nudged hopefully at the dates in the pouch on my belt. As I fed her, the door of the next stall rattled.

'Yes, you were good too, Porcellus,' I said, reaching around to pass him a date of his own.

It was evening and I was lingering over the last of my stable duties, enjoying time with the horses. Training had gone better today and Jewel had been brilliant in her first practice for the channel race, even getting a grudging nod of approval from my grandfather. As I left Jewel's stall, I heard a noise in the corner of the barn. Immediately I thought of Cassius Chaerea and tensed.

'Who's there?' I asked, trying to keep my voice calm.

A slender figure flitted towards me. I let the air out of my lungs.

'I was just looking for the cat,' said Elissa, sounding defensive. 'Have you seen him?'

'Er... no. Not recently.'

I started to sweep up. Elissa hung around and I got the feeling the missing cat had been an excuse. After trying and failing to steal another date from me, Porcellus extended his nose towards her. Nervously, Elissa stood her ground.

'What's his name?' she asked.

'Porcellus. Careful. He's not always friendly.'

But, after satisfying himself that Elissa had no food and wasn't edible herself, Porcellus allowed her to pat his cheek with the tips of her fingers.

'Well done,' I said. 'He must like you.'

Elissa flushed, looking pleased.

'Are you coming in for supper?'

'Soon. Tell them they should start without me if I'm not there.'

As she skipped off, my mind wandered back to when I was her age, hanging around whichever Green charioteer I was desperate to notice me at the time. Papa would tease me about it, though only gently. Thinking of my father brought an image into my head of his kind, weather-beaten face and laughing eyes. When I heard a footstep behind me, I thought it must be Elissa again and I rubbed my face quickly so that she wouldn't see the tears there.

'I'm finishing up, tell your mama I'll...'

But the tall shadow across the entrance to the barn wasn't Elissa's.

'Hello, Dido. It's good to see you again,' said Cassius Chaerea, his blue eyes shining like cold stars in the twilight.

XXI

Instinctively, I moved in front of Porcellus, who was trying to break through the door of his stall. Jewel was watching Cassius Chaerea with suspicion.

'If you come a step closer, I'll scream for help,' I warned.

'Such a girlish threat, Dido,' said Cassius. 'Hardly the way to greet an old friend.' He tilted his head, as though in sympathy. 'But I'm sorry. I seem to have caught you at a difficult moment.'

I dashed away the tears from my cheek with one hand while cradling Porcellus's nose with the other, trying to settle him. I was afraid, but I knew I had to keep my wits about me. I didn't want anyone inside the house to hear the noise Porcellus was making and come to investigate. Not until I could be sure it wouldn't put them in danger.

'Why are you here?' I asked. 'Did you come to find me?'

'As a matter of fact, no, not this time. Although it

crossed my mind you might be here.' He came closer, flicking a speck of dirt off his white uniform. 'Official business, to answer your first question. The emperor sent me to inspect Glabrio's new circus and bring him back a report. He is a little upset, shall we say, by rumours that have reached him of its construction.'

I was relieved, but puzzled.

'That doesn't make any sense. I thought Glabrio was building it in the emperor's honour – why would he be upset?'

'The emperor certainly likes it when people honour him. What he doesn't like is ambition, not in others at any rate. Caligula thinks that by building a chariot-racing stage as big as the Circus Maximus, Glabrio is setting himself up not as an admirer, but as a rival.'

'That… stupid.'

'True, but one should never underestimate the mad workings of Caligula's mind. You know that better than most, Dido. Gemellus Glabrio is an unfortunate and misguided man. He genuinely believes his birthday present will earn him a place in Caligula's inner circle.' Cassius laughed contemptuously. 'Fool. He'll live to regret it.'

I continued to soothe Porcellus, who was still objecting to Cassius's presence.

'What made you think you'd find me here?' I asked.

'Simple. Who else but you, Dido, would have the blind cheek to be planning to race in full view of a circus crowd when the whole empire is looking for you? I like the disguise you've given the emperor's horse by the way. Oh, don't look so worried. It's crude but effective, I'll grant you.'

Cassius let his gaze wander over the other horses in the dim light of their stalls.

'So, these are the headquarters of Muttumbaal of Thugga,' he said. 'Quite a thrill for me, Dido. You know what a lifelong supporter of the Blues I am. Your grandfather was a remarkable charioteer, back in the day. Tell me, how is the reunion between him and Scorpus going? What has it been, fifteen years since Scorpus was last here?'

I was shaken. How did he know about my family? Then again, I thought, Cassius Chaerea always had a sinister habit of knowing more than you wanted him to.

'None of your business,' I replied.

Cassius threw his head back and laughed.

'Very good, Dido. You're determined not to let me know you're afraid, aren't you?' He paused, then, so softly that at first I wasn't sure if I'd heard him properly, he added, 'It's a pity you have no idea how like her you are.'

My hand stilled on Porcellus's nose. He started

to kick the stall door again, but this time I didn't stop him.

'What do you mean?' I asked uncertainly.

Cassius Chaerea just looked at me, a smile playing around his lips. I felt myself getting angry.

'No,' I said. 'Don't. You're trying to get inside my head. You never met my mother. You've no idea if we're alike.'

His next words stunned me.

'You're wrong, Dido. I did know Sophonisba. You might even say we were friends, a long time ago.'

I stared into those mocking blue eyes.

'I don't understand. How… When…?'

Cassius leaned against the wall and folded his arms.

'Funny, the tricks memory plays in old age,' he said thoughtfully. 'Was I leaving the Blues' clubhouse, or just arriving when I first saw her? No matter. She was standing by the door to the stable yard, I remember that. A young woman, barely older than you, Dido, with wild hair and a strong face, like yours.'

I was drawn in by his words, desperate to know more.

'What was she doing there?'

'Asking the grooms for food, I believe. I don't think she'd been in Rome long. It was her voice that made me notice her. So proud and determined, although you could hear the fear in it too. Still, I doubt I'd have given her a second glance if I hadn't heard her say whose daughter she was. I suppose she must have thought her father's name would open doors to her at his old faction. Alas, the groom was a boy and it meant nothing to him. But for a lifelong follower of the Blues, like myself, it had the effect your mother wanted. I saw no harm in giving her a few coins and telling her the name of a woman who gave houseroom to waifs and strays like herself.' He raised an eyebrow. 'You're looking at me with some suspicion, Dido.'

'It just doesn't seem like the sort of thing you would do.'

Once again, he laughed.

'What an ungrateful girl you are. You forget I've saved your life too, more than once.'

I was thinking about the other times he had come close to killing me, but I decided not to bring them up.

'I was a young man in those days,' continued Cassius. 'I'd been a soldier in the army under Caligula's father. I suffered an injury which put an end to my days on the front line and I had to return to Rome. I found the change in my circumstances difficult, and I became somewhat wild, spending too much time in the local taverns. Not long after that first encounter with your mother, I woke in the small hours to find myself lying in the street. I'd been robbed of my purse and badly beaten. Someone was trying to help me up. It was Sophonisba. She'd recognised me as her benefactor and took me to an apothecary. While my injuries were tended, she distracted me from the pain by telling me about her life, about her brothers and the quarrel that made her run away from home. It was obvious she was missing her family. But she saw no possibility of returning.

'After that, out of some sense of gratitude, I kept an eye out for her. I heard of a group of acrobats looking for a new rider for their Circus act. Knowing that this was the world Sophonisba wished to enter, I introduced her to them. A favour I realise you may not thank me for, given what happened later. But of course, it was while performing at the Circus that she met your father. So who's to say you shouldn't be grateful. I leave it to you to decide. None of this, however, is what I came here to discuss with you.'

I blinked, still lost in his revelations about my mother. 'What did you come for?'

'You don't need me to tell you, I'm sure, that there is a substantial reward for your capture. Caligula wants me to keep him informed of how the hunt for you is going. I'm aware of at least six or seven experienced bounty hunters tracking your movements. And I have to tell you, Dido, that at least one of them is getting closer.'

'What do you mean?'

'The crew of the boat that helped you escape from Rome,' explained Cassius. 'One of them has claimed money in exchange for the information that they dropped you off in Utica. So the parameters for the search have narrowed.'

I tried to think calmly.

'It won't matter. Princess Sophonisba doesn't exist any more. There's only Leon now and you said yourself that Porcellus's disguise is good.'

'I also said it was crude. The moment you start racing at the games, the chances increase that someone will recognise him. And if the bounty hunters find their way to Thugga eventually – as they're bound to – you're going to feel the net tightening around you.'

My heart lurched. Scylax. What if he heard the rumour that the princess's last known whereabouts were in Utica? It could get ugly quickly if Scylax turned up in Thugga for the games and started asking questions. I tried to keep my thoughts hidden from Cassius Chaerea, but I could tell he had read something in my face.

'You'd do well to take my advice, Dido. We have

a shared aim in life, you and I. To thwart Caligula of his pleasures, at all costs. The emperor is excited about young Danel coming to race for the Greens in Rome. The only thing that could make him happier is the capture of the fugitive princess. I'll tell you now, if I thought it was going to come down to a choice between Caligula rejoicing in that moment, or making you disappear without trace so those bounty hunters never find you, I wouldn't hesitate to act.'

I found my voice.

'You'd kill me? Is that what you're saying?'

Once again Cassius tilted his head, giving me that sympathetic look.

'It's a pity, isn't it? But yes. That is what I'm saying.'

XXII

'**N**o!' Hanno threw up an arm in exasperation while Abibaal struggled to pull up his team.

'You're going too early, son,' said Scorpus as Abibaal cantered back. 'You have to wait for your brother's back wheels to cross the line in the sand.'

'He's slowing down right before he gets there, to throw me off.'

'I am not...'

Behind them, at the back of the track near the starting gates, Bodo and I circled, trying to keep our horses from fidgeting.

'I suppose you can see why Glabrio thought this event would entertain the crowd,' said Bodo, as we watched Scorpus try to cool the boys' tempers. 'It's certainly different.'

'It's a stupid race,' I answered, urging Jewel to keep moving. 'What's wrong with the usual seven laps of the track?'

We had come to the old abandoned circus on the outskirts of town in order to continue practising for the channel race. A chalk line opposite the turning posts at the near end of the channel marked the point where the first driver's wheels had to cross before the second driver could start their run to the end of the straight and back. Scorpus had told us the trick was to time it perfectly, so that the second person in the team was already cantering towards the line before the first had crossed it. 'That way, you won't lose momentum between each changeover,' he'd explained. But Abibaal, eager to force the pace as always, kept setting off too soon.

As he and Hanno prepared to try again, I noticed a man watching our practice from the road above the circus. It had been several days since Cassius Chaerea's visit to the stable. I'd said nothing about it to Scorpus, knowing his reaction would be to insist on us leaving Thugga. There'd been no sign of Cassius in the meantime and I hoped that meant he had gone back to Rome. But I hadn't forgotten his warning about the bounty hunters on my trail. The man on the road soon moved on and I guessed, from the timber cart he was driving, that he was probably taking building materials to the new circus. I breathed more easily. Moments later, a clanging noise made me jump. Hanno and Abibaal had just failed to complete another changeover, and Muttumbaal, who was watching from next to the starting gates, had hit his walking stick against the rusting metal barrier in frustration. Jewel threw up her head in alarm.

'Steady, girl,' I said.

Muttumbaal came and put a hand on Jewel's bridle. She calmed down at once. It irritated me how easily my grandfather could manage both her and Porcellus.

'Bodo needs to go out second instead of Abibaal,' grunted Muttumbaal. 'Scorpus is a fool if he thinks those two idiots can work together.'

'They're young,' I heard myself saying.

'Young. Why is that always an excuse for everything? If you're young, you should be willing to listen. To learn from your elders, who know better than you.' He jerked a thumb at Abibaal, who was now storming off the track, ignoring his father's attempts to call him back. 'I tell you, if Scorpus or Barca had ever acted that way with me, I'd have taken my whip to them.'

'Look where that got you.'

Muttumbaal's eyes flickered like a guttering candle. I couldn't believe I'd said that aloud. But the thought of my mother gave me the courage to meet his fiery gaze. Then a shout drew our attention to the other side of the track, where Abibaal was pointing to a convoy of horses and chariots approaching. An oath of fury escaped my grandfather's lips.

Zeno was seated astride a big speckled grey at the head of the convoy. He pulled to a halt and waited as Muttumbaal advanced.

'Out!' bellowed my grandfather. 'Go on, get out of here. The circus is ours today.'

'You're not the king of these parts, Muttumbaal,' said Zeno. 'This track belongs to the people of Thugga. We've as much right to practise here as you.'

'You're spying. Trying to get a look at our strategy before the games.'

Zeno shook his head, a pitying expression on his face.

'You're even more senile than the last time I saw you, old friend. No one's interested in your strategy. Your drivers are cubs. You're putting them up against lions.'

He gestured to Danel and Amandio, who now flanked their father. Ordinarily, it would have been the four horses pulling Danel's chariot who captured my attention. With their golden coats, dark legs and manes that cascaded like black water over their necks, they were one of the most perfectly matched teams I'd laid eyes on. The inside horse, Centaur, looked as if he had been carved out of a rockface. But I couldn't stop staring at Amandio's four, who I'd recognised straight away. It was Misty, Storm, Cupid and Psyche.

Scorpus took a step forward. Misty's dark-grey head came up. She neighed in recognition.

'Those horses are stolen,' said Scorpus quietly.

The smile on Zeno's face faded.

'Is that the first thing you have to say to me, Scorpus, after fifteen years? To call me a thief to my face? No one can say you aren't your father's son.'

'All I know is that those are my horses. Stolen from my stable a month ago, by a man who didn't pay for them.'

Zeno frowned.

'These horses are on loan to us from the Greens. They go to Rome with my son once the games are over. If you can prove they're yours, so be it. If not, I'd suggest you don't insult me again with false accusations.'

He gestured to Danel, Amandio and his other apprentices to drive on to the track. Muttumbaal blocked his path as he tried to follow them.

'You were an honest man once, Zeno,' he wheezed.

'And you were a great trainer, my old friend. Time to rest on your laurels. My offer for your stable and your land still stands, at the same price. You could secure your family's future. Think of it as settling your old debt to me.'

My grandfather's eyes narrowed.

'I don't owe you anything. Not a single sesterce, you hear me?'

'At least consider it, Muttumbaal. You're putting a lot of hope in that star charioteer of yours, the one you're boasting about all over town. But you're taking a big risk. Word already reached us from Utica. The boy's suffering from seasickness. Picked it up in the Circus Maximus last summer. It's a shame when a talented young driver flies too close to the sun. You and I have both seen it happen, though. And we both know that often they don't recover.' He nodded at me. 'Don't let your grandfather bully you, boy.'

'He doesn't want your advice,' snarled Muttumbaal.

Zeno shrugged and rode on. His teams were already cantering around the circus. I watched Danel and realised that, with the exception of Scorpus and my grandfather, I was probably watching the best charioteer I'd ever seen. If driving four headstrong horses could be made to look easy, he managed it. His balance was perfect, and he obviously had phenomenal strength in his arms. Encouraged by his father, he was giving the golden horses their heads, flying around the track in a swirl of sand. My heart sank even further. The inside horse, Centaur, was as quick around the turns as Porcellus.

'He's good, isn't he?' said Abibaal, looking crestfallen.

Even Abibaal thinks I don't stand a chance against him.

XXIII

The atmosphere at supper that evening was uneasy. It was humid and flies hovered over the leftover food on our plates. Abibaal had barely eaten, and only a look from Scorpus made him pick up his spoon again and poke at his stew. Hanno was quiet too. On the other side of the table, Elissa earned a mild scolding from Ismene for slumping on the wooden settle.

In his high-backed wicker chair, Muttumbaal glowered like a vulture. Usually, he and Barca and Scorpus would discuss the next day's training, or talk about the other horses and charioteers who would be coming for the games. But tonight, conversation was sparse.

'Can I have some more stew please, Mama?' asked Bodo.

I had a feeling he'd said it just to break the silence. Barca gestured to Ismene to give him a second helping as well.

'Did you see those chariots Zeno's boys were driving today?' he asked, picking up a spoon and dragging it through the sludge of brown lentils. 'Fit for the emperor himself to drive, by the look of them. We should really be investing in some better equipment for the games, Papa. A lot of those wheels in our shed must have seen at least ten years of use.'

He glanced at Muttumbaal, who remained silent.

'Bodo, I'll need you to take the cart to market tomorrow and fetch us more oats from the feed merchant,' added Barca. 'We're running low with the horses on such high rations at the moment.'

'Oh.' Bodo swallowed. 'I... think I might have damaged the cart this morning.'

Barca laid down his spoon.

'You did *what*?'

'I'm sorry, Papa, it's just that I took those harnesses to the tan yard for repair as you asked, and on my way back, Amandio and those boys tried to block my way – you know, to be funny. I tried to go around them but I think I must have gone over a rut, because when I got home I saw that the axle was cracked.'

Barca's face was red now.

'Do you know how much that axle will cost to repair? You realise that everything I'm doing to manage our finances and save this stable is for you? To make sure you have an inheritance. And this is the sort of gratitude you show me?'

Bodo's lip trembled and he stared at his plate. Ismene, who had brought a bowl of pomegranates, laid a hand gently on his head.

'Don't be too hard on him, Barca. Amandio does delight in tormenting him.'

'Then your son should stop being a weakling and stand up for himself,' snapped her husband. 'Remember your place and don't argue with me.'

Ismene's eyes widened. For a moment, I thought she was going to say something. Then she quietly collected the rest of the bowls and retreated to the kitchen. Scorpus looked at his brother, a pulse moving in his cheek.

Elissa, who had sat up hungrily at the sight of the sweet course, took one of the crimson fruits from the bowl and began to prise open the red flesh.

'Papa, who's Sophonisba?' she asked idly.

There was a creak from the wicker chair as my grandfather's gnarled hands tightened on the arms. Ismene appeared in the doorway of the kitchen, looking scared. Only Elissa, busily focused on gouging out pomegranate seeds, seemed unaware of the effect her words had produced.

'Where did she hear that name?'

My grandfather's voice was like a rasp on metal. Elissa opened her mouth. Then she faltered, a look of uncertainty on her face as she realised everyone's eyes were on her.

'I...'

Muttumbaal yanked the sleeve of her tunic.

'Answer me! Where did you hear it?'

He was shaking her like a rag doll. Barca put out his hand in a feeble protest. But it was Scorpus who grabbed Elissa and prised his father's claw-like fingers from her arm. She ran, gulping back sobs, to Ismene who folded her arms around her daughter and led her away. Muttumbaal and Scorpus were squaring up to each other like a pair of bulls.

'Was this your doing?' demanded Muttumbaal, rage blazing in his eyes. 'Did you poison her ears with that word?'

'For goodness' sake, Father, she'll have heard it all around town!' pleaded Barca. 'Everyone's talking about the girl who won at the Circus Maximus, the princess in the poster – they've got the same name!'

Scorpus and Muttumbaal paid no attention.

'You're the poisoner, Father,' said Scorpus. 'Fifteen years on, and you still can't say the name of your own flesh and blood, still can't admit your own fault.'

'I'm not the one who failed. You could have

brought her home when you found her in Rome.'
Muttumbaal jabbed a finger in Scorpus's face. 'It
was your duty, as her brother!'

'She never wanted to leave here in the first place!
You gave her no choice!'

Muttumbaal was starting to wheeze. Barca
looked worried.

'Father, calm down, you need to catch your
breath. Scorpus, stop this.'

'He doesn't care if he kills me!' raged Muttumbaal.
'He's here for his money and then he goes —'

He coughed and started to bring up phlegm. Bodo
slapped him on the back. Eventually, Muttumbaal
recovered. He fixed Scorpus with a baleful stare.

'Once these games are over, I want you out of
this house. Don't even think about coming back.'

He staggered away. A long silence hung in his
wake. Hanno and Abibaal looked upset. Barca
mopped his brow.

'It is strange,' he muttered. 'Both women
having the same name. You don't think there's any
chance…'

Wearily, Scorpus shook his head.

'I know what you're thinking, but put it out of
your mind, Barca. I was there, remember? I saw
Sophonisba fall, I heard her neck break.' His eyes
met mine for the briefest of moments. 'Whoever

that woman at the Circus Maximus was, it wasn't our sister. I can promise you that.'

I left the dinner table as soon as I could. Going past Elissa's room, I heard Ismene murmuring gently.

'But I don't understand where you heard it, darling.'

'It was... you... and Papa.' Elissa hiccuped, through her sobs. 'Yesterday. I heard you. You said... people are asking if it's Sophonisba in the picture. And Papa told you to be quiet... like he always does.'

Ismene didn't reply and I made myself scarce as quietly as I could.

In our room, I found Parmenion counting coins in his palm. My heart sank.

'Where are you going this time?'

'Got a dice game going on with some boys in town. Big money on offer. With any luck, I won't need that career at the Circus Maximus after all.'

He winked, slipped the coins into his pouch and started to climb out of the window.

'You're killing yourself, Parmenion,' I said. 'You have to stop.'

He paused, smiling, but there was accusation in the look he gave me.

'You sound like Scorpus. I thought you were on my side.'

'You know I am. It's why I don't want you to get hurt and I don't want you to give Scorpus a reason to let you go. Come and play dice with me and the boys.'

'Tempting. But Hanno and Abibaal aren't quite rich enough for my blood. Have fun.'

I took hold of his arm.

'Parmenion, I know it's hard and I understand you're in pain. But you're giving up. Scorpus says that if you—'

He shook off my hand with a violence that startled me.

'Every night. *Every* night, I try to sleep and it feels as if someone's stabbing me in the leg, over and over until I think I'm going to go mad. It won't heal, do you understand me? It's never going to heal!'

He was almost shouting. The guilt that had been gnawing at my insides for months now sank its teeth in.

'Parmenion,' I said shakily. 'I have to ask you something and you have to tell me the truth.'

'What?' he snapped.

'Do you hate me?'

The anger on his face turned to bewilderment.

'Of course not. Why would I hate you?'

'Because of what happened. Because you got hurt saving my life. If you hadn't jumped on to Scylax's chariot, if you hadn't... stopped him... he wouldn't have crashed and your leg would still be...'

I couldn't speak through the tears. Parmenion brushed them away with his knuckles.

'Now, you listen to me, Dido. This was not your fault. You understand? Scylax did this, him and those scumbags from the Greens who ordered him to take you out of that race. Don't you ever, *ever* take the blame for this. You hear me?'

He waited until I nodded, then squeezed my hand.

'You saved me too, remember,' he muttered. 'I've never had a friend as good as you. Making sure you lived to race another day was the best thing I ever did.' And with a crooked smile, he was gone.

XXIV

I lay on my bed with the shutters open, staring at the moon. As I fretted about Parmenion, other worries jostled for space in my head. The hatred in Scorpus and Muttumbaal's faces as they hurled insults at each other. The impossibility of beating Danel, especially if I had another attack like the one at my last race in Utica.

It was no use. I wasn't going to be able to sleep. I got up, dressed and crept along the corridor. As I was passing the kitchen, I heard a noise. Ismene was by the stove in the kitchen, a shawl draped over her shoulders. She looked startled when she saw me.

'Hello, Leon. Is everything all right?'

'Yes. I can't sleep.'

'Neither can Elissa. I'm heating some milk for her. Would you like some as well?'

'No, thank you. I think I'll go for a walk.'

She looked out through the kitchen door into the darkness.

'At this time of night?'

I hesitated. Something about her kind, creased eyes made me want to tell her the truth.

'I'm going into town. I need to find Parmenion. He hasn't come back.'

'Oh. Yes.' She took the milk off the stove. 'I'm not surprised you're worried about him. Such a likeable young man. But he's troubled, isn't he? It must be so hard for him seeing you all going out to race every day when he can't.'

I watched as she carefully poured the milk into a cup.

'If you don't find him in town, try the old circus,' said Ismene. 'Amandio and some of his friends go there after dark to race. I've heard that Parmenion's got in with their crowd. Here, take this.' She picked up a lamp and handed it to me. 'It'll be dark on the road.'

'Thank you. Please, could you not tell Scorpus? He'll be angry with Parmenion.'

She nodded. 'I promise I won't. Come and find me if you need help with him when you get back.'

'You don't have to stay up for us.'

'Oh, don't worry about that. These days, I don't sleep much either.' She gave me a weary smile, then disappeared along the corridor.

The main street in Thugga was quiet and the shutters were drawn down over most of the shops. But the slaves at the fullery were still working and the cook shops and taverns were open. I peered into them, searching the crowds of drinkers for Parmenion. There was no sign of him. By the empty shoemaker's, the three old men were having their dice game. I found myself wondering if they ever did anything else.

Following Ismene's advice, I walked towards the north of the town, past temples and tombs where the dead of Thugga were buried. Shadows skulked here, and I was grateful both for the lamp and the gentle companionship of the moon. As I came closer to the circus, I heard whoops and yells. Then there was a smashing sound followed by howls of laughter. I quickened my step. When I reached the grassy bank above the track, I saw that the channel was illuminated by torches from one end to the other. Chariots were circling, driven carelessly by boys taking the turns at the sharpest angle. By the starting gates, a noisy crowd had gathered around a chariot which was harnessed to four horses: Misty, Storm, Cupid and Psyche. The driver standing behind them, holding their reins loosely in his left hand, was Amandio. Behind him, two other boys crouched on the ground. By the light of the moon, I could see something – or someone – lying on the sand between them.

'Well, if it isn't Bodo's boyfriend,' said Amandio as I jumped on to the track. 'You're just in time for the fun.'

Parmenion was lying on his back, moving his arms and legs like an upturned beetle, a sleepy smile on his face. The two boys on the ground were tying a rope to his ankles. The other end was attached to the back of Amandio's chariot.

'What do you think you're doing?' I demanded.

'We're re-enacting the battle of Troy,' said Amandio with an evil grin. 'I'm Achilles and your friend Parmenion here is playing Hector.'

I felt even more uneasy. I had a dim recollection of the story, which Antonius had told me when I was small.

'I've beaten him, because I'm the greatest warrior,' explained Amandio. 'Now to celebrate my victory, I'm going to drag his body three times around the walls of Troy.'

Parmenion, who seemed to have lost his senses completely, giggled.

'Are you insane?' I shouted. 'It'll be like shipwrecking him. His skin's going to come off on that ground.'

Amandio shrugged.

'It was his idea. He wanted to join our dice game, so we let him play. But then he lost and it turned out he couldn't pay his debts. So he said we could do this instead.'

I kneeled beside Parmenion and flicked his face. He mumbled something and I caught a sour waft of wine on his breath.

'Get up, Parmenion,' I urged. 'Come on, you have to get up.'

He responded by trying to hug me. The boys all laughed and jeered. Then they stepped back as Amandio started to wind the reins around his waist. I stood up and held on to Misty's bridle so that he couldn't drive off.

'Three laps of the track,' I said to Amandio. 'You and me. I'll cover Parmenion's bet.'

Amandio looked mockingly at me.

'What, are you going to race me on foot?'

'No. Pick whichever pair you want out of these four. I'll take the other two.' I saw him hesitate, so I threw out more bait. '*And* I'll give you half a lap's start.'

A few of the other boys whistled. Amandio's eyes narrowed. I could see I'd succeeded in irritating him.

'I may not be as good as my brother yet,' he said.

'But I'll be following him to the Circus Maximus soon. Half a lap. That's an insult.'

'Final offer. If you're afraid, let Parmenion go now.'

'I'm not afraid,' he retorted.

'Good. If you win, I'll pay you double what Parmenion owes you. If I win, you forget the debt and you leave Bodo alone from now on too.'

Amandio was silent. Then, aware the other boys were waiting for his answer, he shrugged.

'Done. Let's see how good you really are, Leon of Utica.'

XXV

Howling like wolves, the two boys in charge of opening the gates to Amandio's pen scuttled backwards. Cupid and Psyche sprang on to the track, picking up speed as Amandio brought his whip down on their backs. Seeing their teammates disappearing in a cloud of sand, Misty and Storm called after them, dancing restlessly behind the barrier.

'Easy boys. Easy,' I muttered, working hard to hold them in check. I watched Amandio as he disappeared into the distance. His friends were running along the channel between the torches, applauding and cheering him on. The moonlight added extra illumination to the track but not much. It was going to be difficult judging the turns.

Again, Storm screeched for his teammates.

'Any moment now,' I said, my eyes still on Amandio's receding shape. 'Remember that race you lost to those two at Utica? Time to get revenge.'

Up on the spectator's bank, I could just make out the dark shape of Parmenion. They'd dragged him there and left him sprawled on the ground. He was barely moving. I needed to get this race over with and get him out of here. From the glint of Cupid's harness in the light cast by one of the torches, I could tell that Amandio was about to round the turning post. I squeezed the reins and braced myself. The boys, supposed to be in position to open my gates, were lounging around.

'Come on,' I yelled at them. 'Move!'

Reluctantly, they tugged the gates open. As soon as the gap was wide enough, Misty and Storm leaped into action. Just as I'd been counting on, they were desperate to catch up to their stablemates. Manes flying, they powered into the first lap as if they were reaching the finish at the Circus Maximus. I let them have their heads. This was no time for tactical racing, there was too much at stake.

As I'd expected, the first turn was difficult to judge with only the dancing flame of the torches to light the way. But I did as best I could, and Misty curved round it cleanly. Up ahead, I could see Amandio, still lashing Cupid and Psyche.

'There they are!' I crouched low. 'Let's catch them.'

Excitedly, Misty and Storm extended their noses.

To my left, the faces of Amandio's friends whipped past, their taunts ringing in my ears. Usually, I could feel every bump and rock in my path as the wheels went over it. But Zeno's chariots were so well-sprung, there was hardly any jarring on my knees at all.

We wound round the next post to begin the second lap. Amandio was still a long way in the lead. We'd made up some ground, but not as much as I'd hoped. Steering as close to the channel as I dared, I squeezed the reins, trying to feed the urgency through my fingers to Misty and Storm. I could hear them puffing with excitement. As Cupid and Psyche disappeared at the end of the channel, they quickened their stride. Once again, I relied on instinct as I took the turn. I felt the faintest rattle as my inside wheel skimmed the edge of the channel. But the chariot was sturdy; it didn't lose momentum.

The flames on the torches seemed to be dimming. I was driving into darkness now. If there was an obstacle lying in our path, I wouldn't see it until it shipwrecked us. I didn't care. Amandio was looming larger in my sights. As we cornered for the start of the third lap, I judged that his lead was down to about five chariot lengths. But it was still going to be tough to catch him.

The boys were bellowing at Amandio now, clapping and waving him on. He was still driving well and it crossed my mind that if I'd realised how good he was, I wouldn't have risked giving him such a big advantage. But I wouldn't let the thought of losing even enter my mind. Parmenion was lying on the bank and all that mattered was getting him help. I took the next turn at a dangerous angle, a wheel of the chariot lifting off the ground. Swinging my weight to the other side, I forced the chariot to right itself and urged Misty and Storm on again. With every stride, we were gaining on Amandio and I could see he was struggling to persuade Cupid and Psyche not to hang back for their friends. He hadn't given any thought to what would happen if he went out first.

We were coming up to the end of the channel for the final time. Only half a lap to go. Amandio hugged the inside line. I pulled on Storm's rein and made a quick, darting move, as if to pass Amandio on the right. I knew we wouldn't have the speed to overtake Cupid and Psyche that way. But the looming shadow made Amandio turn and he moved right to block my path, as I'd intended. There was now a gap between the channel and his left wheel. Whether there was space enough for me to pass through, I wasn't sure, but I went for it anyway. It was an even crazier move than the one Abibaal had made at the games in Utica but Misty and Storm tossed their manes as I cracked my whip and eagerly seized the chance to get alongside Cupid and Psyche.

We took the last turn, all four horses side by side. Amandio was breathing hard and swearing, trying to force me into the stone wall of the channel. But it was his chariot that came off the worse in the attempt. As our axles clashed, there was a loud crack. Amandio staggered and seemed to lose his balance. His left wheel had broken and his chariot was listing wildly, the base dragging along the ground. Cupid and Psyche were still cantering, trying to keep up with Misty and Storm. But they were dragging a dead weight behind them. We galloped past the finishing post. The thrill of victory washed over me and I realised something else in the same moment. The curse was finally broken. The race was over and done and the ghosts of my shipwreck with Scylax hadn't come back to haunt me.

When I turned back, I saw that Amandio had managed to pull Cupid and Psyche to a standstill and was on the ground, kicking the broken chariot. His friends were gathering round. I trotted Misty and Storm back towards them and leaped on to the track. I wasn't interested in crowing over Amandio and there would be time to get Parmenion's money back later.

In the darkness, someone was crouching next to Parmenion. I quickened my step and they straightened up, a torch illuminating their face. It was Danel.

'I heard the noise from our stable and I thought I'd probably find Amandio here,' he said. 'Is your friend all right?'

Ignoring him, I kneeled on the cold grass. Parmenion didn't make a sound when I tapped him on the face.

'I need to get him home,' I said. 'You'll have to lend me a chariot.'

'Our stable's closer. You could bring him there.'

'No, thank you. Your family have done enough to him for one day.'

Silently, Danel went and fetched Misty and Storm and brought them over to the side of the track. Between us, we heaved Parmenion on to the chariot. I squeezed in alongside him and took up the reins.

'You don't have to worry about getting the horses back to us right away, or the chariot,' said Danel. 'We've plenty more where they came from.'

'You're too kind,' I snapped. 'But the horses were ours in the first place.' I wheeled Misty and Storm around and set off for home.

XXVI

Just as she'd promised, Ismene was still up when I got Parmenion home. We lugged him to his bed between the two of us, trying not to disturb anyone else in the house. It wasn't easy when he couldn't even stand.

Ismene looked at Parmenion, now snoring on his mattress.

'I suppose you found him at the old circus?'

'Yes. He was with Amandio, like you said. They were playing stupid games.'

'It's always been the place to gather late at night, when you want to hide from your parents. We used to meet down there when we were children. Me, your papa, Soph—'

Ismene stopped herself.

'I think you can say her name now,' I said.

'I'm sorry. It must have been a shock for you, finding out you had an aunt you never knew about.'

'No, not really.'

Ismene's eyes flew to my face. I felt an impulse to tell her everything, every secret that had kept my family quarrelling for so long.

'Scorpus already told us about her,' was all I said in the end.

Ismene sank down on my bed.

'Oh, that makes me so happy!' Realising how loud her voice was in the quiet of the villa, she winced. 'Please, tell me, if you don't mind, what did Scorpus say?'

'Just about why she ran away and what happened to her in Rome. And that you and she were friends.'

Ismene nodded.

'Yes. Ever since we were very young. Sophonisba was the most exciting person I knew. Funny and fearless. I so wanted to be like her. But I never had her bravery. I was the sort of girl who always obeyed my parents and never questioned whether they truly knew what was best for me.'

She lapsed into silence, fiddling with the wedding ring on her left hand.

'Was this her room?' I ventured.

'Yes. How did you guess?'

I went to the cupboard in the corner, took out the wooden box and brought it to her.

'I wondered if this might have belonged to her

once. I thought maybe you had kept the things inside. To remind you of her.'

Ismene's mouth fell open as she lifted the lid. She picked up one of the carved horses and ran her finger over the mane.

'Oh! I never thought I'd see these again! They were her most precious toys. I had my own collection too, not as big as this. But I used to bring them over here and we'd play with them, giving them all names, making them race.' She picked another with a crooked tail and laughed in recognition. 'Scorpus made this one. One of his early efforts with the chisel, not his best maybe. But Sophonisba loved it. She loved anything he gave her.'

She replaced the horse gently in the box and the sad smile on her face deepened as she picked up one of the figurines of the charioteer with the long, curly hair.

'I remember him. His name was Pyramus, I think. An apprentice your grandfather trained. He was quite the local heartthrob around here. Like Danel. Then he went off to try his luck at the Circus Maximus. Sophonisba cried for days when she heard he'd been killed in one of his first races. There was another boy in training at my father's stable, very brash, very full of himself. He stole this from Sophonisba one day and she challenged him to a race at the old circus to get it back.'

'Really? Did she do it, did she race him?'

'Oh, yes. She took a chariot from your grandfather's stable, and his old horse, Tigris, and won by half a length.'

I couldn't help smiling. So did Ismene.

'Your grandfather was furious, though,' she added, shaking her head. 'He used to be proud of her, I think, when she was little, how good she was with the horses. But then there was some talk among the local townsfolk, about Muttumbaal's wild daughter. He started saying she was shaming him. After the race with Tigris, they had an awful fight. She climbed that old cork tree outside and stayed there all night because she knew he'd whip her if she came down.' She stopped. 'I shouldn't be telling you all of this. I don't know why I am.'

'No, please… go on.'

I was trying not to sound too eager. She hesitated, but I could see it was a relief for her to talk about things she'd never been allowed to.

'Well, Scorpus managed to persuade her to come down from the tree in the end. But things weren't right with her and Muttumbaal after that. About a month later, my father told me he was going to be marrying Sophonisba. Can you imagine? My best friend, becoming my father's wife. I was upset. I felt as if Sophonisba was to blame, somehow. We had a fight. She accused me of things too. She said I was weak, that I never stood up for myself. She was right. If only I'd had more courage, if only I'd held out for what I really wanted...'

Once again, I saw her twisting the ring on her finger. A small sigh escaped her.

'Well, no matter now. A few days before the wedding, we heard she'd gone. Run away, and no one had seen her leave. That was the last we heard of her. Until Scorpus came back from Rome and told us what had happened. I never had the chance to make it up with her.'

My senses were drawn towards the place where my mother's lock of hair rested against my heart. I was convinced I could feel a tingling on my skin, as if something had awakened and was struggling to get out. Carefully, Ismene replaced the wooden horses and the figurine of Pyramus.

'It must have been your grandmother who kept all of this. She was devastated when Sophonisba ran away. I often think about how difficult it was for her. Trying to be loyal to her husband, trying to hold her family together. But all the time feeling her heart breaking for what she had lost.'

She closed the lid on the box and stood up.

'You must be tired of hearing about all of these people you never knew. And I'm keeping you from your sleep. I won't tell Barca or Scorpus what happened, I promise.'

She glanced at Parmenion.

'I hope he knows how lucky he is to have such a good friend,' she said with a smile. 'I'm not surprised Elissa's taken such a shine to you. Thank you for being kind to her. Goodnight, Leon.'

After she had gone, I sat watching the shadows from the oil lamp dancing on the wall and feeling as if I was surrounded by ghosts.

XXVII

'Look! Over there.'

It was late afternoon and a long, hot day of training was nearly at an end. We all followed the direction of Hanno's pointing finger, towards the main road on the ridge of the valley, leading to Thugga. A convoy of wagons and horses was coming into view. They didn't get as far as the town gates, turning off the main road and making their way down the side of the valley towards the new circus.

'It's Moses of Thabraca, I think,' said Barca, squinting against the light. 'He's got a lot of greys in his stable. I suppose other trainers will start arriving soon. Good thing we got that early practice in at the old circus.'

We had been in Thugga for almost two months. Some things had changed since we'd first arrived. Others had stayed the same. Scorpus and Muttumbaal's relationship hadn't recovered since the fight at dinner. They exchanged words every now and then, but only when it was something to do with the games. I could tell my grandfather's health was getting worse and I was afraid that time was running out to end the quarrel between them. They were both too stubborn to forgive. Hanno and Abibaal weren't getting on, either, and that led to more flare-ups between Scorpus and Abibaal, who couldn't cope with criticism from his father.

But there were reasons to be hopeful too. My team was coming together well. Porcellus was enjoying his new position alongside Brightfoot and Blaze and the chance it gave him to bully other horses coming up on his outside. Atlas was a good horse, and although I remained frustrated that Jewel wasn't on the inside, she was proving her sprinting speed in the channel race. With Bodo now taking the second leg after Hanno, and Abibaal handing over to me, our changeovers had improved beyond recognition. Best of all was the feeling I had of my strength coming back. My arms and legs were muscled and firm. And, since the race against Amandio, my mind hadn't once taken control of me, forcing me to relive Icarus's death. I felt like myself again, like the Dido – or Leon – of old.

The boys were doing well too. Bodo raced brilliantly whenever his father wasn't around to belittle him. Hanno was making steady progress. But of all of us, it was Abibaal who had come the furthest. He had forged a close partnership with Curly and Thief and was regularly beating his older brother. His turns had come on brilliantly, much to the satisfaction of Muttumbaal, thanks to the wine-jar training. Of all his grandchildren, I sensed that maybe he liked Abibaal the best, and I guessed that Hanno was jealous, which made him get frustrated more than usual.

Now, we watched together as the line of horses picked their way towards the crowded village of stables and tents sprawling around the circus, which was close to completion.

'So it begins,' observed Scorpus. 'There'll be more of them soon.'

He was right. Over the next few days, the streets of Thugga grew busier. I kept my eye out for the sort of men who might be the bounty hunters Cassius Chaerea had described. But as far as I could tell, most of the newcomers were racing fans who had made long journeys over many days to see the new circus and enjoy the games. Every available room in the local taverns sold out and the cook shops did a roaring evening trade. Ticket touts stood at street corners promising seats to the games at triple their worth. Hawkers set up stalls in the marketplace, selling curse-stones and amulets which they promised would bring bad luck upon rival stables.

But the loudest voices about town belonged to the charioteers themselves. New groups of them appeared each day and they roamed the streets in packs, the colours of their tunics proclaiming which of the four factions of Rome their stable had the strongest link to – Green, Red, Blue or White. They liked to gather at the water fountain and flirt with the local girls, who encouraged them from a safe distance before scoldings from the town's older residents sent them on their way. A group from the Thabraca stable had a run-in with Amandio and his friends which ended in a scuffle and some punches being thrown.

Parmenion, to my relief, stayed away from them. I'd spoken to him honestly the morning after the race with Amandio, telling him he'd lose my friendship as well as his job if he didn't change. He didn't say anything at the time. But later that day, I found him in the stables taking the canisters out from under the piles of straw where he'd hidden them and pouring the contents away. He made me a promise then and there. So far, he'd kept it. Every morning we would do muscle training together, bending and twisting to lift stone weights from the ground and lowering ourselves into squat positions, using the long reins to balance against each other. He also admitted that the medication my grandfather had given him was starting to help with the pain.

Ismene kept her word too. She never told Scorpus what had happened that night. I often found myself thinking about the conversation we'd had, the picture she had painted for me of my mother. I also thought about the expression on her face when she spoke of her regret at not questioning what her parents wanted for her. One evening as I came in from the pasture, I spied her and Scorpus through the window of the kitchen. He was smiling and she was laughing, wisps of her black curly hair sticking to her neck as she stirred the contents of a pot. There was a look on both their faces, a happiness that stirred a strange sadness in me. They didn't see me and I vanished quietly before they could.

Three days before the games were due to begin, Barca summoned us at the end of the training session.

'Glabrio's inviting all the competing stables to see the new circus this evening, now that it's finished. They're going to make the draw for the opening day of the games.'

'Can I come?' asked Elissa excitedly.

'Of course not. Now, for the love of the gods, Elissa, don't start whining,' he added, as Elissa looked as if she was going to argue. 'Your job is to stay here and help your mother.'

Seeing that Elissa looked miserable, I tried to cheer her up. 'You can give Porcellus his evening fig for me while we're out, if you like,' I said and immediately her face brightened.

I went to my room to strip off my filthy tunic and replace it for a new one. Sweat had gathered underneath the bands wrapped around my chest and I unwound them so that I could give myself a quick wash. As I was dipping a cloth into the bowl of water, the curtain behind me swished aside. Thinking it was Parmenion, who would usually whistle to let me know he was about to come in, I grabbed the tunic to cover myself and was about to hiss at him to go away.

Then I saw Elissa standing there, the edge of the curtain clutched in her fist. She was staring at me, her mouth open in shock. I was holding the tunic to my front but it was obvious she had already seen what I was trying to hide.

'Wait,' I said, seeing her take a step backwards. 'Wait, Elissa, stop…'

She tried to run but I managed to grab her sleeve and pull her back. She started to gibber and wail.

'Please, you have to be quiet,' I begged.

'You're… you're…'

'Yes. I know.' Gently, I put my hand over her mouth. 'Please, Elissa. Please let me explain.'

She blinked rapidly at me. I made her sit down on my mattress and quickly turned away to put on my tunic while I tried to think of what to say. Then I perched on the blanket next to her.

'You see, I have to wear these clothes and pretend to be a boy,' I explained. 'Or I won't be allowed to race.'

'Does Uncle Scorpus know?' breathed Elissa, still round-eyed.

'Yes.'

'And Hanno and Abibaal? And Parmenion?'

'All of them. But not your parents or Bodo and definitely not Grandpa Muttumbaal. So I'm letting you in on the biggest secret ever and I need you to keep it for me.'

The idea of knowing something that the rest of her family didn't obviously appealed to Elissa. She studied me, her eyes wandering curiously over my face and my hair.

'Is your name really Leon?'

I hesitated.

'No. I can't tell you what it is.'

'Why not?'

'Because there are people looking for me. People who know my real name. They're not very nice and

I wouldn't want to put you in danger. So it's better if I don't tell you.'

'Why do they want to find you?'

'Because I stole something they think belongs to them.'

'What did you take?'

'I can't tell you that either. I'm sorry.'

Elissa was silent for a while. Her fingers twisted together in her lap.

'I always knew you were too nice to be a boy,' she said gruffly and I understood that she was embarrassed.

'Boys aren't so bad,' I said. 'There are plenty of nice ones, like Bodo.'

'Bodo hates me,' she said at once. 'He used to like me but then he stopped. He never wants to take me into town any more.'

'He doesn't hate you. I promise. Once these games are over, he'll have more time for you. You'll see.'

Elissa peered at me again.

'Isn't it frightening, driving a chariot?' she asked. 'Aren't you afraid you're going to die?'

'Sometimes.'

'Then why do you do it?'

Looking down at her puzzled expression, I noticed that although she had Ismene's eyes, she had inherited the strong, proud features of her father's family. My family. Gently, I tucked a stray lock of hair behind her ear.

'Because the circus is the only place where I feel like myself. This is something I'm really good at, Elissa. And I can help Grandpa Muttumbaal and your mama and papa – all of us – by doing it. Will you keep my secret for me?'

Elissa looked awed at being trusted with such responsibility. But she straightened her spine and signalled her agreement to the pact with an emphatic nod.

XXVIII

The sky over the circus was painted with gold and lavender. Birds looped and dived into its torchlit centre as if they were moths drawn by a candleflame. We were standing in a long line leading up to the archway. Beneath the giant statue of Caligula straight ahead of us, we could make out the slender figure of Gemellus Glabrio. Armed guards flanked him as an attendant in black and gold uniform introduced him to each trainer.

'Hector of Bulla Regia,' said Barca, pointing at a thickset man with a bald head, who was surrounded by a bunch of tough-looking boys. 'He'll be our biggest competition, along with Zeno.'

The line shuffled forward. Scorpus was talking to Glarus, who had arrived in Thugga the day before with his apprentices. Watching Glabrio, I noticed he would lean in close when he first met someone, nodding as if they were the most fascinating person he had ever met. Then he would switch his attention to the next face and it was like watching a wax tablet being rubbed clean and presented fresh for the next user.

'Muttumbaal of Thugga,' he said in an earnest voice when it was our turn to be presented. 'Our local hero. My grandfather often spoke of you as one of the greatest trainers in the empire. Welcome. I'm honoured you are competing here.'

Muttumbaal said nothing, eyeing the young Roman like a fox peering out of its burrow.

'And *this*...' Glabrio's lighthouse beam of a smile moved to Scorpus. 'Can it actually be? Scorpus of the Blues. You will not recall, but we have met before. I was just a young boy, visiting this house from Rome and my grandfather took me to the old circus to watch the chariots. It was your last race before you went to the Circus Maximus. I remember thinking then that I had never seen a driver your equal and that I never would again.'

His smile moved fleetingly to Barca, but passed over him quickly without interest.

'These young lads must be your drivers. Future stars of the Circus Maximus all of them, I'm sure. Aha! I see the other home stable is here. What a proud day for Thugga, having not one, but two local stables to represent us.'

It was only then that we realised Zeno was standing right behind us. He was flanked by Amandio, who scowled at me, and Danel, who nodded.

'Good evening,' said Zeno in a hostile tone.

Muttumbaal returned no answer, but stalked through the archway, his walking stick clicking in the darkness. As we followed him, we could hear Glabrio behind us saying to Zeno, 'My grandfather often spoke of you as the greatest trainer in the whole empire. I'm honoured…'

Torches set into the wall flickered as we passed through the long, vaulted archway. My heart beat faster as I thought of the colossal statue of Caligula directly over our heads. Emerging into the open air, the first thing I saw were the gilded turning posts, rising like glittering pines into the fire-streaked sky. I took in the smooth sea of golden sand, the yawning marble channel stretching into the distance and the twin banks of seating which soared above the track on either side, as if they were massive waves about to collide. Alongside me, Bodo, Hanno and Abibaal and the charioteers from the other stables were staring in dazed awe.

'Is it like the Circus Maximus, Dido?' whispered Abibaal, quietly enough so that no one but me could hear him.

'Yes,' I admitted. 'It's just like it.'

As we walked around the echoing stadium, gazing at what that wretched army of slaves had built, I wondered if I'd spoken too soon. The vast starting gates, the towering obelisks along the channel, the seven gold dolphins that dipped their noses to mark the passing of the laps – everything was there that should be. It was as if someone had made a model of Rome's great stadium and brought it here, piece by piece. But something was missing. And I couldn't quite work out what.

From above the archway, Caligula glared at us, his eyes merciless and vengeful. I had an awful feeling, as if his horses were going to come alive suddenly and plunge the chariot on to the track. My stomach churned and I looked away. That pricking feeling was on my skin again. But it soon faded.

The track between the archway and the end of the channel was now seething with a crowd of about fifty charioteers and their trainers. There was a loud blast of trumpets and all heads turned towards Glabrio, who was standing on top of the archway, looking down at us. The oil in his hair glistened in the light of the blazing torches which illuminated the statue of Caligula next to him.

'Thank you,' said Glabrio, that smile still on his face. 'Thank you all for coming here, on the eve of a momentous occasion. As you know, in a few days' time, our beloved Emperor Caligula celebrates his twenty-sixth birthday. Many months ago, I conceived the idea of a fitting gift for a man I am proud to call friend as well as emperor. What better way of honouring that generous patron of the sport of chariot racing, than by building a new circus that will bring the excitement of the Circus Maximus to Caligula's subjects? And what better place to build it than here, in the province of Africa, the breeding ground of the greatest horses and the best charioteers in the Roman Empire?'

An appreciative roar went up from the trainers and drivers. It was then I glimpsed Cassius Chaerea, lurking behind a cluster of slaves. He was watching Glabrio with an expression of undisguised disdain, as the young Roman reverently placed a kiss on the pedestal under the charioteer emperor's feet.

'With your help,' continued Glabrio, facing the crowd again, 'the fame of the Circus of Thugga, and with it, the glory of Emperor Caligula, will spread across land and sea! But before I go on, let me introduce you to some very special guests.'

He gestured to a group of men who had been standing at the back of the archway. All four stepped forward and the colours of their tunics were revealed – red, blue, white and green. A ripple of excitement went through the assembled charioteers. I felt the familiar knot of tension in my stomach. The man wearing green was Scylax.

'You are competing for the honour of your stables and the pride of your home cities,' said Glabrio. 'But I know that every charioteer dreams of his own glory. And so, we have scouts here from each of the four great racing factions of Rome. These men are here looking for new talent. Make sure you impress them. Who knows, you may find yourselves on your way to the Circus Maximus itself.'

The charioteers started grinning and talking up their chances. Scylax had already picked me out of the crowd. He shook his head, a grim smile on his face. I understood his message.

'Tomorrow's racing will be organised in two sessions,' said Glabrio, cutting through the banter. 'Eight stables will compete in the morning and eight in the afternoon. At the end of the first day, I shall host a party in the streets of Thugga, where a fresh draw will be made to decide the running order for the next day. At the end of the competition, the two stables who have won the most victories over the course of twenty races will each put forward their best charioteer to compete for the laurel crown. So, without further ado…'

He reached into the urn and drew out a white ball.

'In tomorrow's morning session, the first of the competing teams, will be...' Glabrio studied the ball and then held it up. 'Glarus of Utica!'

A loud cheer from the crowd around Glarus was drowned out by good-natured heckling from the other drivers. Glabrio selected another ball and then another.

'Atticus of Carthage! Moses of Thabraca! Hector of Bulla Regia!'

Each time he read out the name of a trainer, his words were drowned by hooting acclaim from that stable. Soon, seven of the eight spots in the morning session were filled. Glabrio drew out another ball.

'Muttumbaal of Thugga!'

Hanno and Abibaal cupped their hands around their mouths and made wolf sounds. Barca looked disgruntled.

'Carthage, Bulla Regia and Thabraca all in our half of the draw? That's going to be tough. Zeno's going to have a much easier ride in the afternoon.'

Muttumbaal scowled at his elder son.

'This is why you never got to the Circus Maximus,' he said, cold contempt in his voice. 'You think about losing before you think about winning.'

Glabrio had moved on to the afternoon draw. Zeno's name was called first. Amandio grinned and exchanged backslaps with his teammates. I couldn't see Danel anywhere. But I was uncomfortably aware of the menacing presence of Scylax, the scrutiny of Cassius Chaerea and above all, the inescapable figure of Caligula. My chest tightened. It was getting harder to breathe.

'Where are you going?' muttered Scorpus.

'Just to have a quick look around,' I said. 'Don't worry, I'll be fine.'

Dodging the crowd, I wandered into the deserted darkness of the stadium. My feet sank into the raked sand, which felt cool between my toes. It was better here, away from the crowd. But I needed air, I needed to get higher. In the middle of the tiered seating was the canopied viewing box where Glabrio and his guests would watch the games. I climbed to sit in front of it, leaning against the low stone wall, looking into the darkening sky. Pipe players started up. The draw was over and Glabrio was entertaining his guests.

From the mouth of the box behind me, I heard a slight movement.

'Who's there?' I said, leaping to my feet in panic. My first thought was that it could be a bounty hunter. Then a second, far more terrible fear took hold of me. That somehow it might be the real-life version of Caligula sitting there.

But it wasn't the emperor's pale eyes that peered back at me from the gloom.

XXIX

Danel was sitting in one of the throne-like chairs, like a king.

'Shouldn't you be down there with your team?' I said. 'You missed the draw.'

'What difference does it make?' asked Danel with a shrug.

'You're so arrogant, aren't you? You think you're going to win, no matter what.'

'Does a great charioteer ever think anything else?' retorted Danel.

We glared at each other. Then Danel leaned back and gestured to the chair next to him.

'It's a good view. Come on, come and look at it from here.'

I didn't move.

'Look, I know there's a grudge between your grandfather and my father,' said Danel, sounding irritated. 'But I don't have a quarrel with you and

I don't see why you'd have one with me. Can't we just talk?'

'What do you want to talk about?'

'I don't know. It's not as if we don't have things in common, is it?'

I hesitated. I did want to sit in one of those chairs.

'So,' he said, as I settled down beside him. 'Is it what you expected?' He made a sweeping gesture over the stadium.

'I don't know what I was expecting.'

'Come on, Leon. You know what I'm asking. Is it like the Circus Maximus?'

It was the same question Abibaal had asked earlier. I still wasn't sure how to answer.

'I don't know,' I said. 'The Circus isn't only about the walls and the seats and the track.'

'So, what's missing? The crowd?'

'It might be that, I suppose. When they're roaring you on, you feel... I don't know... like you could do anything.' To my surprise, I realised he was really listening. 'I'm not good at explaining it. That track down there... everything about it's perfect. It's got everything the Circus Maximus has. Except...'

'Blood,' said Danel. 'There's no blood on the track, no sweat. That's what you mean, isn't it?'

I nodded. That was it. No one had ever won

or lost in this circus, no one had ever been shipwrecked. No one would go out thinking about all the charioteers who'd triumphed there before. It was an empty shell.

We sat in silence for a while, watching the antics of our fellow charioteers who were clearly enjoying the party being laid on for them.

'How's your friend?' asked Danel. 'Parmenion, is that his name?'

'He's fine.'

'I'm glad. Grateful too, if I'm honest. Amandio's always been lazy in training. But he's worked hard since that day you beat him.'

He was fiddling with a band on his wrist. Noticing me watching, he held it out to me.

'It's an amulet, with some tail hair from a famous racehorse inside it,' he said. 'My father gave it to me for luck when I was small.'

I pulled out the figurine of Pyramus, which I now wore around my neck alongside the lock of my mother's hair, and explained it was a great charioteer my grandfather had once trained. Danel was silent for a while.

'I wish there wasn't this argument,' he said suddenly. 'Between our families. If you'd grown up around here, we could have pushed each other. Made each other better.'

Something my father, Antonius, once said came back to me. *It's not easy being friends with your competitors.* He'd been talking about himself and Scorpus and their racing days at the Circus Maximus. I thought I'd understood what he meant at the time. That you couldn't be friends with another charioteer if you were also rivals. Now, I found myself thinking about Muttumbaal and Zeno. Maybe what my father had meant was that it was difficult to respect someone who you also wanted to beat more than anything in the world. But also that it was possible.

On the track, two figures had detached themselves from the crowd by the archway. They were standing a short distance apart, looking in our direction. One was leaning on a walking stick.

'It's my papa and your grandfather. They've seen us,' said Danel. 'I suppose we'd better go.'

As we climbed down the steps and stepped on to the track, Danel turned to look at me.

'Maybe one day, once these games are over, you and I can sit down and talk like old friends. Reminisce about our glory days.'

'I think you're the one with the glory days ahead of you,' I said.

Danel shrugged and gave me a little salute, which I returned. Then he went to join his father and they walked away.

'What are you doing talking to him?' growled Muttumbaal as I approached. 'That's the opposition, you don't consort with them.'

His sinewy arms trembled as he fought to keep himself upright with his stick. Suddenly, I realised who he reminded me of. A picture of Sciron came to me, with his grey muzzle and proud stare. I remembered how he wouldn't let me near him when I first went to live with Scorpus. He was a surly beast of a horse then, known for catching you unawares with a vicious kick of his hind leg. Then came the day I saved him from a snakebite. After that, we were firm friends. All he needed was to know he could trust you. I looked into my grandfather's fierce black eyes. I had so many reasons to be angry with this man. But I could see the fear as well as the stubborn rage in him. Like Sciron, he knew he didn't have much time left. But he was fighting death with everything he had.

'Just because I talk to Danel doesn't mean that I don't want to beat him,' I said. 'I do, more than anything. But do I have to hate him as well? Can't you ever be friends with your competitors? You and Zeno were, for a while.'

Muttumbaal said nothing.

'And who knows?' I added. 'Maybe I might even learn something from Danel. Everyone seems to think he's the best there is.'

'Who's everyone?'

'You, for a start. You told me that people would talk about Danel one day instead of Scorpus.'

Muttumbaal shook his head.

'You have something Danel will never have.'

I was surprised and hopeful all of a sudden.

'Me as a trainer.' My grandfather's eyes gleamed as if he had made a joke and was pleased with it. But just as I was thinking that was all he was going to give me, he spoke again, jabbing one finger like a claw.

'All Danel's life, good fortune has come easily to him. Oh, he's worked, done the training. But he always had his father there to guide him and believe in him. He's never questioned his own destiny, never had to struggle. You, on the other hand… you had to wait a long time to find Scorpus, didn't you, to get your chance? There's a look on your face. The look of someone who's had to fight to prove yourself. Danel would be a fool to underestimate that.'

I studied his wizened face and noticed that his grip on his walking stick was still wavering.

'Come on,' I said. 'Let's go home. I'll help you back to the cart.'

'Don't need help,' he grumbled.

But as I put my hand gently under his elbow, he didn't pull away.

XXX

'Hold still, Porcellus. Almost done.'

I applied a spot more dye to the cloth and dabbed it on his forehead. It was only a fleck of white I'd seen showing through the day before. But I didn't want to take any chances, not with Scylax around. Jewel, who was observing the whole operation with interest through her good eye, poked her nose forward and sniffed the dye bottle, which I'd left on top of the gate post.

'No, Jewel. Not for you.'

As soon as I was finished, I gave Porcellus his fig and let him walk away. Jewel followed, and soon they were grazing side by side in the pale grey light of dawn. I looked towards the middle of the plain, where I could just see the distant outline of the circus. Soon, the others would be up and the race-day preparations would begin. I wondered if Hanno or Abibaal had slept. I remembered lying awake all night on the eve of my first race at the Circus Maximus.

For a long time, I sat there on the gate, watching as the sun's first rays began to warm the horizon. Then I felt for the pouch that contained my mother's lock of hair.

'I don't know if you can hear me, Mama. But I know you're going to be with me today.' I clenched my fist. 'I wish I knew what you thought about me coming here. I don't know if your father and Scorpus are going to be able to call a truce. But I hope you think it was the right thing to try to make peace between them. I hope you don't mind that I tried.'

'Where's my whip? Who's taken my whip?'

Abibaal was throwing tunics and breastplates out of the kit chest. He had a panicked look on his face and sweat already marked the arm holes of his blue tunic. Outside the stall, it sounded as if an army was getting ready for battle. Wheels rattled, metal scraped on metal and horses neighed with rib-shaking excitement as men shouted to make themselves heard above the din.

'Your whip's here,' I said to Abibaal, taking it off

the hook on the wall and handing it to him. 'Now, stop making a mess and calm down.'

Abibaal let out a nervous sigh of relief. I put both hands on his shoulders.

'Remember. Bodo and Hanno and I are in this with you.'

'Having you and Bodo helps. Not Hanno.'

'That's not true and you know it. We're a team, Abibaal. We're a family. We win or lose together. So no fighting with your brother today, understand?'

Abibaal made a face but nodded.

We stepped into the blazing heat and were almost knocked over by a groom from Glarus's stable. They were using the stalls next to ours and, like everyone, were rushing to be ready for the procession that would start the games. The charioteers' village beside the circus was a feverish hive of activity. Horses were being assembled in teams of twos and fours, their coats gleaming like metal, their manes woven with coloured ribbons that lifted in the breeze. There were shouts for different harnesses to be fetched, for wheels to be given their final check, and for drivers to get ready.

Beyond the stables, the starting gates of the new circus glittered in the morning sun. Flags fluttered in the breeze from the top tiers and spectators swarmed the staircases as they made their way to their seats. They'd been waiting outside the closed gates when we'd arrived that morning, a huge mass, pouring down the pebbled path from the main road. Now we could hear the simmer of tens of thousands of voices from inside the belly of the stadium, the sound swelling as their numbers increased.

Scorpus came up to us.

'Are they ready?' he asked Barca, who was helping Bodo attach a trace to Ocean's bridle.

'Nearly. Where's Father?'

'In the stands, scoping out where the most dangerous sections of the crowd are likely to be, so we can warn our boys to watch out for things being thrown at them. It's like a snake pit in there. The Bulla Regia supporters are already spoiling for a fight.'

'I'm not surprised. Is it a good crowd, though?'

'Too good. Looks to me like they've sold more tickets than there are seats. People are blocking the exits. Are this lot nearly ready? The procession's about to start.'

Porcellus strutted into harness alongside Brightfoot, Blaze and Atlas. I had plaited his mane and twisted blue ribbons around the dark coils. As he lifted his powerful forelegs and pawed the ground, I saw the attention he got from some of the other charioteers and team trainers. Gently, I smoothed down his black forelock.

'Remember,' I whispered. 'We want everyone looking at the team, not at you. You can't outrun Atlas, even if you think he is going too slowly. Got it?'

He nudged me impatiently with his nose as if to say that he understood perfectly and there was no need to remind him. I took the reins from Parmenion, stepped on to the axle and bounced up and down on my heels a few times to stretch out my legs. From the corner of my eye, I could see Abibaal copying me.

'Here we go, then,' I said.

A throng of chariots was starting towards the great archway, where the opening procession would begin. As soon as Hanno, Bodo and Abibaal were ready, we joined them, riding four abreast. We were dressed in the racing tunics Ismene and Elissa had sewn for us. They were made of undyed wool and had sky-tinted stripes around the neck and sleeves of the tunics. Elissa had made a mistake adding the colour to Bodo's, so the blue had bled messily on one side. Ahead of us were the drivers from Bulla Regia. Their helmets were decorated with a picture of a leering serpent.

People still waiting to get inside the stadium started pushing as they saw us approach. There was a roar inside the stadium as rumour spread that the charioteers were on their way. Food-sellers who had set up stalls under the vaults scrambled to meet the demand from customers wanting to get back to their seats. Three supporters in red tunics were having an angry confrontation with the guard at the foot of a staircase. The men's shoes were tattered and their clothes sweat-stained, as if they had travelled a long way. The guard was refusing to let them in without a ticket, but while he was distracted, I saw another group of young men sneak past him and disappear into the circus.

At the archway, we found a colourful cast of performers had gathered for the opening procession. A team of acrobats were flexing their muscles to warm up, while musicians blew practice chords through their flutes and pipes. Someone in a boar's costume was pretending to charge at a man wearing a lionskin and holding a club. There were real animals too, pink-skinned pigs flapping their ears, and huffing bulls with garlands of flowers over their horns. Waiting to lead them into the circus was Gemellus Glabrio himself. He was standing beside a jewelled chariot drawn by a pair of dapple greys and he wore a black breastplate and a sword belt. A slave was combing his hair.

As the charioteers slowly assembled, I struggled to control Porcellus, who had taken against the man in the lionskin. A team of four gold horses pulled up close by. Danel held their reins easily in one hand. On his other side was Amandio. They both wore emerald green tunics and their chariots were painted green too, with wheels picked out in silver. Porcellus and Centaur flattened their ears at each other.

Finally, Glabrio mounted the chariot. He shouted something, but we couldn't hear him over the spectators. They were chanting and stomping their feet on the ground. It almost seemed as if the walls of the circus were shaking. Then, the massive gate under the archway swung open and the two dapple greys cantered forward; Glabrio raised his arm as if he was leading his troops into battle. He was followed by the first wave of entertainers, tumbling, dancing, waving to the crowd.

'Good luck,' said Danel, giving me a brief salute before urging his four into a canter. He disappeared through the archway along with Amandio and his teammates, and I couldn't stop Porcellus plunging after them. We cantered through the long tunnel, the clatter of wheels both ahead and behind echoing through the dark space. Then we were out into the dazzling light of morning, an oval of perfect blue sky above us, and I saw faces, thousands and thousands of them, gazing down on us.

I waited for Bodo and the boys to come alongside and we cantered slowly down the long golden length of the track. As the teams in front curled around the turning posts at the far end, they fanned out like autumn leaves caught in a gust of wind. Porcellus's ears were pricked and I could sense him longing to stretch his legs and overtake those horses. A large section of the crowd rose to their feet, chanting.

'Danel! Danel! Danel!'

It was the Thugga supporters, standing to applaud their local hero. They were surrounded by visitors from Bulla Regia who booed and tried to drown them out. I saw a scuffle erupt, which was speedily broken up by Glabrio's guards.

Glabrio had now reached the post which marked the finish line, below the grand spectators' box where Danel and I had sat three nights earlier. A slave came forward to take his horses and as Glabrio went to take his seat, his guests applauded him. They were richly dressed – men in striped tunics, women in colourful gowns with their hair arranged in rows of tight curls. In the corner of the box were the faction scouts, in their red, green, blue and white tunics. I tried not to look at Scylax, who was chewing relentlessly. At the back, I spied the white uniform of Cassius Chaerea, standing watchfully in the shadows.

The acrobats and musicians left the circus and the charioteers were instructed to draw up in front of Glabrio and his guests. A priest bowed several times to the statue of Caligula above the archway. Then the animals in their garlands were led forward. The priest produced a huge knife and sacrificed one of the bulls. As the crowd hissed and cheered, I stared at the blood flowing across the sand, like a bright red snake.

My vision clouded. I was back at the Circus Maximus again and it was Icarus lying on the track, not the slain bull. The blood was his. Or was it Parmenion's? Or Scylax's? Or mine?

The wasps were crawling across my skin again.

I can't do it, Mama. I can't do it. I'm going to let them all down.

XXXI

'Four-horse race! Number one drivers! Charioteers to the gates!'

Inside the circus, the crowd roared. Glabrio's games were about to begin.

Parmenion led me into the pen, settling Atlas and Porcellus who were both excited by the sight of the golden track. He checked the harness for the final time. Then he leaned over the chariot guard rail, whispering so that no one else could hear.

'No secrets. I know you're scared. But you can do this. Show them who you are. Understand?'

I bit my lip and nodded. The gate closed behind us and we were in darkness with only the jangle of harnesses in the pens on either side for company.

I tried to distract myself from the fears raging in my head by going through all my usual checks, bracing my feet against the sides of the chariot, winding the end of the reins tighter around my waist, checking the knife was correctly stowed in my breastplate pocket. As my fingers touched the handle, my heart seemed to push out of my chest.

Then another voice rose above the others. The tone was hoarse and rasping.

Fear is just another opponent. To be faced down, then defeated.

A blast of trumpets cut through the tangle of my thoughts. The horses squealed in excitement. Porcellus kicked the gates and Atlas nodded his head. I bent my knees and waited. They held us a long time, the noise of the crowd rising. Then, with a violent clang of metal, the way ahead was suddenly clear.

A wave of heat and noise hit me in the face. The other drivers were lashing their horses in order to pick up speed. As we reached the break line where we could leave our lanes, the charioteer on my right made a move to try and cut across my line. Without hesitating, Porcellus rammed his inside horse with his right shoulder, knocking him off his stride. The Thugga supporters bellowed their appreciation.

My heart lifted.

Come on, Dido. It's you against everyone. Just like it's always been. Show them who you are.

The statue of Caligula loomed as we approached the gold posts at the end of the channel. One of Glarus's drivers took the lead as we came off the turn. Porcellus tried to catch up, but I held him back.

'Not too soon,' I warned. 'Plenty of time to show them what you can do.'

Curse-stones and rocks had already started to fly past my head. I realised now that the seats were closer to the track here than they were at the Circus Maximus. It felt as if those watching from the front row could reach and grab you if you steered too close. Scorpus had been right. The stands were full to bursting. No attempt had been made to separate the supporters from different towns. No matter where you were on the track, there was someone cheering for you and someone else who wanted you to be shipwrecked.

But it didn't matter. I had sand in my eyes, pain in my legs and all I felt was excitement. Porcellus and I were racing together in front of a huge crowd, like I'd always dreamed. There was nothing else to think about, except plotting a path to victory.

We made it to the end of the fourth lap. Glarus's apprentice still held the lead. The Bulla Regia charioteer suddenly sped past us, whipping his horses. Porcellus's ears were flicking back and forth. I could tell he was waiting for my signal. We curved around the next turn. Two laps to go.

I lifted my whip, deciding it was time. But before anything could happen, I felt something slam into the side of my head. A rock had flown out of the crowd and struck me on the ear, below my helmet. Through the pain, I heard a howl of protest from the Thugga supporters followed by the thunder of hooves coming up fast behind me. There was going to be a crash.

I tasted iron and dirt in my mouth.

Cut the reins.

The faces of the crowd swam out of focus. I blinked, trying to keep my balance. But it was as if the chariot was deliberately trying to throw me off its back. I had the vision of Scylax's face again, watching me being dragged along the floor of the Circus Maximus. Pain was coming, pain worse than any I'd known since my father's death...

Then I saw my own shadow on the ground. The clear dark shape of a chariot and horses against the golden sand. I remembered Parmenion, leaping on to Scylax's chariot to save me. Refusing to let him win.

Sensation returned to my fingers. I shook my head and the noise of the crowd flooded my ears.

'Come on!'

Porcellus heard me. His neck lengthened, his knees lifted and the other three took their lead from him. Within half a lap, we were close behind the three leaders.

Around the circus, people were on their feet, craning their necks. I steadied Porcellus, all too aware of Scylax in the front row of Glabrio's box, not wanting to make it look too easy. But my opponents were tired now and not difficult to catch. We passed the third-placed charioteer, swerving round him like a stream flowing between rocks. Then we overtook the second. Only the driver from Bulla Regia stood in our way, with the last turn to go. I kept Atlas on a tight rein as we closed the gap. We were going to win, we were going to score the first victory of the games...

Then, as we were about to make the pass, my left rein snapped clean in half. Atlas stumbled going around the posts, landing on his knees. He picked himself up and Porcellus carried the team forward. But I'd lost momentum and the Bulla Regia team had already moved away from me. We crossed the finish line in second place, just holding on from the driver coming up behind.

The booing went on all through prize-giving ceremony. The Thugga fans were crying, 'Foul!

Foul!' A scuffle broke out in that section of the crowd.

I looked up at the hateful eyes of Caligula. They smiled mockingly at me.

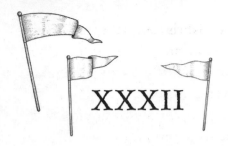

XXXII

Scorpus finished examining the harness and sighed.

'Old leather. Too much wear on it. Just gave out. I don't think anyone tampered with it.'

'I wouldn't be so trusting,' growled Muttumbaal. 'Zeno could easily have got to it.'

'No. We should have invested in some better harnesses. That's all.'

Barca kicked the stable door in frustration and aimed a filthy look at his father.

It was Hanno next, for the first of the two-horse events. He went into the pens with a look of fierce determination and I knew he was desperate to score a win and get one up on Abibaal. He made a good start and went straight to the front, shadowing the lead charioteer from Bulla Regia. The other drivers bunched close behind them and there were some reckless manoeuvres, which resulted in a broken wheel and a scattering of debris across the track. But Hanno kept out of trouble and at the start of the fourth lap, he took the lead with a daring overtake of the Bulla Regia driver.

'Too early,' said Scorpus through gritted teeth, in the competitors' stand next to me. 'He's pushing it too hard.'

Eagle and Dagger held their form, though. Soon, Hanno was a good two lengths ahead. He was driving much more aggressively than he usually did. More like Abibaal, in fact.

'How much if he wins?' I asked.

'Fifty thousand sesterces,' said Muttumbaal, who looked as tense as Scorpus.

I was starting to believe it was going to happen, that we were going to get our first laurel, when it all went wrong. Hanno made a mistake on the turn into the final lap and the Bulla Regia driver took back the lead. Scorpus groaned in frustration.

'That's it. Look at them, they're going backwards now. He took too much strength out of them on those early laps.'

Hanno looked despondent as he came off the track. Scorpus crossed the second line off on his tablet. Another chance of prize money gone.

It didn't help Bodo, who was in the next race, that he had his father in his ear until the lane stewards called them in. Nor that he got left at the start after the gate mechanism jammed, which cost him at least two strides on the other drivers. There were angry demands for a recall from the Thugga supporters, but the stewards ignored them. Bodo fought to make up the lost ground, but he kept making mistakes on the turns, taking them so fast that he couldn't keep control of Ocean and his other horses. On the fifth lap, a curse-stone flew out of the crowd and hit him. I was certain it had been thrown from the area of the competitors' stand where Amandio was sitting, but I couldn't be sure. After that, Bodo went to pieces and he trailed in next to last.

Abibaal had asked me, rather than his father, to come with him to the start. I'd agreed, although I could tell Scorpus was hurt that Abibaal didn't want him there for the biggest race of his young life. Now, as the other teams were loaded into the pens, I thought how small Abibaal looked compared to his opponents. He was obviously thinking the same thing.

'How old do you think he is?' he said, nodding to one of the charioteers from Bulla Regia, who did seem to have a lot of facial hair for someone competing in the boys' races.

'Who knows? Don't think about anyone else, race your own race and remember what

Muttumbaal and Scorpus have told you. Wait for the right moment.'

I put my hand on Curly's bridle and waited for the steward's signal to lead him forward.

'Ready?'

Inside the circus, the crowd were clapping and stamping their feet. I led Curly and Thief up to the entrance of the stall, then stepped back.

'Good luck,' I said, smiling at Abibaal to try and give him courage. 'Be patient. Look after your horses and they'll look after you.'

He nodded, but he looked deathly pale. The dark cell swallowed him up and the gate swung shut with a bang. I went to find Scorpus and Muttumbaal in the stands.

'Is he all right?' asked Scorpus. He looked ill with worry.

'Yes. Like an old hand,' I lied.

There was a long hold at the start. Glabrio was standing at the front of his box, gesturing angrily at the stewards. But they were still having problems with the mechanism which opened the gates. The crowd, who had been clapping and cheering, started to whistle. A few rocks flew on to the track. I thought of Abibaal inside that dark, airless pen and, all of a sudden, I wanted to tell Scorpus to go and get him out of there.

Then they were ready. Glabrio raised his hand and dropped the white cloth. There was a clang of metal as the gates flew back and hit the walls on either side. The charioteers and their horses surged on to the track like a river bursting its banks and the whistles from the crowd were drowned by a roar of excitement. I leaped to my feet along with Scorpus.

'Come on, Abibaal!' he shouted.

Muttumbaal was on his feet too, his black eyes eagerly tracking the moving pack. I could see Abibaal in the middle of the swarm, a tiny figure in his blue striped tunic, his shoulders hunched to his ears. They were scrapping for position, wheels clashing, whips flying. The older driver from Bulla Regia muscled his way to the front with his red roans, and reached the golden posts first. The rest of the field bunched close behind him.

'Hard right on the rein, don't get boxed in,' bellowed Scorpus. But Curly and Thief got Abibaal out of trouble. Soon, they vanished in a cloud of dust on the other side of the circus. Scorpus let out his breath and glanced at his father.

'How did you used to do this when we were growing up? Didn't you ever worry one of us was going to break our neck?'

'If you had, it would have been because you hadn't listened to something I'd told you,' said

Muttumbaal, his eyes still fixed on the drivers' progress.

All the young charioteers were determined to prove themselves and there was a lot of reckless driving on display during the first half of the race. The boy from Bulla Regia still held the lead and had pulled two lengths clear. In the group behind, Abibaal's blue stripes were often lost among the red, white and green tunics. At the start of the fifth lap, there was a huge crash. Several wheels bounced over the channel and pieces of wood went flying into the air. Someone was being dragged by his horses.

'Who is it? I can't see.'

Scorpus was on his feet, cupping his hands around his eyes in desperation. I pointed.

'It's one of the drivers from Thabraca. Abibaal's still up. Look, you can see him.'

Stewards managed to stop the bolting horses, rescuing the shipwrecked driver who was stretchered off. Two laps to go. The challengers weren't making any impression on the leader from Bulla Regia, who could smell victory.

One lap to go. It looked as though the only fight would be over second and third place.

Then I saw it. A darting flash of blue.

'Look!' I said, grabbing Scorpus by the arm. 'He's going for it!'

Abibaal burst out of the chasing pack. Curly and Thief had their noses forward, their manes and tails flying. They were gaining on the red roans with every stride and within half a lap they had closed on them. Sensing the danger, the Bulla Regia driver tried to move out to block any overtake. But all my grandfather's wine-jar training paid off. Abibaal swerved and nipped past on the inside before the leader knew what had happened. Abibaal had timed his run to perfection. As he crossed the finish line, the Thugga crowd roared their approval and Abibaal punched the air.

Scorpus watched in delighted pride as Abibaal took his lap of honour.

'Fifty thousand sesterces,' he said. 'That should buy you some new harnesses at least, Papa. And maybe put a new roof on your stable.'

'No,' answered Muttumbaal. 'Better it goes to helping you rebuild yours. He's your boy. He'll be proud to think he was able to help you.'

They looked at each other. I saw a softening of Scorpus's eyes.

'Thank you, Papa. You inspired him. More than I ever could.'

XXXIII

Back in the charioteers' village, we found Abibaal being slapped on the back by Parmenion and Bodo. Abibaal was wearing the laurel wreath of victory on his head and was smiling from ear to ear. Some of the other trainers stopped my grandfather to congratulate him.

'Well done, Abibaal!' I punched him on the arm and he grinned at me.

'Thanks for coming in with me at the start. I was almost sick on you. Did you see the way I went past that big ugly lad from Bulla Regia? He was so angry afterwards.'

Hanno was standing behind me. I could see that this was difficult for him, after the disappointment of his own race. But he swallowed his pride and nodded at his brother.

'Well done,' he said. 'Great victory.'

'Ha,' said Abibaal rudely. 'Now you get to see what it feels like to be second best for a change.'

Scorpus had been about to take his turn to embrace his youngest boy. But now the smile on his face faded.

'It was a good win, son. But a champion doesn't gloat.'

'You always made me grovel to him when he won and he used to gloat every time.'

'No, I didn't,' protested Hanno.

'Yes, you did…'

'Enough,' said Scorpus, an edge creeping into his voice. 'Abibaal, you've won the race. Act like a winner.'

Abibaal took off the laurel wreath and threw it on the ground.

'You're never happy unless you're telling me what I've done wrong. Why can't you be proud of me, for once?'

He stalked off and Hanno disappeared as well. Muttumbaal, who was still talking to the other trainers but had seen the quarrel, was frowning. Barca muttered something.

'What was that?' snapped Scorpus.

'Nothing.' Barca shrugged. 'I just said it was interesting.'

'And what's that supposed to mean?'

'I was thinking about all the times you beat me and never let me forget it. You've got a short memory, Scorpus.'

'Maybe I took it too far sometimes. But I never refused to shake your hand after a race, Barca.'

'What about when that scout came to sign you for the Blues?' Barca chuckled as if it was a joke, but we could all see it wasn't. 'You couldn't resist rubbing it in. That I'd never been picked to go to Rome and you had.'

'Why should I spare your feelings? You never cared about mine.'

'What's that supposed to mean?'

'You were jealous of me a long time before that scout came by. Why else would you have taken advantage of the one thing you had over me?'

Barca tensed.

'I don't know what you're talking about.'

'Oh, yes, you do. You were the eldest. With all the privilege that went with it.'

For a moment, I thought they were going to draw their fists on each other. Muttumbaal stepped between them.

'Stop this,' he growled. 'Do you want to disgrace me? Bodo, Leon, go and get ready for the channel race.'

As we went to collect our horses from Parmenion, I could see that Bodo was upset. I had a feeling that, like me, he knew the reason why Scorpus and Barca had quarrelled.

We entered the stadium and lined up. Jewel chewed on her bit purposefully. Some of the spectators in the front rows pointed and laughed when they saw her missing eye. Our opponents in the first race were the team from Carthage and we knew that if we beat them, it would be Bulla Regia that we would face next. Abibaal was holding the reins with swaggering confidence. But Hanno was clearly nervous and he got off to a sluggish start, leaving Bodo with some ground to gain. The crowd were fired up, excited by the brute simplicity of the event, which was all about speed. Bodo's horse, River, had a long stride and he gained quickly on his opponent, reaching the end of the track at the same time. The Thugga supporters roared him on. But, in his eagerness, Bodo misjudged the turn and smashed his wheel against the post. His chariot was destroyed. Carthage completed their final two legs at an easy pace while our race was already over, before Jewel had even had the chance to show off her paces. I saw Scylax laughing and sharing a joke with the other three scouts from Rome.

Afterwards, Barca yelled at Bodo all the way back to the stable, leaving him in tears.

We sat together in the stands to watch the afternoon's events in a state of gloom. As soon as Danel came out of the starting gates, it was obvious that every other charioteer in his race was competing for second. He took the lead from the start and extended it every lap. Centaur and the gold horses outside him charged around the track with their dark manes flying. They looked as if they could have run all day. But Danel controlled them with a mixture of aggression and grace that was beautiful to watch. In the end, he won by almost a full lap. The Thugga supporters were ecstatic. Amandio and Zeno's other apprentices won their events as well and later, all four came out together for the channel race. The apprentices took the first legs. They made seamless, well-executed changeovers as they crossed the chalk line. Amandio then extended the lead before Danel took over. He was driving a black horse with a white stripe that reminded me of Porcellus. Victory was quickly secured and they went on to knock out the other two teams they faced. Scylax cheered home every victory from the front of Glabrio's box, punching his fist in the air with satisfaction. On the other side of the trainers' stand, Zeno's face was the picture of pride and satisfaction.

The victory lists were finally closed. With seven wins out of seven, including the channel race rounds, Zeno's stable was the most successful of the opening day. They were followed by Hector of Bulla Regia and Atticus of Carthage with four laurels apiece. At the bottom of the list were the stables with no victories at all. And around halfway up was us, with Abibaal's win.

'Offer still stands, Muttumbaal,' murmured Zeno as he walked past. 'But the price I'm prepared to pay is going down by the hour.'

My grandfather swore at him.

XXXIV

In the distance, we could hear shouts and laughter from the direction of Thugga's main street. The remains of the supper Ismene had cooked lay on the table before us. No one had eaten much.

'Are you sure none of you boys want to go and watch Glabrio's parade?' asked Ismene, clearing away the half-empty bowls of chickpea soup. 'I hear there are going to be acrobats there.'

None of us answered.

'I'm not sure any of them are really in the mood,' said Scorpus.

'I don't see why I can't go,' said Abibaal. 'I was the only one to actually win my race.'

'As you keep reminding us,' muttered Hanno.

Barca entered the courtyard from the kitchen. He had been into town to watch the draw for the second day.

'Well?' asked Scorpus.

'We're in the afternoon session,' said his brother grimly. 'And we've got Zeno in with us this time.'

Scorpus ran a hand over his head.

'Well. That's it then, isn't it?'

'Maybe. Maybe not,' replied Barca. 'Zeno's out of reach, but if we can put together two or three tomorrow, and get deeper into the channel race, we should make enough money to keep at least one of our stables going. Who knows, we might even be in with a chance of getting into the race for the laurel crown, so long as Carthage and Bulla Regia both have bad second days. With Leon in our team, we can do it.'

'Leon can't carry this on his own,' said Scorpus. 'Besides, you're forgetting something else. We'll have Zeno's drivers in all our races, with their horses and those chariots. Ours are almost falling apart after the beating they took today.'

In his high-backed chair, Muttumbaal said nothing. His chest heaved, the sound of his breathing was laboured.

I listened to the cheers and music drifting over the olive grove. The whole population of Thugga was probably out on the streets, celebrating the victories of Zeno and his stable. If only that rein hadn't broken. I'd listened to my grandfather and his advice had worked. I faced down my fears.

But it was too little, too late. I couldn't see how I was going to get the chance to beat Danel now. He was going to the Circus Maximus to become a champion. And I'd be left behind, no one ever knowing my name.

Ismene came into the courtyard. She said something, so quietly at first that none of us heard her.

'Scorpus.' The fear in her voice made us all look up. 'Someone wants to see you.'

From the dim interior of the house, Scylax appeared. Scorpus put a hand on Hanno's shoulder.

'Go inside. Take your brother and Elissa with you.'

But Scylax raised a hand and we saw that he was holding a knife.

'No, no. Everyone stay where you are. Don't want to interrupt the family supper.'

He eased into Ismene's place, next to Elissa. She shrank from him, moving closer to Bodo. Scylax laid down the knife, picked up the cup nearest him and drained it. I saw Muttumbaal and Scorpus exchange glances. My grandfather's look was hard and questioning. Scorpus shook his head slightly and I knew he was warning his father not to react.

'Ah. That's better,' said Scylax, setting the cup down. 'Been a busy day. Just seen those boys from Bulla Regia. Offered two of them the chance to come and race for the Greens. Bought some horses off them too. The emperor's going to be very happy.' He patted the seal on the scroll at his waist.

'What can we do for you?' asked Barca, nervously.

Scylax leaned back in the wooden settle.

'Came here to ask your brother a question. Came here to find out why he lied to me.'

'About what?'

'He knows. Don't you, Scorpus?'

All eyes turned to my uncle, who was still gripping Hanno by the shoulder.

'I haven't a clue,' he said.

There was a horrible, knowing look in Scylax's eyes.

'I think you do.'

'He's already told you. He doesn't,' said Parmenion. 'So why don't you slither off?'

Under the table, I pressed my knuckles warningly against Parmenion's leg.

'Brave lad.' Scylax bared his brown teeth. 'But you're not going to distract me this time. I want to know why Scorpus here lied to me about the girl and I'm not leaving until I find out.'

'What girl?' demanded Barca.

Still, Scorpus said nothing. Scylax leaned

forward, the light from the candles illuminating his harsh face.

'You're wriggling like a fish on a hook, my friend. You know full well which girl I mean, don't you, Scorpus?'

His fingers toyed with the blade by his hand. Elissa pressed herself even closer into Bodo's side. My heart was thumping.

'Wasted a lot of time, this summer,' said Scylax, the light from the candles illuminating his face menacingly. 'Looking for leads at every stable I came to. Turns out, this was the place I should have been sniffing round all along. Interesting town, Thugga. People around here have got long memories. I got talking this evening with some fellows playing dice on the main street. They tell me this old-timer, here' – he nudged Muttumbaal with his toe as he said it – 'used to have a daughter. And you'll never guess what her name was.' Scylax picked up a morsel of bread on the tip of his knife, brought it to his lips and ate it. Then he looked around at us with a triumphant smile in his eyes. '*Sophonisba.* Would you believe it? But Scorpus here, when I asked him a couple of months back, he told me he'd never heard of any woman of that name.'

'If my son did say this, he was obeying my wishes.' Muttumbaal spoke suddenly, in his low rasp. 'My daughter disgraced her family. We don't speak her name here.'

'That's convenient, isn't it? Point is, Scorpus lied. Now, I want some honest answers.'

He brandished the knife threateningly so that it caught the light. Elissa cried out in terror and grabbed for Bodo, who moved to her other side, so that he was sitting between her and Scylax. Ismene gasped and covered her mouth with both hands. I tried to catch Scorpus's eye.

'This is ridiculous,' protested Barca. 'If it's the girl from the Circus Maximus you're looking for, you're chasing ghosts by coming here. My sister has been dead for fifteen years.'

'I know she has,' said Scylax, not taking his eyes off Scorpus. 'It's her daughter I want. Antonius's girl. You're hiding her and I want to know where.'

Muttumbaal's chest stilled, his breathing suddenly quiet. Ismene and Barca looked as if they'd been struck dumb. But out of the corner of my eye, I could tell that Elissa was staring at me. I felt dizzy with fear. By the pressure of his hand, I knew Parmenion was telling me to stay quiet. But I couldn't let this go on much longer. I'd rather go back to Rome and be Caligula's slave for the rest of my life than let Scylax hurt any of the people around this table. Cassius Chaerea could choke on his threats for all I cared.

A sound on the wind caught my ear. For a moment I thought it might have been the echo of wheels. But now there was silence again. Scylax's eyes were still fixed on Scorpus.

'So? It's no use telling me you don't know where she is. I'm not leaving here until I get some answers.'

The edge of the blade caught the light as he tilted the knife. I willed Scorpus to look at me. *Stop this. Stop it now.* Across from me, Elissa was starting to squirm, unable to control herself.

'What's going on with her?' asked Scylax. 'You know something, little girl?'

Elissa pursed her lips and shook her head desperately.

'Leave her alone,' said Bodo.

But Scylax hadn't lost the ability to sense weakness in his opponent. It had once made him one of the most ruthless charioteers at the Circus Maximus. Ignoring Bodo, he reached past him and stroked Elissa's cheek with the edge of the knife. She whimpered in terror.

Barca and Scorpus sprang to their feet at the same moment Bodo grabbed Scylax's arm. But Scylax was too strong for him. Ismene screamed as Bodo was forced on to his back under the weight of Scylax's body, the point of the knife pressed into his throat.

'No!' Barca stopped and held Scorpus back too. 'Not my son. Please!'

I shook off Parmenion's hand, which was trying to keep me in my place. *Stop. It's me you're looking for.*

But the words I was about to say died in my throat. Someone else spoke ahead of me.

'Stand away from him!'

XXXV

D anel stood in the light from the doorway into the house.

'You heard me,' he said sharply to Scylax. 'Stand away from him.'

Scylax hesitated. Then he stood up and Bodo was dragged into an embrace from his mother and sister.

Danel turned to my grandfather, who was sitting in his chair, his face white, his hands trembling.

'Forgive me. I know ordinarily I would be forbidden from setting foot here. But I have business to discuss with you.'

Muttumbaal seemed unable to speak.

'This man thinks we're hiding the princess,' said Scorpus in a low voice. 'The one on all the posters in town. We've tried telling him that she's not here but he refuses to believe us.'

Danel stared at Scylax.

'You must be drunk. This lady here is my sister.

How dare you insult her? These people are telling you the truth. I'll speak for it.'

'Stick to racing, lad,' snarled Scylax. 'You don't know what you're talking about.'

Danel regarded him coolly.

'No? I do know that I'm supposed to accompany you back to Rome once the games are over. I've had a letter from the emperor himself, telling me how much he's looking forward to me coming to race for him. Would you like to be the one to inform him why I'll be declining the invitation?'

Scylax licked his lips. There was a long pause.

'You're conspiring,' said Scylax, finally. 'The lot of you. I'm going to find Antonius's daughter and I'm going to bring her in and get my hands on that reward money. And when I do, I'm going to prove that you've all been hiding her. Then you'll see what the emperor does to you.'

He disappeared into the shadows and moments later, we heard his horse's hooves cantering up the track. Ismene took Danel's hand and kissed it.

'Thank you, brother,' she said, her eyes shining with tears.

'It was nothing. What was that lunatic talking about?'

'Who knows?' said Scorpus. 'But you came along at just the right time.'

'I'm glad. I brought something which I hope might… But forgive me… is your father all right?'

Muttumbaal was leaning over the table, his knuckles pressing into the wood. He was struggling to breathe. Scorpus went to him at once.

'Papa?'

Muttumbaal's eyes were bright with alarm. Barca came to help. Between him and Scorpus, they persuaded their father to sit down. His awful panting didn't stop.

'He needs the physician when he gets as bad as this,' said Barca. 'I'll ride into town. Get him to bed. Ismene, fetch the ephedron.'

But Ismene was trying to comfort Elissa, for whom the emotion of the evening had become too much.

'I can find the ephedron,' I said. 'I know what it looks like.'

I found the bottle in the medicine cabinet. As I hurried along the corridor, I realised we had abandoned Danel. But there was no time to think about that now. Pausing by the door of the bedroom next to Barca and Ismene's, I could hear Muttumbaal still struggling for breath.

'Easy, Papa. Easy,' said Scorpus.

He came to take the ephedron from me and I watched as he went to the low bed in the corner and put the bottle to Muttumbaal's lips. Slowly, painfully, the awful gasping noise eased. Scorpus laid a hand lightly on his father's back, stroking it as he would a nervous horse. I watched them for a moment. Then I drew the curtain back across the doorway to give them privacy. But no sooner had I turned away than I heard my grandfather's croaking voice.

'Why... did you... never... say...?'

I stood still as a statue, every muscle in my body tensed as I waited to hear what would come next.

'When you... came back... when you... told us what had happened... you never said... Sophonisba had a child.'

It was the first time I'd heard my grandfather say my mother's name.

'You'd already told me she was dead to you,' said Scorpus quietly. 'I didn't think you'd be interested. And, maybe, I didn't want to give you the chance to reject the child too.'

'So... it's true?'

'Yes. A girl, if you must know. Born a few months before Sophonisba died.'

The wheezing started up again, loud and painful. Scorpus urged my grandfather to open his mouth and he must have given him more ephedron because soon the room was quiet again.

'When I... saw those posters around town, I

thought… maybe… you lied to me. Maybe… you told me Sophonisba was dead… all those years ago… to punish me.'

'Barca wondered the same thing. I wish I could tell you that's what happened. But I didn't lie. She's not coming back, Papa.'

There was a long silence, broken only by the soft sucking sound of my grandfather's lungs opening and closing.

'I'm going to see if there's any sign of Barca with the doctor,' said Scorpus. 'Don't try to get up.'

Scorpus came to the doorway. He saw me standing outside.

'Scorpus…'

My uncle turned his head, his hand still on the curtain.

'Yes, Papa?'

I caught one word. *Name.*

Scorpus glanced back at me. He hesitated before answering his father.

'Dido,' he said. 'They called her Dido.'

This time, there was no reply.

'Was I right to tell him?'

We were outside, a cool breeze blowing in our faces

as we watched the track that led down to the house. Thin purple clouds prowled the horizon. Scorpus repeated his question. I shrugged, feeling helpless.

'I wish there didn't have to be any more secrets. I'm so tired of hiding, Scorpus.'

'I know. I'm sorry.'

He squeezed my shoulder.

'Is Danel still here?' he asked, after a while. 'What did he want?'

'I'm not sure. I think he's gone. Zeno probably sent him. To offer to buy the stables again.'

'Maybe.' Scorpus sighed. 'I'd better go back and sit with your grandfather. Go and see if Ismene needs any help with Elissa, would you? There's nothing you or anyone else can do until Barca gets back.'

I heard Ismene moving about in the kitchen and went to peek in Elissa's room. She was curled up in some blankets, but she sat up when she heard the curtain twitch.

'Mama's heating some milk for me,' she said. Her face was tear-stained. I went and gave her a hug and she clung to me with her thin little fingers.

'You were so brave not to give me away,' I whispered. 'But don't you ever put yourself in danger protecting me again, you hear? I'd sooner die than let anyone hurt you or Bodo.'

She nodded and peered at me.

'Was that man right?' she asked. 'Are you really Aunt Sophonisba's daughter?'

I took out the pouch from around my neck and showed her the curl of hair inside.

'This was hers. People sometimes tell me I'm brave like her. Now I know it's in you too.'

She smiled and after giving her another hug, I left her playing with the toy horse from my mother's collection that I'd pressed into her hand.

There was no sound from the boys' room and Parmenion wasn't in ours either. I went outside and listened for the doctor's cart. Music was still drifting over the olive groves. Then I heard noise coming from the stable yard. It sounded like laughter.

'Look what Danel brought!' said Abibaal happily, when I came around the corner.

They were all there – the boys, Parmenion, Danel – crowded around a cart drawn up in the middle of the yard. Chariots were tied to the back of it, carefully secured with rope so that they wouldn't roll off. I watched in bewilderment as Danel carefully passed each vehicle into the waiting arms of Hanno and Abibaal. Parmenion was crouching on the ground, inspecting the wheels and axles.

'Aren't they amazing, Leon?' said Bodo. 'Danel's lending them to us.'

From the cart, Danel gave me a sideways look.

'Why?' I demanded.

'Because yours aren't fit for competition, to be blunt,' he said. 'These were made by the finest race engineer in Africa.'

'We don't need your charity. Besides, how do we know you haven't tampered with them?'

'My thoughts exactly,' said Parmenion.

Danel jumped down and set the last chariot on the ground before straightening up and looking me in the eye.

'You don't much like trusting people, do you?'

'I've never had much reason to,' I replied.

'Well, here's something you can be sure of. I'm planning to beat you for the laurel crown tomorrow. And I want you to use these chariots so that no one can say I had an unfair advantage.'

I shook my head in disbelief.

'You can't possibly still think I'm going to be in that last race with you. You saw what happened today. We're nowhere. I lost.'

'You were unlucky, that's all,' said Danel. 'You'll come back. I'd put money on it, after the way I saw you drive against Amandio.'

We eyed each other for a while.

'I don't see you offering to give us back our stolen horses,' I said. 'And what's your father going to say when he sees us driving these?'

'The horses I can't do anything about. But I want my father's victory over Muttumbaal to be as sweet as possible and that's what I'll say to him. Look,' said Danel, pushing back his hair. 'You don't have to trust me if you don't want to. I'm not trying to be nice here. If I'm going to go to Rome and call myself the best charioteer at the Circus Maximus, let alone the number one driver for the Greens, I need to *know* for myself that it's true.'

He climbed on to the cart again and nodded at the chariots.

'Use them. Don't use them,' he said to me. 'Just make sure you get to that final.'

XXXVI

A red sun was rising behind the circus. Against the fiery sky, we could see the shapes of people waiting in huge lines outside the staircase entrances. It was early but there were thousands of them.

'It's even worse than yesterday,' observed Barca. 'Those ticket touts are going to do good business.'

Porcellus pranced and tossed his head. I rested my hand on his withers to soothe him. Parmenion and the boys were bringing the rest of the horses. Scorpus drove the cart with our equipment. Muttumbaal sat alongside him. We'd disguised the loaned chariots by covering them with piles of harness. Neither Barca nor Scorpus had any qualms about accepting Danel's gift, but we knew my grandfather would see it differently. In his weakened state, though, he barely seemed aware of his surroundings. But he wouldn't hear of staying behind at the villa.

As we passed the circus, the smoke from eggs being fried in chicken fat filled the air. The snack vendors were already busy.

'I hope Glabrio's got enough manpower on hand to protect those staircases,' said Scorpus, nodding at a group of men who were arguing with a guard, trying to persuade him to let them through.

Next to him, Muttumbaal started to cough, then retch. He was wrapped in a blanket, but it didn't stop him from shivering.

'Are you all right, Papa?' asked Scorpus, drawing the mules to a halt. 'I'm not sure this was such a good idea. Shall I take you back?'

'Stop your coddling,' muttered Muttumbaal. 'Just let me down here so I can get to my seat.'

He climbed off the cart, assisted by Barca, and hobbled towards the staircases, supporting himself with his stick.

'I'll see that he makes it safely,' said Barca, handing Ocean's reins to Parmenion. 'Give me the ephedron in case he needs another dose. You go and start preparing the horses.'

At the charioteers' village, there was a watchfulness between the teams who still had a good chance of getting their charioteers into the race for the laurel crown. Hector of Bulla Regia was barking orders at his grooms. I saw Danel, stretching the muscles in his legs. We acknowledged each other with a look, but didn't speak.

I put Porcellus and Jewel in the stalls next to each other, then brushed each of their coats in turn while they ate their breakfast.

'Big day today,' I said to Porcellus, combing his mane so that it gleamed like silk. 'I'm going to need you to be at your best, you know that?'

Porcellus blew out through his nostrils and nudged me.

'I see. You'll be on your best form, but only if I give you a fig. Is that it?'

Clearly pleased that I understood the situation so well, he chewed up the sweet fruit I held out to him, making a smacking noise with his teeth.

'Good boy, Porcellus,' I said, rubbing his nose and giving it a quick kiss.

A loud banging made me jump. Jewel had spooked at something and was pacing her stall. I went in and found that she had kicked her water bucket over. Her eye was bulging with alarm and I could see the white around it.

'Easy girl,' I said. 'Easy.'

She calmed down, but her ears were still twitching. I looked around to see what could have frightened her, but there was no sign of anything unusual. The stall next to hers was empty.

We watched the morning session from the stands. The team from Carthage was racing. They already had four laurels from the first day, and we knew that if we were going to have any chance of getting into the top two places in the victory lists, we couldn't afford for them to do well. When they won the first race of the day, our hearts sank. But their luck ended there. Their drivers suffered one mishap after the other. The channel race had been a strength of theirs from the day before. But in their opening head-to-head, Glarus's team came through and denied them the prize.

As the Thugga supporters celebrated, Scorpus exhaled.

'That was close. I'm going to owe Glarus a drink when we get back to Utica.'

With half the day's races run, Zeno was still top of the standings. But the second spot in the race for the laurel crown was open. The Circus was bubbling like a cauldron and the mood was getting bad-tempered. People without tickets had been pushing their way into the stadium all morning. Gemellus Glabrio's guards had tried to hold them back, but they scaled the walls and were hauled up by friends. People behind us were complaining that they were being crushed. Scuffles between rival supporters were frequent, with the worst clashes between those from Thugga and Bulla Regia. I saw Glabrio come to the front of his box and raise his arms, trying to persuade the crowd to calm themselves.

After a break for lunch, the trumpets sounded to summon the eight stables competing in the afternoon session. My heart leaped. At last, I was going to get my chance to pit my skill against Danel. Even better, I was going to do it with the team I'd always wanted to drive in the first place. Apart from Parmenion, I hadn't told anyone about my plan to substitute Jewel for Atlas on the inside of my four. I knew she was the right horse and with my grandfather safely in the stands, he wouldn't be able to protest.

But when I got to the warm-up track, there was no sign of Danel. Parmenion came to adjust a strap on Jewel's bridle.

'Your rival has scratched,' he said. 'Resting those gold horses of his, or so their groom tells me. For when he gets to the final.'

I ground my teeth. *So that's how you want to play it. Fine by me.*

The lane stewards called us in. Scorpus came to wish me luck. As soon as he saw Jewel, he opened his mouth. Then closed it again.

In the darkness of the pen, I tickled Jewel and Porcellus's backs to let them know to be ready. They nodded their heads eagerly and the trumpets sounded again. It felt so different to have such a beautifully sprung chariot floor to stand on. The countdown started and the crowd bellowed in anticipation. This time, the gates worked and as soon as there was daylight ahead, I roared at my team.

'Go!'

We plunged on to the track with the other teams. As soon as we'd crossed the break line, the Bulla Regia driver in the lane inside me pushed to get to the front. I let him go, tucking in close behind. Scorpus and I had already agreed on the tactic before the race. By sticking close to my opponent, I would make his supporters think twice before throwing a rock or curse-stone that might go astray.

Three laps went by in a blur of sand and heat. Even though they'd never raced together competitively as a four, there was already an understanding between my horses. Porcellus and Jewel controlled the pace, Brightfoot and Blaze kept perfect rhythm. Jewel's ears were pricked. She was loving the atmosphere of the big stadium. The leader and I were now clear of the rest of the field. He whipped up his horses on the fourth lap, trying to put clear distance between him and me. I let him go but not too far ahead. Behind us, I heard a crash. For a moment, I had that feeling of something crawling on my flesh. But I focused on the lock of my mother's hair resting against my breastbone. Soon, my mind was clear again.

Mid-way through the sixth lap, I tapped Jewel once on the flank. It was time to make our move. With a gleeful snort, she stretched her neck. Brightfoot and Blaze kept the chariot steady as we came to the turn, and Porcellus worked skilfully to keep us moving around it with no loss of speed. We came up fast on the leader. A chant began to bounce off the high walls of the circus.

'Thugga! Thugga!'

The Bulla Regia driver glanced around in surprise. He'd probably thought he had this sewn up, with Danel out of the race. Raising his arm, he cracked his whip. But Jewel's red coat was already skimming his outside horse's shoulder. We sped past on the outside and soon we were clear.

For the final half-lap, I let my team have their heads. I wanted to be sure of victory, but I also wanted to send Danel a message. Porcellus was flying on the outside. But it was Jewel who the Thugga crowd was cheering as she coiled around the turns like an eel. As we crossed the finish line, I clenched my fist and celebrated with them. Then, tucking my hand inside my tunic so that no one would see, I stuck a finger up at the statue of Caligula.

Lining up in front of Glabrio for the presentation of the laurels, I noticed that Scylax wasn't in his seat next to the other scouts from Rome. For some reason, this made me uneasy. But I told myself there was no point in worrying. My grandfather was right.

All that mattered now was winning. Winning and family.

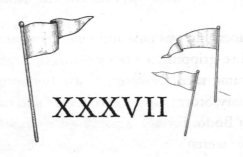

XXXVII

Try as he might, Hanno couldn't get us another win in the two-horse event. But he did manage to snatch second place on the line and, in the channel race, we knocked out the team from Thabraca. In the next round, we'd face Bulla Regia, and if we beat them, there was a good chance we'd be up against Zeno's stable for the final round. By now, Jewel had captured the hearts of the Thugga crowd and as we came off the track, they were chanting her name. Some of the schoolboys who usually followed Danel thronged around us and asked if they could stroke her. According to Scorpus, my grandfather had cursed when he saw her on the track instead of Atlas in the first race. But after we won, not another complaint had escaped his lips. And if he'd noticed the new chariots, he wasn't saying anything about those either.

It was Bodo's turn next in the second of the

four-horse races. He was pale and tense, his hands gripping and re-gripping the reins. Amandio, who was in the same race, drove on to the warm-up track with Misty, Storm, Cupid and Psyche. He said something to Bodo. From the smirk on his face, I guessed they weren't words of encouragement. Then Barca summoned Bodo over to the fence. He listened to his father for a while, nodding along obediently. Then suddenly he drove away, leaving Barca mouthing in mid-sentence.

'Are you all right?' I asked as he caught up with me.

'Yes,' said Bodo. 'I just needed to get him out of my head.'

Then stewards called them in. The teams were loaded, the crowd started to chant and after a long delay, we heard the clang of the gates flying open. I was still on the warm-up track, cantering Atlas who I'd decided to race in the next round of the channel race in order to give Jewel a rest. For the first half of Bodo's race, I had to rely on the noise of the crowd to work out what was going on. When a gleeful howl scared the roosting birds off the top of the circus wall, I couldn't stand it any more and handed Atlas's rein to Abibaal.

'Big smash on the turn,' said Parmenion, as I joined him and Barca who were watching from the starting gate. 'Three charioteers down, there's wreckage all over the track. But Bodo's still up and he's into third. Just over a lap to go now. Here they come.'

With a thundering of hooves, the leading group of drivers approached the end of the channel nearest to us. Amandio was in front. I felt furious as I saw him lashing Cupid. He took the turn well. But Bodo was driving brilliantly and he steered Ocean on an even tighter line around the posts. Alongside me, Barca's knuckles were white as they gripped the metal railings of the gate.

'Come on, son. Come on,' he muttered.

The last golden dolphin dipped its nose. The charioteers were galloping away from us now, disappearing in a cloud of sand, and it was impossible to see what was going on at the far end of the track. A roar of 'Thugga! Thugga!' echoed around the stadium. But we had no way of knowing if it was Amandio or Bodo the spectators were cheering for.

'They're on their way back,' I said, squinting into the distance. 'I can't tell who's in the lead. There's only two of them at the front now, I think. Wait… is that… yes! It's Bodo! He's into second! And he's catching Amandio!'

Amandio's chariot was starting to weave across the track. It was a desperate tactic, something you did when you knew the charioteer coming up behind you had more speed and your only option was to block them. We watched, our hearts in our mouths. Bodo was trying to find a way past.

'Yes, go on, Bodo, go on...'

Amandio glanced over his left shoulder, then his right. Both chariots were almost at the turn. Again, Bodo moved wide as if he was going to attempt to overtake. Again, Amandio steered right and covered the move. Suddenly Ocean swerved, slicing through the narrow gap that Amandio had left open. There was a nail-biting moment as Amandio tried to swing back and shipwreck Bodo against the channel wall. But Ocean held firm. Cupid and his teammates were spent and Amandio could only watch helplessly as Bodo galloped clear, crossing the finish line a full length ahead.

Barca was shaking the bars of the gate as if he was a man trying to break out of a cage.

'He did it. He won, he won, he actually won!'

When Bodo emerged from the circus and saw his father and I coming towards him, his face split into a beaming smile.

Barca put his hands on the guard rail of the chariot. Eventually the words came out.

'You did well, son. The way you took that last corner, it was just like... just like watching your grandfather...'

Barca's chin dropped. Emotion was making his body shake.

Bodo leaned forward and gently put one arm across his father's shoulders.

Spurred on by his victory in the four-horse, Bodo raced brilliantly in the channel race against Bulla Regia, handing me a lead that Atlas and I were easily able to convert to a victory. Meanwhile, Danel led his stable to a huge win in the other round. It would be us against them in the final.

With two laurels left to win, Zeno was still a long way out in front in the overall standings. Hector of Bulla Regia's stable had five laurels and two second places, as did we. If Abibaal could finish ahead of his opponent from Bulla Regia in the last of the boys' two-horse events, the result of the channel race wouldn't matter. I would be going up against Danel for the million sesterces that would save both Scorpus and Muttumbaal's stables.

Scorpus and I stood either side of Abibaal's chariot, waiting for the lane steward to summon him forward. Curly and Thief were pawing the ground and shaking their heads.

'Remember, son,' said Scorpus. 'It's not all

about speed. Keep your eyes open, watch your competitors, pick your moment…'

'I know, Papa, I know.' Abibaal was bouncing up and down on the springs of his chariot, gnawing on a piece of straw tucked into the corner of his mouth. 'Trust me. I can do this.'

He hadn't objected to Scorpus coming down to the gate with him this time. The steward gave the signal.

'Remember, second place will be enough to keep us in it, even if Zeno's driver wins,' said Scorpus, walking alongside the chariot as the wheels rolled. 'Manage your horses, use your ears as well as your eyes, keep your knees soft and don't…'

But his words were lost. The gate had slammed shut behind Abibaal.

'Nothing else you can do,' I said to Scorpus.

He let the breath out of his lungs.

'No. Just pray.'

The chariots broke in an even line. Abibaal was in a strong position at the end of the first lap, behind the two leaders. Scorpus and I were watching from the competitors' stand alongside Muttumbaal.

'Good line,' I said as Curly and Thief swept around the turn. 'He's keeping them together nicely.'

On the second lap, the pace slowed. The whole field was bunched together. There was a lot of scraping and swearing as the chariots clashed. Miraculously, no one was shipwrecked. Then Zeno's young apprentice whipped his horses aggressively and moved to the front. Abibaal stayed close to him, but to my relief, he didn't attempt to go past.

'Yes! He's learning, Scorpus, he definitely is.'

Scorpus chewed his lip and said nothing.

The golden dolphins continued to dip their noses. As the race unwound, Zeno's apprentice and Abibaal gradually began to put distance between themselves and the rest of the field. The Thugga supporters were split along faction lines, the Greens cheering for Zeno's stable, the Blues for Muttumbaal's.

On the sixth lap, the charioteer from Bulla Regia made a quick, darting bid to get to the front. But Abibaal covered the move and his opponent fell back. On the next turn, Zeno's apprentice made a mistake, drifting wide.

'Now, Abibaal, now!'

As if he had heard me, Abibaal crouched low and tried to go for the gap. Curly and Thief stretched their noses, galloping at full pelt. But they didn't quite have the legs. Scorpus let his head drop in frustration.

'It doesn't matter,' I said to him. 'That Bulla Regia driver's not going to catch them. If it stays like this, we're through. Just hold your position, Abibaal.'

But Abibaal was desperate for the win. You could see it from the way he was pushing Curly and Thief, cracking his whip over their heads. They were hurtling down the home straight for the last time. Zeno's apprentice hugged the line closest to the channel. Try as he might, Abibaal couldn't get around him. Then, as they prepared for the turn, the tiniest of gaps opened up on the inside. Abibaal's eyes fixed on it.

I caught my breath and I heard Scorpus doing the same. We could both see what was going to happen.

'No, don't be an idiot, you can't do it...'

It was too late. Abibaal was trying to force his way through the gap. But there was no room. His left wheel shredded on contact with the wall of the channel. The chariot tipped sideways and Abibaal disappeared.

'No!'

Scorpus had already climbed over the barrier and was charging across the track. He got to Curly and Thief as they rounded the turn, dragging the shipwrecked chariot behind them. They were confused and willingly came to a stop as Scorpus grabbed for their reins. Drivers thundered past, almost colliding with the wreckage. I dodged between them and found Scorpus kneeling on the track. He was desperately trying to revive Abibaal, whose twisted body was lying half-in and half-out of the chariot.

'Wake up, son. Come on. Wake up.'

Stewards ran over to us. Around the circus, people were standing up, trying to see what was going on. There were a few cheers for the winner as he crossed the finishing line.

'Abibaal, it's me, come on, son. It's Papa.'

A trickle of blood seeped from under Abibaal's helmet, soaking into the sand. His eyes didn't open.

The stretcher-bearers took Abibaal to the medical tent. We crowded in too, staring at Abibaal's lifeless face. The physician, a man in a blood-stained apron, examined the head wound. Then he prised open Abibaal's eyes and peered into them.

'Not good. Probably a skull fracture.'

'What can you do?' asked Scorpus.

'See if he wakes up. If not, we can try opening his head. See if that makes the swelling go down.'

Hanno stumbled out of the tent and I heard him retching.

'What are the chances he will wake up?' asked Scorpus through gritted teeth.

The physician scratched his head.

'Hard to say. I've seen it happen. Sometimes the damage is so bad though, you think it would have been better if they hadn't.'

He shrugged and busied himself with another patient on the other side of the tent. Scorpus sank to the ground next to Abibaal's stretcher. Barca gripped his shoulder.

'He'll be all right, brother.'

'What if he isn't?' There was a crack in Scorpus's voice. 'It'll be my fault. You were right. I made it too hard for him. He was so desperate to make me proud.'

A muscle was pulsing in Muttumbaal's jaw. I could still hear Hanno being sick outside and I felt like joining him. Abibaal looked so pale, so cold. I was terrified that life was escaping from his body, even as we watched. Then Ismene appeared at the opening of the tent. She went straight to Abibaal and kneeled beside him, taking off her mantle and tucking it around his skinny frame to keep him warm. Leaning across, she reached to Scorpus, who briefly clutched her outstretched fingers. Barca's eyes followed the movement of their hands, but he said nothing. Elissa, who had come in with her mother, was standing next to me. I felt her cheek brush against my arm.

'Muttumbaal of Thugga?' The starting steward had entered the tent.

'What do you want?' croaked my grandfather.

'We need your team for the final of the channel race. The track's ready.'

There was a long silence.

'Perhaps we could find another driver, to make up the four,' said Barca. 'One of the other teams might let us borrow someone...'

'Not possible, I'm afraid,' said the steward at once. 'Rules are clear. Teams can't mix.'

'Can't you at least give us more time,' pleaded Barca. 'The boy could wake up soon.'

The steward looked at Abibaal and scratched his head.

'Doesn't look likely. I'm sorry, but I need to start this race, or declare your opponents the winners.'

We all looked at each other.

'We'll be ready. Here's your fourth charioteer.'

Parmenion had picked up a racing breastplate discarded by an injured charioteer and was putting it on.

XXXVIII

Doubt was written across the steward's face.

'Not sure if you're allowed to substitute one driver for another mid-competition. It's a new event for me. I'll have to check in the rules.'

He took out a corded set of tablets and started to rifle through it. Scorpus looked at Parmenion.

'You could lose that leg if you have another shipwreck.'

'I know. Then again, it might be the last chance I ever get to race again. At least this way, I can try to make it up to you, Scorpus. For what happened.'

'You're not in debt to me, lad.'

'Yes, I am,' said Parmenion. 'For a lot of things. I'm sorry I didn't listen. I'm working hard to get better at it.' He glanced briefly in my direction. 'You kept faith with me, Scorpus, when I didn't deserve it. Let me do this, for you and your family.'

Scorpus was silent for a moment.

'We've all had some lessons to learn lately,' he said at last. 'But there was nothing I could ever teach you about courage.'

I saw the gratitude and relief in Parmenion's eyes as he gripped Scorpus's outstretched hand.

There was a swish of canvas as the flap of the tent was pulled back again. Gemellus Glabrio himself entered. He had a sheen of sweat on his high forehead.

'What's going on?' he demanded. 'That crowd's going to rip my stadium apart if we don't give them some more entertainment soon.'

'Thugga team wants to make a substitution,' explained the steward, still studying his rulebook.

'And I want this race underway, so hurry up.'

'Ah!' The steward tapped the tablet in triumph. 'Here it is. Says in the event of a charioteer being injured during the rounds for the channel race, you can swap in another driver from the same stable, so long as the opposing trainer doesn't veto.'

'What? That's absurd. No trainer's going to miss his chance to veto when he can claim victory without even having to race. Who wrote such a stupid rule?'

The steward scratched his cheek.

'Begging your pardon, Master Glabrio. This is the rulebook your people gave us.'

Glabrio sank on to a bench and ran his fingers through his oily hair.

'The idea for the race was mine. I left the organisation to others.'

'Ah,' said the steward. 'Always best to oversee such things yourself, if you don't mind me saying.'

Muttumbaal turned to Bodo.

'Find Zeno. Bring him here.'

Bodo ran fast. Within moments, Zeno was entering the tent. His eyes went at once to the stretcher, where Abibaal lay motionless between Scorpus and Ismene. The furrows in his brow deepened.

'I'm sorry, Scorpus,' he said gruffly. 'Hope he'll pull through. Gave my lad a lesson in courage.'

'Thank you,' said Scorpus, tersely.

'They want to swap in another driver for the channel race,' explained the steward. 'Says in the rules you can veto it if you don't like it.'

Muttumbaal and Zeno eyed each other.

'Well?' rasped Muttumbaal. 'What about it?'

Zeno said nothing. My grandfather's shoulders dropped, as if in exhaustion.

'Give me this, Zeno,' he mumbled. 'If we lose, I'll sell you the stables and the land. At the price you wanted.'

Barca opened his mouth, then closed it again.

Ismene's eyes were fixed on her father, silent and pleading.

'No veto,' said Zeno at last.

Glabrio looked relieved.

'Good. Now get your teams to the start, I beg of you.'

The steward followed him out.

'Thank you, Papa,' said Ismene quietly. Zeno just nodded.

There was no time to warm up our horses. A slow hand-clap in the circus turned to ecstatic roars from the Thugga crowd as we entered, and boos from the Bulla Regia supporters. They knew that the outcome of this race would dictate whether their stable or ours made it into the race for the laurel crown. Porcellus danced on the spot as the breeze lifted the ribbons in his mane.

'Easy, boy, easy,' I said.

I knew what a risky thing I was doing, putting him in for Jewel. There would be no other horses either side to take the attention away from him, nothing to distract Scylax from his speed. But we had to win this final. And as good as Jewel was, there was no horse faster than Porcellus. A picture of Abibaal's bloodless face kept swimming through my head, the damp curls clinging to his neck like tiny strangling snakes. *Hold on, Abibaal. Please hold on.* I had the idea that somehow, if I could go back and tell him we'd won, he would come back from wherever he was.

Zeno's team were ready. It looked as though they were switching tactics and putting Danel on the first leg. That meant they were planning on trying to gain a big lead which we then wouldn't be able to make up. Amandio was driving Cupid, which rubbed salt into the wound.

I went up to Hanno, whose face was tinged green. Rocks thrown by the Bulla Regia supporters were hitting the sand close to Eagle's hooves.

'Remember what Grandpa Muttumbaal always says,' I shouted over the din. 'Don't leave anything behind you on the track. You can do this, Hanno. Think of what Abibaal's going to say if you go back and tell him you beat Danel.'

Hanno nodded, his teeth chattering.

They lined up behind the chalk lines drawn either side of the first turning post, Hanno with Eagle on the left of the channel, Danel with his black horse on the right. The Bulla Regia fans were making noises to put Hanno off. Glabrio had appeared on to the track to start the race from the channel itself. Alongside him were the stewards who would judge whether there were any fouls on the changeovers. Glabrio raised the white cloth.

'Charioteers, ready!' he shouted but we could barely hear him over the baying of the crowd. Hanno clenched his jaw. The flag dropped. Eagle leaped off the line as if someone had set fire to his tail.

'Come on!' I yelled.

For the first length they were neck and neck almost the entire way. I could tell that Danel had underestimated Hanno, who was driving as though his brother's life depended on it. As they approached the turn, Danel curled around it almost lazily. Then he picked up the pace and his black horse pulled away from Eagle, extending his lead with every stride. But Hanno clung on valiantly, like a boy holding a lion by its tail, and the gap wasn't as big as it could have been by the time they came back.

The changeover was close. Bodo crossed the chalk line at almost the exact same moment Hanno's wheels went over it. There were loud cries of 'foul' from the Bulla Regia supporters and I tensed as the stewards conferred. But they didn't raise the red flag, which would have ended the race there and then.

Now it was Bodo against Zeno's apprentice, who was almost half-way up the track by the time Bodo got River into his stride. As they disappeared into the mist of sand blowing across the circus, Parmenion and I circled Atlas and Porcellus. Although he had his leg strapped up, I could see Parmenion wincing every time he had to make a turn. He caught me watching him.

'It may not be pretty, but I'll make it back, I promise,' he said. 'Just be ready to clean up after me. It's going to be up to you to finish this.'

Bodo had come off the turn. His opposite number in green still held the lead, but Bodo was cutting into it. I could see Zeno on the far side of the track, urging his apprentice to use his whip. Parmenion moved to the start line, holding Atlas in check. Eyes fixed on Bodo, he waited until his wheels were about to cross the chalk. Then with a shout, he let Atlas have his head and they sprang forward.

All the way up the straight, it was like watching the Parmenion of old. The Thugga supporters roared as he edged ahead. I felt a wave of emotion, thinking what he must be feeling, hearing that sound for what he knew might be the last time. On the sharp turn at the end, though, I could see him struggling to keep his balance and the chariot nearly tilted on its side. Zeno's driver was already on his way back down the track, being cheered on by his teammates.

But Parmenion was there, holding on. Dragging Atlas around in a sweeping circle, he pointed him back down the track. As his chariot barrelled towards me, I braced myself, holding Porcellus on a short rein. Amandio was already off the start line and on his way. Parmenion was almost there. I saw the pain etched on his face.

'Go!' he yelled.

Our wheels crossed safely. Porcellus was quickly into his stride. The wind caught the edges of my tunic, pushing my sleeves up my arms. Something flew past me – a rock, thrown from the crowd. Ahead, Amandio was pushing Cupid without mercy. He had a lead of about five lengths and was trying to build on it. Porcellus snorted as he saw his old stable companion on the other side of the track. This was like play for him. I felt the speed building under my wheels. The gap was rapidly closing.

We coiled around the turning post. Amandio's lead was down to three lengths. I gave Porcellus his head. Free at last to run, he stretched his neck. I could almost hear the gasp around the circus. Amandio's lead lessened to two lengths in an instant. Then one. Then nothing. The contest was over with half the straight still to run. And still we were going faster. The Thugga crowd were on their feet, celebrating.

We crossed the finish and I just managed to pull Porcellus up before we crashed into the wall at the far end. Parmenion and the boys greeted me with howls of triumph. The circus echoed to the ecstatic roar of the Thugga supporters who now knew they would have two local drivers in the final. But the Bulla Regia supporters were furious and still calling foul on Bodo's changeover.

Back at the medical tent, it was eerily quiet inside. Ismene and Scorpus were sitting either side of Abibaal. There was no one else there. The physician must have gone to watch the races.

'We won,' I said.

Ismene smiled at me.

'Glarus came to tell us. Well done, Leon.'

I sank down next to Abibaal.

'Has there been any change?' I asked Scorpus, whose eyes were fixed on Abibaal's face.

'Very little. I squeezed his hand a moment ago and I think he squeezed back. But I'm not sure.'

I leaned forward and spoke into my sleeping cousin's ear.

'Abibaal. Wake up. We won. Just like I told you we would. We're going to race for the laurel crown.'

Behind me, I heard the tent flap open. Barca came in, followed by Muttumbaal.

'There you are. They need you for the last race, Leon. They want you and Danel to do a parade lap for the crowd. Parmenion's getting your horses ready.' He looked elated, but his expression changed when he saw Scorpus's face. 'Still nothing?'

'No,' said Scorpus.

I rested a hand on the top of Abibaal's head.

'Abibaal?' I said louder. 'We need you to wake up. We won, Abibaal, we won!'

His eyelashes twitched then lifted, like clamshells opening. Abibaal looked at me out of a silver fog. Recognition dawned. He croaked one word.

'*Dido.*'

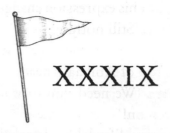

XXXIX

There was a long silence in the tent. Ismene, who had gasped in delight when Abibaal opened his eyes, looked confused.

'What did he say?' she asked.

Abibaal was squinting at me. I could see the fear and confusion in his eyes and I knew I had to reassure him, to stop him from slipping away again.

'Yes. It's me,' I told him, wrapping my fingers around his. 'It's Dido. Everything's going to be fine. Just lie still and keep squeezing my hand. Don't let go, you hear?'

I felt his nails dig into my palm.

'Where's Papa?' he whispered.

'I'm here, son,' said Scorpus, his voice shaky with relief. He leaned forward so that Abibaal could see him. 'I've got you safe.'

'My head. It really hurts.'

'I know. But it's going to get better. I promise.'

Ismene was sitting back on her heels now. She was staring at us, her hand raised to her mouth.

'Of course,' she whispered. 'I see it now. I always knew there was something... but I couldn't quite... oh, how could I have been so blind?'

I dared to meet her eyes and saw that they were full of tears. But she was smiling too.

'You look so like her, you know,' she choked. 'It's your expression, I think. That same direct look. Oh, Scorpus. How could you have kept it from us this long?'

She glanced to the back of the tent, almost fearfully. Barca didn't seem to have fully understood what was going on. My grandfather's face was ashen. He stared at me as if I was a ghost. I didn't know what to say. So I just went on stroking Abibaal's hair. He was blinking like a newborn foal.

'Did you really win, Dido?' he whispered. 'Did you beat Danel?'

'Not yet,' I said. 'But we made it to the final. Parmenion took your place and I raced Porcellus.'

His eyes brightened.

'Was Porcellus really fast?'

'So fast. Our wheels almost left the ground.'

He beamed happily. Then a look of worry crossed his face.

'But no one knows, do they? They don't know the secret?'

'No. No one knows.'

Abibaal looked reassured. Barca, on the other hand, seemed almost fearful.

'But it's… it's not possible. You can't mean, that man was right? This is Sophonisba's child? And…' He peered out of the tent flap to make sure no one was listening. '*She*'s the girl who won at the Circus Maximus?'

'This is Dido,' said Scorpus. 'Let's not be afraid of saying names in this family any more, Barca.'

'But there's a price on her head! For her and the little black horse! And she's—'

'*She*'s the one who just won that race for you and might be just about to save your stable as well as mine. More importantly, she's your niece, Barca. And your granddaughter, Papa. Nothing else matters.'

The frail hand clawed around the top of my grandfather's walking stick was trembling.

Parmenion ducked into the medical tent. His knee was badly swollen.

'They want you for the last race,' he said to me. Seeing Abibaal was half-awake, he grinned. 'I don't know. Some people will use any excuse for a nap.'

Abibaal smiled sleepily. Parmenion sensed the tension among the rest of us. He nodded at me.

'Danel's waiting. I've got the horses ready.'

I stood up and confronted my grandfather. His black-eyed glare scurried across my face, like the movement of a beetle.

'You're the one who says that there's only two things that matter in life,' I said. 'Winning and family. I can do the first one on my own. But not the second.'

Still, he said nothing.

'It's your stable,' I went on. 'You make the decisions. Do you want me to race for you?'

His breath was shallow and ragged. For a long time, we stared at each other.

'Grandfather?'

He gave me the tiniest of nods.

The noise from the stadium was deafening.

'Thugga, Thugga, Thugga,' the local supporters yelled, stamping in time with their chant. Some of the Bulla Regia followers had left the stadium in disgust. There were empty areas where they'd been sitting. But others were staging noisy protests. A group of men had managed to get on to the track and were lying in the sand, trying to stop the race from starting. Danel and I had to wait while they were dragged away.

We cantered side by side for the lap of honour, behind Glabrio, who was driving his chariot and grey horses again. He saluted the crowd, waving and flashing his dazzling smile. Some of the spectators applauded. Others heckled. Almost all of them laughed when he had to duck as a well-aimed pomegranate just missed hitting him. Danel and I kept our distance, but Porcellus and Centaur were already eyeballing each other, snatching at their bits, eager for the fray.

We went into the starting gates. As the charioteer with the most laurels, Danel had been allowed to pick his lane first. He chose to go on the inside, just as I would have done. Final adjustments were made, axles checked, harnesses secured. Then we were alone and in darkness, with the waning sunlight of the late afternoon illuminating the sandy track. A metal grille between the stalls separated me and Danel. But we could hear and see each other.

'Told you it would be us,' he said, his voice barely audible over the chanting of the crowd.

'You're a fortune-teller,' I replied, gritting my teeth as I tried to hold Porcellus in check and stop him from kicking the gate.

Danel laughed. 'That would mean I can predict the result.'

He thought he could. I knew it by the confidence in his voice. For all the talk about rivals being friends, this was what he'd been waiting for. The chance to beat me. To fulfil his destiny.

Trumpets sounded. Porcellus and Centaur tensed, their eyes fixed on the track. Jewel flared her nostrils. Brightfoot and Blaze were calm. I took up my starting stance, gripping the reins.

'Good luck, Leon,' said Danel as the countdown began. 'May the best man win.'

XL

The gates cranked open and light flooded in. Jewel tripped as we burst on to the track and I had to use all my strength to hold her up or the race would have been over before it started. The crowd sucked in its breath. But Porcellus steadied the ship. Soon we were galloping in a steady rhythm down the opening straight, Brightfoot and Blaze keeping perfectly in stride. Danel was already a length ahead, and he moved close to the channel as soon as we were allowed to break from our lanes. I pulled out so that I wouldn't get hit in the face by the dust flying from his wheels. We both took the first turn neatly, keeping an eye on each other all the way down the long straight on the other side. The first lap was over. One golden dolphin dipped its nose.

The noise in the stadium was like a clash of weapons. The crowd was divided – not just the locals from Thugga, but also the spectators from the visiting towns who now had to throw their support to a rival stable. Cries of 'Leon' and 'Jewel' rang out from those wearing blue. Followers of the Greens were mostly shouting for Danel. Meanwhile, the protesting Bulla Regia fans still refused to be drowned out.

As we passed the competitors' stand, I glimpsed Zeno and Muttumbaal. They were sitting some distance apart, given pride of place in the front row as the two trainers competing for the laurel crown. I caught sight of Scorpus sitting behind my grandfather. My heart lifted. If Scorpus was there, that must mean Abibaal was well enough to be left on his own with Ismene.

Danel moved slightly ahead as we came to the turn. I could tell he wasn't pushing too hard yet. He knew exactly where I was and had no intention of either letting me get ahead, or wasting his horses' strength. If there was going to be a sprint finish, he would be ready for it. Normally, I would have backed Porcellus and Jewel against any team, even one as good as I was facing. But they had both already raced two or three times that day. Centaur and the gold horses were fresh.

The second golden dolphin flipped. Two laps down.

All the way around the next circuit and the one after, I watched Danel like a fox, ready to pounce if he drifted even a tiny bit away from the channel or left a gap on one of the turns. But he didn't make a single mistake. If anything, he was edging further ahead off each turn, driving in that supremely relaxed, confident style of his. I was tempted to surprise him and overtake with a burst of speed on the outside. But I knew he'd be waiting for me to do that and that he'd fight not to give up the lead. Even if I did make it past him, there was a big risk that the effort would tire my team out and Danel would pass me again before the finish. We were playing a game of cat and mouse and I'd never faced anyone more skilled at it.

I glanced into the competitors' stand on the fourth lap. Zeno was shouting encouragement to Danel. Scorpus was on his feet as well. He clapped and clenched his fist at me, but I could tell he was worried. Muttumbaal was like a statue. He hadn't moved for the entire race.

Another two dolphins down. Three laps left.

The Thugga supporters yelled angrily as a Bulla Regia protestor, carrying a blazing torch, suddenly ran on to the track. Danel's outside horse flinched, but accelerated past the man, who then turned and brandished the torch at me. His face was twisted with rage. My team swerved like cats, and I cracked my whip above the man's head for good measure, making him duck. The crowd cheered and the danger was past. But now we had lost even more ground on Danel.

The gilded turning posts flashed past. It was the start of the sixth lap. If I was going to win this race, I had to do something now.

I moved to the outside, trying for a quick overtake. Jewel and Porcellus lengthened their stride hungrily. But Danel whipped his four in an instant. We battled for supremacy over a full half-lap, gold, black and brown noses darting in unison. The noise of the crowd was like the roaring of the wind. But Danel had the inside track, which gave him less ground to cover. Realising we weren't going to get past, I dropped back. My supporters groaned and Porcellus snorted, as if he was annoyed at me for giving way.

Now, I didn't know what to do. My team still had fight in them. But the gold horses were just as strong, and I'd never raced an opponent with the tactical skill of Danel. There were only a few turns left. Maybe Danel really was a fortune-teller. Maybe he'd been right all along to believe he would beat me.

Are you giving up?

My gaze was tugged towards the competitors'

stand. It was as if I could feel my grandfather's piercing black stare boring into me. The words he'd said to me in that first training session with Porcellus echoed in my head.

They're coming for you now! They can see you're beaten! What have you got left?

A picture formed in my head. The first time I'd seen Muttumbaal drive, the day we arrived in Thugga. I remembered the way the wheels of his chariot sliced the sand, turning with impossible speed as he switched direction, first one way, then the other... and I thought of what he'd said to me about Scorpus. *I taught him to be a circus warrior. To take the race to his opponent. Never accept defeat.*

Switching stance, I tugged on the right rein. Porcellus's ears twitched in surprise, but he obeyed the command. We veered right, into the empty, smooth sand in the middle of the track. The crowd reacted. Danel turned his head warily as he sensed me drawing almost level. His eyes dared me to try to pass him.

But I wasn't planning an overtake.

The turn was approaching. I moved further to the right so that Danel would think I was still going to attempt a pass on the outside. I tried to remember the way my grandfather's hands had moved. Precision was going to be everything.

Jewel's rust-red ears were pricked. Like the old cavalry horse she was, she waited for the command.

Danel squeezed his inside rein for the turn. Four gold muzzles moved left, nosing their way around the posts. Now Danel had his back to me.

'Now! Come on Jewel, fly!'

The mare's yellow mane caught the breeze like the crest of a wave. We tore across the track at a sideways angle, moving fast from right to left. Danel was completing the turn. There was a narrow gap of track on his left between him and the edge of the channel. Too late, he saw me coming straight at him.

Centaur's eye widened. But Jewel had no intention of backing down and neither did I.

Danel swore. I pulled my team up just in time to avoid a collision and immediately hauled left, my wheels scraping inside Danel's. Porcellus and Centaur clashed shoulders and bared their teeth at one another. We were battling for space on the track now, our wheels running dangerously close. But I'd stolen the inside line. The noise in the stadium was at fever pitch. There was under a lap to go.

All the way along the last long straight, we fought. Neither of us used our whips. Our horses didn't need them. They were as caught up in the battle as we were. Centaur got his nose in front. Then Porcellus. Then Centaur again. The gold horse had the advantage in size. But Porcellus was his equal in strength. As we came up to the gilded turning posts for the final time, the focus switched to Jewel. Danel was applying the pressure. But Jewel's one good eye never left the channel. She nosed around it like a red hound on a scent, the other horses dancing around her in a perfect curve.

Now Glabrio's box and the finish line were straight ahead. We both attacked it with every last scrap of strength we had. The crowd screamed us home. I sensed Danel edging ahead on my right in the last few strides. He'd saved something right for the end.

Then Porcellus poked out his nose as we flashed across the line.

I collapsed on to the guard rail of the chariot. Danel had cantered ahead, but I knew he was completely spent as well. Both sets of supporters were claiming victory. The stewards were in a huddle. As they approached Glabrio, Danel turned back and pulled alongside me. Our horses were too exhausted to snipe at each other any more. We waited, our eyes following Glabrio as he stepped on to the track and walked towards the competitors' stand. When he approached Zeno first, my heart sank. Then I saw that he wasn't congratulating Zeno, but patting him on the back and saying a few words to him. The trainers behind my grandfather stood up as Glabrio moved towards him. Scorpus helped him to his feet. Then Glabrio took Muttumbaal's hand and raised it to the sky.

All around the circus, the crowd erupted.

I ran to my horses' heads and hugged them in turn, Porcellus the longest. Then I turned to Danel, who had stepped off his chariot as well. He had taken off his helmet and was scooping sand into it from the track. Then he walked over to me. Sweat streaked his face and hair.

'Hold out your hands,' he said.

I did and he poured the sand over them, so that the grains ran in rivulets through my fingers.

'Feel that?' he said. 'It's different, isn't it? More like the Circus Maximus. Know why?'

I shook my head.

'Because it's had a great charioteer race on it. And I'm the lucky one who got to lose to him.'

He gave me the helmet and smiled. It might have been the hardest thing he'd ever had to do. And I knew then, whatever life held for me, that if any young driver of the future asked me what made a great champion, I would remember what Danel did that day.

I took off my own helmet and offered it to him in return.

'You can't be a great charioteer if you don't have a great rival,' I said. 'Another time, the result might be different.'

'I hope so. But you won today. Well done, Leon.'

The head steward came up and instructed us both to go to the victory podium in front of Glabrio's box. Jewel was unharnessed and brought forward with me, as the victorious inside horse. Porcellus stamped his foot, irritated at being left behind in the care of the circus officials.

Glabrio was waiting for us. It was only then I realised that Scylax was back in his seat, right behind him. And that, like Glabrio, he was smiling.

XLI

'Congratulations, Leon of Utica,' said Glabrio. A smell of scented hair oil mixed with sweat wafted from him. 'You've brought honour to your grandfather's stable.'

He waited for me to bow, then laid the crown of laurel leaves on my head. The roar of the Thugga supporters echoed around the circus. Danel, who had tucked his own, smaller palm of victory under his arm, applauded. And so – to my unease – did Scylax, who was still lurking behind Glabrio. What was he doing there? Why did he have that look on his face? He should be annoyed – Danel, the new star of the Green faction, had just lost. I searched for Cassius Chaerea, in the box behind Glabrio. His face was as inscrutable as ever.

Encouraged by Glabrio's hand on my shoulder, I turned to face the crowd on the other side of the track. It was a wild sight. Ecstatic chants of 'Thugga,

Thugga' filled the stadium. People were dancing to
the beat of drums. Blue banners were being waved.
But there were still protestors from Bulla Regia keen
to make themselves heard above the noise. A mob
of about thirty of them had climbed on top of the
archway. One man was seated astride Caligula's lead
horse, as if riding into battle. Above the emperor's
bronze head, the sky was beginning to darken.

On the track, Jewel, as the winning inside horse,
had been garlanded with flowers, which she was
trying to eat. Behind her, Porcellus gnawed his bit
and stamped his foot alongside Brightfoot and Blaze.
I glanced over to the competitors' stand. I could
just see my family. Bodo and Hanno were jumping
up and down in time with the drums. I wondered
if Abibaal could hear the noise from the medical
tent. Parmenion was there too, talking to Barca. He
waved and punched the air when he saw me looking
their way. In front of everyone stood Muttumbaal
and Scorpus, side by side, watching me. They were
too far away for me to see their expressions. I lifted
a hand, trying to signal, trying to point to Scylax.
Help, I wanted to say. *Something's wrong.*

A hand gripped my shoulder. I flinched.

'You must be feeling as if your cup is full, Leon,'
said Glabrio, leaning in to speak loudly in my ear.
'But wait. I have exciting news for you.'

He beckoned to Scylax. My stomach lurched.

'You know who this is?' asked Glabrio, smiling encouragingly at me as if I was a child.

I nodded warily as Scylax bared his brown teeth.

'Well, then you know he is a man of influence. He was telling me, before the race, about your experience at the Circus Maximus. It seems you've shaken off the seasickness that made him reluctant to recruit you to race for the Greens before.'

'I...'

'Well, that's all changed now,' said Glabrio. 'He wants you to go back to Rome with him. To race for the Greens alongside Danel. What do you say to that?'

My throat seemed to close up.

'No,' I croaked.

The dazzling smile dimmed.

'I can't go back to Rome,' I said. 'Please, I don't want to race at the Circus Maximus.'

'Nonsense.' Glabrio laughed. 'Of course you want to go. What charioteer doesn't? And when you get to Rome, you will give the emperor my best regards. Tell him about my circus!'

Scylax took hold of my wrist. He led me forward to the front of the podium, produced a green tunic and wrapped it around my shoulders. A roar went up from the Green supporters in the crowd as they understood what was happening. They started to unfurl their banners, pointing in triumph at the Blues.

'Listen to me and listen carefully,' Scylax growled, as he acknowledged the cheers of the Greens. 'You're not going to make any fuss. You're going to come with me, and you're going to come quietly. Because if you don't, if you try to escape, I'm going to have that demon black horse of yours skinned and fed to the ocean on our way over to Rome.'

I stared at him in terror.

'Saw you this morning,' he said, chewing hungrily, the orange glare from the torches around the circus reflected in his eyes. 'Feeding him figs. That's what did it. That's what made me remember. Every night, you used to feed him those figs. Like you were a mother eagle with a chick.'

Then I understood why Jewel had been frightened in the stables earlier. She'd seen Scylax and remembered him from the day of the fire.

At Scylax's signal, two of Glabrio's guards came and took hold of Jewel's bridle. She threw up her head in irritation. Another group of soldiers had circled Porcellus, Brightfoot and Blaze.

'You and that black horse are coming back to Rome with me right now, along with those others,' said Scylax. 'And I'm going to claim that reward from the emperor.'

'No!' I tried to prise his fingers from my wrist. 'You can't, please. I won't go, I won't race for the emperor, I won't let him have Porcellus.'

'Oh yes you will,' he hissed, tightening his grip. 'Or it's not just your horse that'll suffer. You'll do everything the emperor wants, or I'll tell him about how Scorpus and that cussed grandfather of yours harboured a fugitive. Caligula will have your whole family slaughtered.'

Danel came forward. He wore a rueful smile and clearly had no idea of what was going on.

'It'll be good to be on the same side,' he said to me, clapping me on the shoulder. 'Rivals and friends, I hope. Like we talked about. Congratulations, Leon.'

I shook my head wordlessly, trying to let him know with my eyes that something was wrong, desperate for anyone to help me. But he didn't understand and I couldn't make a run for it. I knew Scylax wasn't lying about his threats. Danel retreated again and I turned to Glabrio's box, to the last person who might be able to help. But Cassius Chaerea was leaning against a pillar, giving nothing away.

'Let's go,' said Scylax and he walked me down on to the track, nodding to the soldiers to take the horses first. Porcellus's hackles went up as soon as he saw Scylax and it took the efforts of the entire group of guards to stop him from charging forward, dragging Blaze and Brightfoot with him.

The mood in the circus was changing. It wasn't just the Bulla Regia supporters protesting now. Angry whistles rang out all around. Hometown loyalties were forgotten. It had become about the factions and the Blues were furious that the Greens were stealing a driver they thought of as their own.

As we moved towards the archway, two figures leaped from the competitors' stand and started running across the sand towards us. It was Scorpus and Parmenion. I shook my head, desperate to tell them to stop, that it was no use and not to put themselves in danger, but they kept coming. Glabrio's guards intercepted them and there was a violent struggle. Scorpus was hit.

'Keep going,' snarled Scylax as I cried out and tried to free myself from his cruel grip.

A small blaze had broken out in the stands. Someone had set fire to the wooden seating. Spectators were scattering from the flames. Panic set in. The aisles were full and people were being trampled in the rush. In their bid to find safety, some climbed on top of Caligula's arch where the defiant crowd of men from Bulla Regia still staged their protest, stamping their feet and banging their drums. We had almost reached it.

'Here, we'll go through first,' Scylax said to the soldiers, who were struggling with Porcellus. 'That should make the black horse follow.'

We passed into the shadowy tunnel, our feet crunching on the pebbled sand. Screams from the panicking spectators echoed through the darkness along with the stamping feet of the protestors above. Scylax still had my arm in a pincer grip. Half-way through, he realised there was no sound of hooves following and turned back. I could see Porcellus was desperate to get to me. But Jewel was blocking the path, refusing to go into the tunnel.

'Come on,' bellowed Scylax. 'Use a whip on her.'

Jewel was rearing now, fighting the guards. Every time Porcellus tried to go around her, she swung her haunches and stopped him.

Something tickled my face. I looked up and realised it was dust, raining lightly from the underside of the arch.

I looked back at Jewel. Her good eye was open very wide at me.

Snatching my wrist from Scylax's grasp, I dived and rolled across the ground into the narrow opening of the stairwell. Rolling myself into a ball, I covered my head with my arms. Scylax was grabbing at me, his fingers clawing blindly.

Next moment, it was as if the sky had fallen. A huge wave of stone and surge of sound, crashing to earth like a wave. I cried out, feeling the ground shake as the archway disintegrated under the weight of screaming people and the great statue on top of it. The noise seemed to go on forever.

And then, there was silence.

XLII

I opened my eyes and immediately started to blink.
Dirt was trapped between my lashes. The skin on
my face felt tight and I could taste wood shavings
and cement dust. For a moment, I was confused.
What had happened? Why was my head dark and
empty of thoughts? I blinked again, tears mixing
painfully with the grit, trying to wash it out. Then I
saw the white of Jewel's eye, the look of panic on her
face. She'd been warning me to get out. A terrible
sound echoed through my ears. I'd heard it as the
arch tumbled. It was the sound of a horse screaming.

I flinched violently and knocked my head against
the cold stone where it rested. Porcellus! Jewel! My
horses. My brave horses. Where were they? I had
to get to them. What if they'd been caught in the
collapse? What if Scylax's soldiers had taken them?
I started to struggle. But the whole of my left side
was encased in the flood of rubble now filling the

tunnel. By moving, more of it tumbled into the niche, like a creeping wave. I felt it slipping down the neck of my tunic.

Stay still, Dido. Don't move.

I tried to breathe. There was an awful pressure on my chest and my throat was dry. Water. I wanted a drink of water so badly. How long had I been here? Hours? Days? Had they abandoned me here, thinking I'd been buried? Everything was so terrifyingly quiet. *Breathe, Dido. Slowly, just breathe.*

I wiggled my right foot. There was space there. I could feel my outside toe rubbing against the wall. Then it touched something else. Something soft and warmer than stone. I pulled my foot back with a cry of fear. It was flesh I could feel against my toes. There was a person there. A body.

Straining my ears, I listened for any noise that might give me hope. I could make out a few sounds now. Distant shouts. Someone crying. Was it another survivor? Some of the men from Bulla Regia must have been killed when the archway came down. A smell reached my nostrils. Bitter, acrid. I realised it was smoke. Panic flooded my chest again. The fire in the stands, what if it was still burning?

There was the shouting again. It seemed closer this time. There was another noise as well. A rattling echo.

Then I heard it.

Dido.

Someone was calling my name.

I opened my mouth to shout back. But no sound would come out. My throat was too parched. Frantically, I started to move my foot, tapping it against the wall. There was a scrabbling sound, like a rat moving through a pipe. It got louder and as it did, I kept rattling my foot, hoping it would help guide whoever was coming towards me. I could hear them coughing. Then the weight holding my left arm pinned to my side seemed to lessen. I felt a breath of cool air against my skin. I turned towards it just as someone's fingers tugged at my sleeve.

A pair of jewel-black eyes glinted at me.

'Give me your hand,' croaked my grandfather.

They had made a clearing through the rubble, digging with their bare hands, using horses to tow away what they couldn't shift on their own and – as I learned later – ignoring advice from rescuers who had long since abandoned the scene, believing there could be no survivors. A heavy beam had fallen sideways against the wall, sheltering me from falling rafters but stopping them from going further. The only way to get to me was for someone to crawl under the beam and dig a path through the debris.

Muttumbaal shuffled backwards on his elbows and stomach, never letting go of my hand as I crawled after him. The dust in the narrow space was thick and I could hear him choking, almost vomiting, as he struggled to breathe. But he didn't stop moving. I could hear voices, smell the fresh air. Then we were through and Scorpus's face was above mine. I felt him smearing away the dirt from my cheeks and eyes before he pulled me into a hug, his palm supporting the back of my head.

'Porcellus?' I whispered. 'Jewel?'

'They're here, Dido. We got them all out. They've been helping us find you.'

I felt a soft muzzle brush against my cheek. Bursting into tears, I reached for Porcellus, who was now looming over me. I stroked his soft cheek and kissed his nose. On my other side, Jewel was licking my face. I tried lifting my other hand to stroke her too, but someone was holding it tight.

'You almost had us worried there,' said Parmenion. He looked exhausted, his brow covered in sweat. I noticed a cut on his neck.

'You're bleeding,' I said.

'Tried fitting into that tunnel to get you. But it was too narrow. We were arguing about who should try it next when we realised your grandfather had disappeared. Went in before any of us could stop him.'

I turned my head. Barca and Bodo, who, like Parmenion, both looked bedraggled and sweat-stained, were kneeling next to Muttumbaal. My grandfather was lying on his back, his chest rising and falling like a failing set of bellows. His eyes were half-open and fixed on the stars. But he turned his head as he heard me crawling across the ground to be beside him. His thin lips parted. No sound came out. There was hardly any air left in his lungs. Then I saw a flicker of interest in his eyes. They were fixed on the figurine of Pyramus the charioteer, which had slipped out of the neck of my tunic. I pinched it between my fingers and held it up to the light of the torch that Barca was holding so that Muttumbaal could see it.

He stared. Then his lips curved in a gummy smile. Suddenly, I realised who had kept the wooden box in my mother's room all these years.

Reaching for the pouch tied alongside the chain, I took out the curl of Sophonisba's hair and pressed it into my grandfather's palm. A silver gleam appeared in his black eyes. Then he started gasping for air and his frail hand fell back against his chest, the curl enclosed tightly in his fist.

Bodo stood to make way for Scorpus, who crouched to lay a hand on his father's shoulder.

'Papa…'

Muttumbaal pulled Scorpus towards him. He spoke in a whisper. Barca and I both leaned in to listen.

'Told… you… so. Winning. And… family.'

And then my grandfather seemed to sink into the ground. His shoulders dropped and the breath left his chest in a long sigh. His eyes were still half-open. But there was a look of calm on his face. As if all the anger that had been trapped in the lines and furrows had escaped. The lock of my mother's hair still lay hidden inside his palm.

Gently, Scorpus pressed his father's eyes shut. We were all silent. Bodo wiped a tear from his cheek with the back of his hand. Even Porcellus and Jewel stood still and solemn like sentries, the gentle night breeze ruffling their manes.

A strangulated cry made us all turn.

Scylax had crawled out of the tunnel my grandfather had made. He was bleeding from the head and he looked confused. But he had drawn the long knife from his belt and was staggering towards me.

'Princess Sophonisba…' he leered.

Porcellus reared and prepared for the attack.

But Scylax had only got half-way towards us when he stopped. His eyes glazed, his mouth drooped and he fell to the ground, landing face down in the dirt.

And it was then that we saw Cassius Chaerea behind him. The blade of his sword gleamed red in the moonlight. He wiped it on the inside of his white cloak before placing it back in its scabbard and strolling over to where the huge statue of Caligula was lying in the rubble of the archway. Placing his foot on the emperor's bronze neck, he let it rest there, a look of pleasure in his cold eyes. Then he turned and smiled blandly at us.

'What a mess. Truly, I shouldn't like to be Gemellus Glabrio when he has to explain to Caligula what happened to his birthday present.'

XLIII

'Please accept my condolences, Scorpus. To you and all your family.'

'Thank you, Danel. I hope you find good fortune at the Circus.'

The funeral was over. We had passed in a long, silent procession along the road out of Thugga towards the burial ground near the old circus. Ismene and Elissa walked with some of the women of the town at the front. They wore their hair long and unpinned and sang mourning songs. Behind them, Scorpus, Barca, Bodo and Zeno helped carry the wooden bier on which my grandfather's body lay, wrapped in a shroud. Hanno, Abibaal, Parmenion and I were in the crowd that accompanied the second bier for the other person being buried. We wore red clay masks which were supposed to ward off evil spirits and completely covered our faces.

The two shrouded figures were lowered into the burial chamber. Ismene placed offerings for the afterlife. An amulet my grandfather had worn for luck when he was a young charioteer at the Circus Maximus. His walking stick. The figurine of Pyramus that had belonged to my mother and which I had shown Muttumbaal before he died. I had retrieved the lock of her hair from his fist but left a few precious strands tucked inside. Elissa then brought the rest of the goods and laid them by the second figure. A blue racing tunic. A whip. A driver's helmet. As she stepped back from the tomb, I noticed her sneak a quick look in my direction. But she continued to play her part well.

When the ritual was complete and the tomb sealed, officials from the town began to set the grave marker in place. Zeno stood at the side of the road looking at it for a time, Danel and Amandio standing respectfully by his side. As they left, Danel stopped to exchange words with Scorpus.

'Will you be going to Rome soon?' my uncle asked.

'Yes. In a few days. Glabrio has offered me passage on a ship. I think he's anxious that the emperor should be pleasantly distracted before he hears what happened to the circus. And his statue.'

'I'm sure you'll be able to divert his mind. My

father greatly admired your skills as a charioteer. I've no doubt you will win many races for the Greens.'

'That's good of you.' Danel looked back at the grave marker. 'But no matter how many times I win, it won't change anything.'

'What do you mean?'

'I'll always know I wasn't the greatest. That there was someone else who deserved that title.'

Scorpus laid a hand on his shoulder.

'Greatness isn't just about victories won on the track. Leon would have been the first to say that.'

'Thank you. Will you be staying on in Thugga?'

'No. We begin the journey home to Utica tomorrow. I have a stable to rebuild. And we made a promise to someone back home.'

I waited for Danel to leave. Then I went to stand next to the rest of my family. The officials had set the grave marker in place now.

'Tell us again what it says, Papa,' said Abibaal.

Slowly, Scorpus began to read.

'To all who pass by this place. Here lies Muttumbaal of Thugga. Trainer of great horses and charioteers. And his grandson. Leon. Champion of the Circus Maximus.'

Epilogue

The wind had picked up. Autumn was still clinging by its golden fingertips to the fields around Utica, but the wheat and olive harvest had been gathered in. On a table outside the kitchen, where Anna and I were sitting, there were wooden racks of figs, drying in the sun. A layer of cloth protected them from the bees. I watched as Anna nursed the newborn infant in her arms.

'Scorpus said that his brother and your aunt and cousins may come to visit in the spring,' she said.

'Maybe. If Barca's managed to find some new apprentices by then who can manage the stable.' I tickled the baby's tiny brown foot, watching it curl up like a slug. 'Have you thought of a name for her yet?'

'Yes.' Anna smiled. 'We were thinking, if you wouldn't mind, that we'd like to call her Dido.'

The little girl opened her eyes, shiny like raisins, and gazed at me.

'Just don't expect me to teach you how to drive a four-horse chariot before you're ready,' I told her, pinching her toes gently. 'You've got to learn to walk before you can run. Any trainer will tell you that.'

After Anna had taken the baby inside for a sleep, I wandered out to see how the building work was going. Scorpus and the boys had started putting the new roof on the stable the day before. But I found the construction site deserted, tools abandoned on the ground. Shielding my eyes, I soon spotted them, three figures standing by the edge of the wood. Scorpus had an arm resting around both Hanno and Abibaal's shoulders. They were looking at their mother's grave, a short distance from Sciron's.

Porcellus and Jewel came trotting to the pasture gate. I plucked a clump of grass for them from the other side of the fence. They took turns to share it, bumping noses as they ate. More horses grazed in the field behind them. Behind me, someone approached with a cheery whistle.

'Stable's coming on well,' I said. 'You'll have somewhere to sleep again soon.'

'I hope not,' said Parmenion, dumping a pile of hay over the fence for the horses. 'Indoor life suits me, I've discovered. Hanno and Abibaal want to share the roof space when the thing's finished, I think.'

He wiped the sweat from his brow and picked up a canister that was resting against the fence post. Catching me observing him, he smiled.

'Just water,' he said, before taking a long swig.

'How's your leg today?' I asked.

'Not bad. Not good. Certainly won't be taking the corners at the Circus Maximus any time soon. But I can manage the pain better than I used to.'

'At least both of us got to go out on a win,' I said. 'Not many charioteers can say that of their last race.'

'The last race? For you? Come on.'

I shook my head.

'Leon's dead. Princess Sophonisba's still out there somewhere. But I'm Dido and I want to enjoy being her now. I was always going to have to live with regrets, Parmenion.'

He looked disgruntled but didn't argue the point. Taking another swig of water, he gestured to Scorpus and the boys by the grave.

'What about Scorpus? You think he has regrets?'

'I'm sure he does. But he and Muttumbaal were close again for that moment at the end. That means everything to him, I think.'

'If I'm honest, I was talking about your Aunt Ismene. Don't tell me you never realised there was some kind of history between them.'

'Of course I did. Scorpus told me about it on the

way home. He and Ismene planned to be together one day when they were old enough. But Barca was jealous that Scorpus was a better charioteer. So he told Muttumbaal he wanted to marry Ismene. Being older, he got the first choice. Ismene was too afraid of her father to refuse.'

'So? Do you think he wishes things had been different?'

I thought about this.

'I can't speak for him,' I said eventually. 'I know for certain he loved Hanno and Abibaal's mother. If anything, I think it's harder on Ismene. But then, it always is for women. We don't get to make the choices we'd like to.'

Parmenion rested his elbows on the fence.

'If you could make any choice you wanted, aside from being a charioteer, what would it be?'

'I've been thinking about that a lot,' I admitted. 'You know what I'd really like?'

'What?'

'I'd like to be a trainer.'

Parmenion didn't laugh, as I'd expected him to. Instead, he looked thoughtfully at me.

'Interesting idea. You'd probably need a front man.'

'A what?'

'A front man. Someone to pretend to be the

one in charge, negotiate with the breeders, take all the glory in public, that kind of thing. Meanwhile, you'd be the one running everything behind the scenes.'

I raised an eyebrow at him...

'You know someone who'd be prepared to do that?'

'I might. I just might.'

Porcellus and Jewel were cantering away across the paddock now, Jewel the pursuer, while Porcellus flicked his tail in glee.

'Glory,' I said, mulling over the word Parmenion had used. 'It's funny, isn't it? You spend your whole life hungering after it, working for it. But you do it knowing that you'll never be able to hold on to it. It can't ever last. You have to move on and find a way to live with just the memory of it. Start thinking about the next thing.'

'That's life, I suppose,' said Parmenion. 'It's all about the next thing.'

At the other end of the field, Porcellus and Jewel were now grazing peacefully. I watched them, enjoying the warmth of the sun and the feeling of just being myself.

Author's Note

Rivals on the Track is set in AD 38, the second year of Emperor Caligula's reign. As with the first title in the series, *Race to the Death*, most of the situations and characters in my story are fictional, with the exception of Caligula himself and Cassius Chaerea, a member of the Praetorian Guard, whose job was to protect the emperor. But my reconstruction of the world of Roman chariot racing and its setting in the landscape of north Africa is based on careful historical research.

Chariot racing was already the Romans' favourite form of mass entertainment by the time Caligula came to power. The young emperor's passion for the sport only boosted its popularity. He was famously a supporter of the Green faction, whose top drivers he hero-worshipped the way a football fan might idolise Messi or Ronaldo. During Caligula's four-year rule, the number of chariot races typically held in a single day at the

Circus Maximus – Rome's equivalent of Wembley stadium – increased from twelve to as many as forty on special occasions, such as Caligula's birthday. With each race lasting around ten minutes, and time needed to clear the track between events – not to mention the acrobatic displays on horseback which were staged at intervals to vary the entertainment – that meant a day of non-stop action from sunrise to sunset. It's no wonder Roman spectators needed to take cushions into the circus with them, or that the snack vendors outside, selling street food such as hot sausages and fried chickpeas, did steady business.

The Circus Maximus was not just the oldest chariot-racing arena in the Roman empire, it was also the biggest. As many as 250,000 spectators could be seated inside it, which is twice as many as the world's biggest sporting grounds today. The Colosseum – perhaps the most iconic ancient building in Rome – where gladiator fighting took place, only held a maximum of around 50,000 people, reflecting the superior appeal of chariot racing.

During the first and second centuries, there was a boom in circus building around the Roman empire, from Spain in the west to Syria in the east. Some of the best preserved are in north Africa, a large area of which came under Roman control following their destruction of the city of Carthage (in modern Tunisia) in 146BC. The remains of more than two dozen circuses have been found in this region alone.

In *Rivals on the Track*, we see wealthy Gemellus Glabrio attempting to impress Emperor Caligula by building a new circus on the same scale as the Circus Maximus in the valley below the town of Thugga, (known today as Dougga). No circus of that scale ever existed on this site, or any other outside Rome, although there was a racetrack on the outskirts of Thugga, in the same location where Muttumbaal and Zeno's stables go to practise before the games. Another invention of mine is the 'channel race', where teams race head-to-head down either side of the central barrier. But we do know of a special event where the top two drivers would compete against each other for glory, and I have borrowed that idea for the climax of Glabrio's games (though not the additional detail that they apparently took turns to drive each other's horses).

Roman chariot racing was a big business. It provided a livelihood for thousands of people, from the trainers and breeders who worked for the top teams, to the architects and engineers who designed the circuses. For ordinary Romans, a day out at the games provided an exciting escape from their everyday lives. But it was also an industry that relied on the exploitation of slaves, from the ones who did the back-breaking, unpaid labour of constructing the stadiums to the majority of the charioteers themselves. For every driver who earned enough to buy their freedom and maybe even become a legend of the track, there were thousands whose careers were ended by injury – fatal, in some cases – and who never tasted fame or glory. In this most dangerous and cutthroat of sports, success wasn't just about winning honour for you or your faction. It was a matter of life and death.

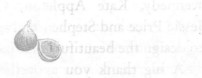

Acknowledgements

They say that second novels are hard to write. Over the past twelve months, I've gained a good insight into what they're talking about. Fortunately, I've had incredible support along the way, helping me and Dido make it to the finish line.

My first and last thank you, as always, is to my husband Julian. Whenever I fell down the rabbit hole, he dug me out and always made sure there was a delicious supper and a glass of wine on the table at the end of the day when I needed it. I truly couldn't have written this book without him.

I am very lucky to work with one of the best editors in the business, Fiona Kennedy. With her unerring eye for detail and her finely tuned ear for the heartbeat of a character, she is an inspiring writing mentor. I am so grateful for her ongoing support and belief in Dido and her story. All of the team at Zephyr/Head of Zeus have been brilliant, including Megan Pickford, Jade Gwilliam, Topsy

Kennedy, Kate Appleton, Clemence Jacquinet, Jessie Price and Stephen McNally, who stepped up to design the beautiful book jacket.

A big thank you as well to Fritha Lindqvist, my tireless and brilliant publicist, and to all of the bloggers, reviewers and booksellers whose support and enthusiasm for *Circus Maximus* has meant more to me than I can say. In this hardest of years, I've really appreciated the chance to connect online with other children's authors, both established and new to the game, and am hugely obliged for their support and encouragement. Hope to meet you all in person for a cup of tea and a slice of cake one day. My friend and fellow classicist, James Wall, was kind enough to be an early proofreader once again. Fingers crossed we'll get back to Italy. And a special thank you to my pupil, Josh Hull, who came up with the name 'Atlas' for one of the horses in the story.

Finally, a massively grateful shout-out to my agent, Nancy Miles, who always talks great sense down the phone from Wales and has been a rock of support.

Although this is a tale of high-octane racing action and adventure, at its heart it's a story about family, in particular the special relationship between fathers and their sons, and between mothers and their daughters. Growing up, I was incredibly fortunate to have a mother who would do anything for her children, and still would to this day. Among countless gifts, she shared her love of horses with my brother and me when we were young, giving up her own time to drive us to riding lessons, shepherd us to competitions, and even do the mucking out for us when we were too lazy. This book is dedicated to her, with endless gratitude and love.

Annelise Gray
Dorset
August 2021